UNBOUND GIFTS

UNBOUND GIFTS

DOUGLAS YOUNG

Library of Congress

Published by AK Classics

PAPERBACK

ISBN-13: 979-8-9878326-3-9

Cover Design - Marcia Noisette (NoisetteInk.com)

Layout Design - Kim Hall

Printed in the U.S.A.

AK CLASSICS®
Publishing

P.O. Box 77203, Charlotte, NC 28271

www.akclassicstories.com

DEDICATION

This book is dedicated to my family, and specifically to my wife and best friend, Pam. For many reasons this was a difficult book to write, and there were several times that I almost quit. Pam encouraged me to continue, and with her support I was able to keep going. For that, and for countless other blessings she has given me over the years, I love her and I'm in her debt.

ACKNOWLEDGEMENTS

There are many people I would like to thank for their help and support during the writing of this book.

I am indebted to my fellow authors Ron Ancrum, Anthony Carter, Patrick Diamond, Diane Flynt, Katherine Heath, Gus Parker, Ossian Wynn and Paul Young that provided me with invaluable information and encouragement during my writing journey.

I would like to thank my reviewers Katherine Disher, Adelle Harris, Pamela Harris-Young, Georgianna Jackson, Priscilla Rosenfeld, Alan Slaughter and Blair Young for taking the time to read my manuscript and provide me with honest and insightful feedback.

Michael S., my editor from Reedsy, was very thorough and did a wonderful job of providing structure to my prose.

Eric Hight is an educator and Civil War historian that reviewed the chapters that took place during the war. His enthusiasm and insights were very much appreciated.

I would also like to thank my publisher, Helen Kimbrough of A.K. Classics for her many recommendations and for turning my manuscript into a book.

Finally, I would like to thank my late mother, Lovie Young, for instilling in me a lifelong love for education and reading.

PROLOGUE

We moved through the trees single file, trudging slowly along a narrow path. No one was in a hurry to begin the day's work. There were nine of us in the burial detail that morning, each carrying a pickax or shovel. A Confederate in a tattered gray uniform led the way, while an armed soldier kept watch from the rear.

I couldn't yet see the battlefield, but I knew it wasn't far away. Though a wet cloth covered my nose and mouth, the stench of the place was already seeping through the fabric, causing me to gag. We were close now. The smell of gunpowder, blood, human waste, and decay combined to form a miasma that hung over the entire valley. Morning sunlight shone through gaps in the trees, and as we moved past, I noted beech, cedar, chestnut, oak, spruce, and several types of pine. Before the war, I would have happily walked a path such as this, finding enjoyment in the quiet of the woods. But death had touched this place, as it had so many others, and I knew it would be a long time before anyone could walk this ground again without remembering what had happened here.

When we finally stepped from the trees I froze, taking in the hellish scene before me. To my right, my friend Louis's complexion had taken on a sickly pallor. I followed his gaze, then looked away quickly, feeling my own bile rising.

"You boys keep moving up there," snapped the soldier behind us, and with great reluctance, I started walking again.

The area ahead was strewn with hundreds of bodies, their faces and limbs contorted by the rigor of death. For many, the damage was so severe that the end must have come quickly. For others, it seemed life had slipped away more slowly, for their hands were still pressed to wounds that no longer bled, or clutched photos of loved ones they would never see again.

By that point in my life, I had already seen too many people die. When I closed my eyes, I could still see their faces. I could still hear their voices. But these deaths were different. This was the needless destruction of countless lives in the space of a few hours, sometimes minutes. The men who covered the field had died alone, far from home with no one to comfort them. This was death on an industrial scale, random and impersonal. This was not a good death.

Some of the Confederates, who had fought so hard for this ground only the day before, were now laying out their dead in neat rows at the far end of the field. The Union corpses, stripped of anything useful, were left to rot where they fell. When the Confederates lost a battle, it was their dead that were left unburied. Even in death, I thought, winning was preferable to losing.

We made our way forward, but progress through the ruined field was slow. I considered each move carefully, not wanting to step on a corpse, or fall among the dead. I felt something tug at my leg and realized that my pants had snagged on a jagged bone protruding from one of the bodies. As I reached down to free the fabric, I saw that much of the man's face had been destroyed by shot or shell. He had only one eye left, and that lone eye was looking straight at me.

I woke with a start and lay awake in the darkness, waiting for my heart to slow. It took some time for me to realize what had happened. I'd been asleep, but it hadn't been a dream. Well, certainly not a dream in the usual sense. It was, in fact, a memory from many years ago. It had really happened, and instinctively I reached for the place on my leg where the sharp bone had punched through my pants.

There were no sounds in the house, save for the rhythmic breathing of my wife, asleep next to me. The room was dark, and I sensed that dawn was still several hours away. Feeling certain I would sleep no more that night, I decided to get up. I swung my legs to the floor and, as quietly as I could, moved toward the bedroom door. As I reached for the knob a floorboard creaked, and I winced at the sound. I looked back to the bed, but there was no movement. Our dog, Rex, who had been sleeping in the corner, stretched languidly and fell in beside me. I hadn't meant for him to come, but I was nonetheless glad for his company. I moved through the house slowly, navigating by memory and the pale moonlight that shone through the front window. When we arrived at my workroom, I lit the lamp on the desk. After looking up at me questioningly, Rex settled comfortably at my feet. Absently stroking his fur, I reached for my quill and ink. I had put this off long enough.

* * *

My name is Henry Freeman, and by almost any reckoning, I have had a remarkable life. I was born a slave, but now live as a free man. My mother was a Negro woman and my father, who is unknown to me, was white. I never had the opportunity for a formal education, but I don't think it boastful in the least to say that over the course of my life I have learned a great many things.

Most of the people I've encountered over the years were not educated. In the case of the slaves this was by design. In fact, when I was a young man, it was illegal in North Carolina to teach a slave to read, or write, or do arithmetic. Though there were a great many deplorable things about slavery, systematically denying education to an entire group of people to keep them subjugated stands as one of the vilest features. History will never know what God-given gifts lay undiscovered and undeveloped within the enslaved population. So, although most of the people I have known were not educated, in this book I *choose* to recount their words not as they were, but as they might have been. As they should have been.

Why have I decided to write my story? Quite simply, it has become a burden to me. Every night as I try to find solace in sleep the words, sounds, and images come back to me unbidden. The recollections are so vivid that I am forced to relive these events again and again. I earnestly hope that the process of transferring my story to paper will reduce this profusion of memory, thereby bringing me peace. However, I have no wish to get ahead of myself. Let me start at the beginning.

TABLE OF CONTENTS

PART 3

PART 4

PART
1

CHAPTER I

PLANTATION

1842

I was born into slavery on a twelve-hundred-acre planta-tion that bordered Little Sugar Creek, about ten miles south of Charlotte, North Carolina. There were more than sixty slaves on the plantation that did whatever the owner, Dr. Robert Parker, or his overseer, Mr. Fox, said had to be done. Over the years I learned that Dr. Parker's grandfather, Mr. Augustus Parker, carved the farmstead out of what was then the North Carolina wilderness. Augustus was an officer in the Continental Army and fought against England in the War of Independence. As a reward for his service, he received a large grant of land in the Piedmont region of North Carolina, near what was then the small crossroads town of Charlotte. He and his wife moved to the area in 1784, a year after the war ended. Five years later, George Washington was chosen as the first president of the United States, and later that same year, North Carolina became the twelfth state in the union.

In contrast to his father and grandfather, Dr. Parker was never very interested in being a planter. Instead, he had always been fascinated by natural science and medicine. As a young man, he read any books or articles on the subject he could find, and still he pressed his tutors for more information. By all accounts his father, Charles, was a practical man who saw little benefit in Robert's pursuits. He believed that the sole purpose of education was to prepare a man for the challenges of business, nothing more. Charles and his son quarreled often, until begrudgingly he relented and allowed Robert to travel to Philadelphia to study medicine, a decision made more palatable because his oldest son was still living on the plantation.

But sadly, during Robert's absence, a tragedy was visited upon the Parker family. In 1834 the plantation house caught fire and burned to the ground, with Robert's parents, his older brother, and a beautiful young slave named Bella still inside. The house burned so quickly that some suspected the fire had been set intentionally, but it was never proven. Though it was whispered among the slaves that Bella was unhappy with the unwanted attention of Robert's brother, they said nothing. The possibility that a slave intentionally killed herself, and took an entire white family with her, was something that no one wanted to talk about.

Upon hearing the news, Robert immediately returned to Charlotte. This was many years before the railroad came to town, so the trip overland took several weeks. By the time he arrived, his family was already buried on a small hill overlooking the north side of the property. The plantation had been his father and brother's dream, but it was not a dream he shared. So, after settling his family's affairs and beginning work on reconstruction of the main house, Robert turned over day-to-day farm operations to Mr. Fox, moved to Charlotte, and began referring to himself as Dr. Parker. Soon after arriving in Charlotte, the new Dr. Parker met Mary Higgins, the daughter of a prominent local family. The couple were married in the spring of 1836, the same year I was born.

* * *

Like many farms in the Piedmont region, the Parker Plantation was planted with several crops, including cabbage, cucumbers, squash, sweet potatoes, wheat, and cotton. Hogs were raised for meat. Ironically, it had been Dr. Parker's idea to plant cotton. Though he was not interested in farming, he had a keen aptitude for business and predicted that the already strong demand for the fiber would continue to increase.

It was not a popular decision with the slaves, but of course we had no say in the matter. Cotton was a difficult crop. It was hard to plant, challenging to maintain, and laborious to pick. During the harvest slaves worked from sunrise to sunset, bent low over the hated plants, adding cotton to a sack looped over their shoulders that they pulled along behind them. Each downy white tuft was surrounded by a sharp boll, and after my fingers had been pricked dozens of times, they bled, throbbed, and ached constantly. As with most children on the plantation, I went to work in the fields when I was five years old. I worked next to my mother, who showed me how to pick the cotton without getting stuck.

When a picker's sack was full, it was emptied onto a large burlap blanket. Each of us had our own blanket, and in that way the overseer, Mr. Fox, could judge our output. Time in the fields passed slowly, and most slaves sang as they picked. It seemed to make the time pass a little faster. Someone would call out the verse, and everyone would sing a response. I didn't know the songs when I started working the fields, but I soon knew them well enough.

My mother, Emaline, was a petite woman with sharply defined features, high cheekbones, and dark, inquisitive eyes. Her skin was a rich shade of brown, and she had short, curly hair, which complemented and framed her face to advantage. She seemed always to be in motion, and I loved watching her brisk, economical movements.

She was also a skilled seamstress who made all our clothes with whatever bits of cloth she could find. She also made quilts, tablecloths, curtains, and all manner of other decorative items for the Parkers. But her most important job, the one she treasured above all others, was to grow and collect medicinal plants and look after the plantation's sick or injured slaves.

They would come to her in the evening, after the day's work was done, or on Sunday, which was our free day. Sometimes she would visit them in their cabins. They came with all manner of complaints. Fevers, pain, breathing or stomach ailments, cuts, burns, broken bones, anything really. She also ministered to those that had been whipped or punished by Mr. Fox.

Some folks called her a doctress, which was not accurate as she rarely invoked charms or spells. But like her mother before her, and her mother's mother, she was from a line of healers that went back many generations. Back to a time before they were brought to America.

The sickest slaves would be kept in the plantation hospital, a small wooden structure that sat alone between the slave quarters and the main house. The building, which had a noticeable lean, had been constructed haphazardly, as if neither it nor its inhabitants were expected to last for very long.

The plantation was less than a two-hour ride from town, and when Dr. Parker was in residence, he took over the medical care of the slaves. His treatments, which included bloodletting, purging, and violent emetics, were much more aggressive than those employed by my mother. Knowing this, unless they were very ill indeed, most folks tried hard to get back on their feet before Dr. Parker came calling. In his absence, he depended on my mother to keep the slaves healthy, knowing she was considered a healer in her own right.

One afternoon, while my mother and I were in the fields, Mr. Fox felt that a boy named Peter was not working quickly enough. I knew Peter well. I was six and he was perhaps two years older than me. It was a hot, cloudless day, unseasonably warm for October, and the sun bore down on us relentlessly. For some time, Peter had been suffering from stomach worms. My mother had treated him with Jerusalem oak seed tea, and he'd expelled many of them, but the experience had clearly left him drained. Working just two rows from me, Peter was moving slowly, stopping from time to time to catch his breath. Everyone could see he was struggling to keep up.

Suddenly Mr. Fox rode up to Peter, looming over him on his tall gray horse. He unfurled his whip and lashed down at him. Everyone froze, but we quickly returned to our work, not wanting to invite the same type of attention. Peter fell to the ground, stunned, but he was too slow to rise. For his sluggishness, he was rewarded with two more lashes.

Later that night, after we'd finished a supper of pork and flour cakes, my mother went to check on Peter. When she got back to our cabin, she called for me. "Henry, come inside. I need to talk to you."

We shared a one-room wooden shack situated at the end of the row of slave cabins, near the hospital. I was kneeling on the ground a few feet in front of the cabin, poking a fat black beetle with a long twig. When I heard my mother call, I picked up a mussel shell lying nearby and placed it over the beetle, hoping to detain my prize for later examination.

The cabin we shared had a narrow bed in one corner, a straw pallet where I slept, and a single window, just to the right of the door. A table and two chairs sat in the middle of the floor. A large fireplace, built of big, rough-hewn stones, was on the back wall. But the cabin's most striking feature, the one most often discussed, or ridiculed, by other inhabitants of the slave quarters, was my mother's huge plant collection. Nearly every interior wall of the cabin, excepting where the fireplace and windows were, was covered with plant specimens. All manner of bark, leaves, stems, flowers, and seeds lined the shelves on the walls, while mushrooms and roots hung in bunches from the ceiling. A few were freshly cut, but most were dried or had been ground to powder. There were samples of barberry, candle bush, horsemint, juniper, manroot, wormseed, elderberry, goldenseal, coneflower, false unicorn, asafetida, burdock root, witch hazel, and dozens of others. Like me, my mother couldn't read, but she knew the name and use of every plant in the cabin.

When I got to the door she looked up and said, "Come in here and sit down, Henry." She was at the table, and I could tell from her stiff posture that something was bothering her. The only movement in the room came from the burning logs in the fireplace, which cast long shadows that writhed and danced across the floor. She repeated her request, more gently this time. "Come here, Henry. Come on now." I crossed the last few feet to the table and sat down.

"What's wrong, Momma?"

She looked at her hands, and after letting out a sigh looked directly at me. "It breaks my heart to see you working the fields like me." She got up and poked at the fire before continuing. "I've seen what happens to people that spend their life in the fields. Skin baked hard like leather, fingers and hands twisted, and backs so bowed they can hardly stand up straight. I don't want that for you."

I thought about some of the older slaves on the plantation and frowned. "That's not going to happen to you, is it, Momma?"

"Don't worry about me. I'll be all right," she said with a slight smile. "But you're just a boy, you shouldn't have to work like me. You understand what I'm saying?"

I thought for a moment before answering. "Yes, Momma, I think so. You don't want me to work in the fields anymore."

For an instant, she looked as if she might cry. "No, Henry, I guess I don't. But there is nothing we can do about that right now. You've got to work in the fields because that's all they think you can do. But they're wrong." She considered me in silence for a moment before continuing. "You're my only child. I don't think I'll ever have another," she said sadly. "Besides, I'm not getting any younger. It's past time I started to teach you what I know about plants. I wasn't much older than you when I started learning. I'm going to teach you everything my mother taught me." Then she smiled and added conspiratorially, "I'm even going to show you a few things I learned on my own, things even my mother never knew."

I shifted in my chair but said nothing.

"What's the matter, Henry? Don't you want to learn?"

I looked at the floor and said, "Yes, Momma."

"Well then, what's wrong with you?"

"I thought healers had to be ladies like you," I said. I was startled by my mother's hearty laugh.

"It's true, most of the healers in our family have been women, but some were men," she said with a smile. "In fact," she added, rubbing her chin thoughtfully, "there may be more men that are healers than women."

I brightened for the first time since entering the cabin. I knew the story of our family, having heard my mother recite the names of our ancestors many times. In fact, I could remember all the names myself. Somehow, it hadn't occurred to me that a man could be a healer, but I found that I liked the idea. My mother was known by all the slaves on the plantation. Though some of the more superstitious folks feared her, she was respected by most. Even Dr. Parker recognized her deep knowledge of the natural world.

"All right, Momma, I want to learn."

She nodded slowly. "Good, Henry, that's good. Tomorrow is Sunday, so we don't have to go to the fields. We'll get started after breakfast."

CHAPTER 2

SOJOURN

October 1842

The next morning at sunrise we shared a bowl of corn meal porridge, seasoned with a small slice of pork fat. After breakfast, my mother put on a broad straw hat and picked up her collecting bag and walking stick. Inside the bag she carried her mattock, a small tool she used for digging up roots. Some of the plants were for her own use, but most of what she collected was for Dr. Parker, though she said she wasn't sure what he did with them.

"When I was about your age, my mother started teaching me how to use what nature provided to keep healthy."

"Dr. Parker doesn't mind if we leave the plantation?" I asked.

She shrugged. "I suppose he tolerates it because healthy slaves do more work than sick ones," she said, with a trace of bitterness in her voice.

Although I had left the working portion of the farm to walk the broader property with my mother many times, doing so always filled me with apprehension. While in many ways the plantation was an oppressive place, it was also my home, the only home I had ever known, and I was not at all comfortable leaving to trek into the wilderness. In contrast, my mother was never more at ease than when she was in the woods, surrounded by the trees and plants she loved.

The other reason for my discomfort was that it was possible that we might encounter a local slave patrol. This was particularly true on Sundays, when slaves weren't working in the fields and the patrols were most active. The patrollers operated in teams of three or four men. They had been given authority from the local magistrate to search for and apprehend runaways. If they encountered a slave without a pass, they could punish them immediately with up to thirty-nine lashes. But in truth, they could whip the slave as much as they liked, if they took some care not to kill them. My mother knew the borders of the plantation well and was careful to never leave the Parker property. But the patrollers didn't always respect property lines, so we were always cautious.

It was a crisp, clear morning, and the sun was still low in the sky when we left the cabin. A few of the slaves were already outside, and they watched as we walked past the quarters. Some spoke as we passed.

"Morning, Emaline."

"Emaline, where you off to?"

"Emaline, if you see any rabbits out there, put one in your bag for me."

Other slaves simply regarded us in silence. Some of them didn't approve of her work, or her association with Dr. Parker. But I also suspected many of them wished they could also walk the grounds as freely as she did.

My mother returned all the greetings, and she even stopped a few times to inquire about someone's health. She then went to the slave hospital to look in on her patient. On that day, the hospital had only one occupant, a withered slave everyone called Old Tom. He didn't stir when we came in. His daughter, Rachel, was lying in the next bed, keeping vigil. She watched as my mother checked on the old man and tried to get him to take some water or eat a bit of the corn porridge she had made earlier. But he seemed beyond caring about such earthly things as food and water. She left the porridge with Rachel, and we continued on our way.

"Momma, what's wrong with him? Is he going to die?"

"He has something eating away at him from the inside. There is nothing we can do now, except try to ease his pain."

Soon the quarters were behind us as we headed west along a track that cut across the cotton fields. The path ended at a copse of woods that marked part of the boundary of the plantation. We then turned south, walking parallel to the trees, before cutting through an open meadow. My mother set a steady pace and I had to walk fast not to fall behind. Without warning, she turned west again and picked up a trail that was barely discernible. When we finally crossed Little Sugar Creek, we disappeared into the trees.

Entering the woods was like stepping into another world. Outside, the morning sun shone hot under a bright blue October sky. But once inside, the sky gave way to a dense thicket of leaves and branches, dappled here and there with a diffuse light. Many of the trees were hung with thick vines that completely obscured their trunks. It seemed to me that they were being slowly devoured and one day only the vines would remain. An assortment of low plants covered the ground, and as we passed, I could hear the rustle of countless unseen creatures moving through the undergrowth. After a short time, we reached a small clearing, and my mother stopped before turning to me.

"Listen to me now, Henry. You been to the woods with me plenty of times, but it takes a long time to *know* the woods. We're blessed because the Lord has put so much here for us. Still, you have got to know what to look for, where to find it, and how to use it." She reached down and picked a handful of small green leaves. "We can get almost everything we need from these woods, but medicine and food are the most important." With that, she put some of the green leaves into her mouth and started chewing. She handed a few to me, and after a pause, I tried them as well.

"There are a lot of plants, berries, nuts, and roots out here that are edible. Knowing what you can eat just might save you one day. There are also a lot of things that can make you sick, or even kill you. The trick is to know the difference. This is chickweed. It grows all around here, and you can eat it."

She started walking again and I stuffed another handful of the small green leaves into my mouth before running to catch up. As she moved through the trees, she continued speaking.

"Most days I come out here looking for something special. Don't get me wrong—if I see anything else I can use I will take it too. Today we need to find some holly bark, flagroot, and dogwood."

"What do we need those for, Momma?"

"Well, Sissy's baby girl is colicky, so I'm going to make some dogwood tea for her. The flagroot is for Benny. He's having stomach trouble again and chewing flagroot seems to help. Now, a holly bark tea can help stop coughing, and right now, we've got plenty of folks in the quarters with a cough."

For several hours my mother and I collected samples. We found a young holly and stripped off some of the bark before moving on and locating the flagroot and dogwood she needed. She also collected some sicklepod, pennyroyal, kola seeds, and bloodroot for Dr. Parker. As we moved carefully through the trees, my mother explained everything she was seeing and doing. She had been learning about plants and their medicinal uses since she was a girl, and it was evident that she knew her subject well.

As she worked, she told me what each plant and root was used for, how to recognize them, when to collect the material, and how it should be stored and prepared. My mother's features became animated as she described the natural world. She had honed her skill with plants over a lifetime, and I was her first student. Perhaps then, it wasn't surprising that she would be excited to finally share her knowledge with someone, particularly her son. I certainly wanted to learn, and I tried hard to pay close attention to her lessons. However, I was still a child, and like most children I was easily distracted.

"Henry, are you listening to me?"

Startled, I looked up quickly while the object of my interest, a large orange-and-black butterfly, drifted away on the breeze.

"Yes, Momma, I'm listening."

Her eyes narrowed as she studied me. "It doesn't look like you're listening. If you want to learn you have to pay attention!"

"I know, Momma, I've been listening. I heard everything you said."

She put her hands on her hips. "All right then, Henry. Why don't you tell me what I was saying?" she challenged.

I didn't want to disappoint her, but I didn't see how I would ever be able to remember everything. She had been talking all morning. Nonetheless, I tried to recall what she had said. I squeezed my eyes shut and tried hard to remember all that had happened since we entered the woods. As I concentrated, I drifted deeper and deeper into my memories, until the physical world fell away. Then suddenly, as if a locked door had been thrown open, something remarkable happened. With effort, I found that I could remember everything that my mother had told me. Everything, every single word! I could clearly see all the events of that morning, strung together like beads on a necklace. The past came rushing back to me, whole and intact. Most startling of all, as I continued to concentrate, I could even recall things my mother had said weeks, or even months ago. It was an odd, disorienting sensation.

My mother looked at me with concern. "Henry, are you feeling sick? You lost all your color."

The sound of her voice pulled me roughly back to the present. "I'm all right, Momma. I'm fine. It's just that, well, I remember what you said. I remember everything you said."

Her brow furrowed as she studied me with a critical eye. Finally, satisfying herself that I was not ill, she assumed the posture of a teacher addressing a willful student. "Well, go on then, Henry, what did I say?"

I closed my eyes and once again connected to the memories. It was a little easier this time. Taking a deep breath, I slowly started to recite my mother's exact words, everything she'd said since we entered the woods that morning. Once I tapped into the past, I became little more than a vessel, a passive conduit through which the words flowed. I'm not sure how long I spoke, but I eventually became aware that my mother was repeating my name and shaking me.

"Henry, Henry, stop!" I opened my eyes to find her looking at me with a mixture of fear and astonishment. Releasing me, she sat down heavily with her back against a thick oak. I tried to say something more, but she held up her hands for silence, lost in her own thoughts.

I sat down beside her, and we didn't speak for some time. Finally, she seemed to come to a decision. "It's a gift, Henry, a gift from God," she said, looking at me directly. "I don't know why he chose to give you such ability, but I know that he must have had a good reason. The Lord doesn't make mistakes."

* * *

We didn't talk much on the way back to the plantation. However, when we were back in our cabin, she put a hand on my shoulder. "You listen to me now, Henry, because this is important. You understand?" she asked seriously.

"Yes, Momma." I nodded.

"You can't tell anybody about how you can remember things. Do you hear me? You can't tell any of your friends, or that girl Marcie that you trail after all the time. You can't tell anybody." She took my face between her hands for emphasis. "You have to promise me."

"All right, Momma, I promise. I won't tell anybody."

"That's good, Henry, because folks won't know what to make of this, and there could be real trouble. People are superstitious, and it doesn't take much for them to blame their problems on someone else, and I don't want that someone to be you."

CHAPTER 3

REVELATION

May 1843

My training progressed quickly then, particularly after my mother learned how best to use my "gift," as she had taken to calling it. In time, she trusted that she could tell me the name of every plant and root she knew, and she marveled that no matter how much information she presented to me, I could recall exactly what she had said. However, over time, we came to realize that there were clear limits to my abilities. Although I remembered everything she said, I did not necessarily understand the *meaning* behind her words. For example, she might tell me that we use jimsonweed for rheumatism, or a mustard plaster to treat pneumonia. Though I could repeat her words verbatim, I would not have been able to describe the features of either disease. I might know how to treat dropsy, but I had no idea how to recognize it in an affected person. Still, I was only six years old, and my mother felt that I was making remarkable progress. She also believed that, with time, my depth of understanding would improve, and that we would have many more years to continue our lessons. It turned out that, on this last point, she could not have been more wrong.

As I have already recounted, on many Sundays my mother and I would typically rise with the sun and, following a light meal, head into the woods to collect the specimens she required. However, on those Sundays when Dr. and Mrs. Parker were at the plantation, all the slaves were required to gather on the broad lawn in front of the main house for Sunday morning service. In truth, it wasn't much of a service, but rather consisted of Mrs. Parker reciting a few verses from the Bible. She would stand on the front porch, at the top of the stairs, and read to all of us below. Mrs. Parker seemed more comfortable with the Bible than Dr. Parker did, and though he was always in attendance during Sunday services, he never read from Scripture.

The two of them, standing side by side on the porch, presented quite a contrast. Dr. Parker was a large man with a broad face and penetrating brown eyes. His thinning hair was always a bit too long, and in constant need of attention. He was known to be a man of considerable learning and intellect, who had the ability to focus intently on those things he found interesting. In contrast, Mrs. Parker was a slight woman, with a narrow face and small, hard eyes. She was born into privilege, and her usual expression suggested a slight distaste for everything and everyone around her. She kept her hair pulled back tightly into a bun, and although her clothing tended toward the drab, she was always neat and tidy in appearance. They had one child, an energetic little boy named Matthew, who stood to the left of his father, partially hidden behind his nanny's skirt.

The overseer, Mr. Fox, was also a constant presence at Sunday services, though he was not there as a worshipper. Instead, he stood at the far-left corner of the porch watching us intently. Perhaps he was concerned that we might suddenly all decide to revolt, as Nat Turner had done eleven years earlier. Of course, at the time none of us knew anything about Nat Turner, his ill-fated rebellion, or the chilling effect it had on the psyche of slaveholders.

Mr. Fox had stringy black hair partially covering a tanned, angular face, with narrowly spaced, hooded eyes. He had very large hands and forearms, and a barrel chest. He liked to describe himself as a fair man, and he would often repeat this adage as he was meting out punishment to some unfortunate soul. He seemed to always be in a bad humor, with one notable exception. His mood was noticeably lighter when he was in the process of inflicting pain on someone.

I remember that Sunday vividly. It was a clear, crisp spring morning, and as we stood in the grass waiting for Mrs. Parker to begin, I listened to birdsong coming from the trees that flanked the house. The grass was cool and damp beneath my feet, and I wiggled my toes, waiting. My friend Marcie stood next to me, swaying slightly from side to side.

Finally, Mrs. Parker stepped to the top of the stairs and gave us all a wan smile. She said she would be reading a selection from Ephesians. I had heard this text before, and of course, I already knew it forward and back.

> *And, ye fathers, provoke not your children to wrath: but bring them up in the nurture and admonition of the Lord;*
>
> *Servants, be obedient to them that are your masters according to the flesh, with fear and trembling, in singleness of your heart, as unto Christ;*
>
> *Not with eyeservice, as menpleasers; but as the servants of Christ, doing the will of God from the heart;*
>
> *With good will doing service, as to the Lord, and not to men;*

*Knowing that whatsoever good thing any man
doeth, the same shall he receive of the Lord,
whether he be bond or free.*

Even now, I have no explanation for what happened
next. It was early in the day, and perhaps I was still a
bit drowsy. Alternatively, I might have been distracted,
because as Mrs. Parker spoke the birds sang even louder,
as if they too were vying for our attention. It's also
possible that I was trying to impress Marcie. I can't say
why I did it, but I do know I felt a sense of anonymity,
standing among so many others on the lawn. I certainly
didn't think I would be noticed.

In any case, as soon as Mrs. Parker started reading, I
closed my eyes and began quietly reciting the verse with
her. At least, I thought I was being quiet. With my eyes
shut, still repeating the lines from Ephesians to myself, I
didn't immediately notice that Mrs. Parker had stopped
speaking altogether! It was only the urgent hiss of my
mother's voice that broke through my reverie.

"Henry, be quiet!"

When I opened my eyes, I saw that everyone was
looking at me curiously. Mrs. Parker closed her Bible
slowly and regarded me coldly.

"What is your name, boy?"

I looked to my mother for help, and she said, "He
didn't mean any disrespect, missus, he's just a boy."

Never taking her eyes from me, Mrs. Parker said, "I wasn't talking to you, Emaline. I asked the boy his name."

My mother looked down and said, "Yes ma'am," before prodding me to answer.

Feeling very uncomfortable at being the center of attention, I managed to stammer a reply. "Hen-Henry, ma'am, my name is Henry."

"Well, Henry, how is it that you know this verse?"

I wasn't sure how to respond. I desperately looked again to my mother for guidance, but it was clear that she could not help me. I could feel everyone watching expectantly to see what I would say, to see how this would end. Marcie backed away from me.

"Has someone been teaching you to read?" she asked pointedly, her attention shifting to my mother.

Bringing her head up sharply, my mother shouted, "No ma'am, he can't read. He works in the fields all day. No one has taught him to read!"

Mrs. Parker snapped, "Emaline, you be quiet now. I'm not going to tell you again. I asked the boy a question." Returning her gaze to me, she said, "I'm going to ask you once more. How is it that you know this verse?"

What could I say? How should I respond? We all knew that reading was a serious offense, ensuring a swift and severe punishment. I didn't know how to read, and I was afraid of being punished, particularly for something I hadn't done. For some time, I didn't say anything, but as Mr. Fox started moving toward me, I found my voice at last.

"I remember it, ma'am."

"Remember it? Remember it from where?"

"From you, ma'am. I heard you say it before."

I heard low snickering from nearby slaves, and Mr. Fox, who had now reached my side, took a rough grip on my arm. "The boy is lying! Leave him to me, Mrs. Parker, and I'll soon get the truth from him."

"Thank you, Mr. Fox. I'll let you know when I require your assistance." Mr. Fox said nothing more but maintained his hold on my arm. Now I was genuinely terrified. I knew that no matter what Mrs. Parker said, if this man wanted to hurt me, there was nothing anyone could do to stop him.

"What do you mean you heard it from me?" Mrs. Parker looked at her husband, who was taking in the entire scene impassively. "I haven't read that particular verse for"—she paused—"many months." Would you have us believe that you remember it from so long ago?"

I blurted out, "No ma'am. I mean, yes ma'am. I remember it. I remember everything you said. I remember all sorts of things." I desperately wanted to run away and hide in the brush behind our cabin, or even in the woods. But after risking a glance at Mr. Fox, I knew there was no escape.

Mrs. Parker seemed on the verge of exasperation, but before she could respond, Dr. Parker spoke for the first time. "Henry, is it? You're Emaline's boy, aren't you?"

Dr. Parker had never spoken to me directly. My mouth and throat had gone bone dry, and I needed to swallow several times before speaking. "Yes sir."

He consulted briefly with his wife before continuing. "Well, Henry, Mrs. Parker has not read that passage for quite some time. I don't think it likely that you would remember it from so long ago. Perhaps someone else has been reading the Bible to you? You can tell me about it. No one will be in trouble. I can't very well be angry with someone for reading the Bible, can I?" He shared a look with Mr. Fox, who smiled unpleasantly, flashing a gold tooth. "Has someone been reading the Bible to you, Henry?"

"No sir, no sir. I remember what Mrs. Parker said."

Dr. Parker regarded me for a moment before continuing. "I won't tolerate lying, do you understand?" Although he was speaking to me, the tone of his voice suggested he was addressing his comments to everyone assembled.

"Yes sir, I'm not lying. I remember what she said." My legs were shaking so badly now that I might have collapsed, had it not been for the firm grip of Mr. Fox.

Dr. Parker looked at me evenly. "Very well, we will put an end to this nonsense. Mrs. Parker read another passage that day. I suppose you remember it as well?"

Everyone was quiet as they waited for my answer. Even the birds had stopped singing. Looking back on my life, I now recognize there are times when you reach a crossroads. This was such a time. Answering no to Dr. Parker would have earned me a beating, likely a severe one, but my life on the plantation could have continued. In contrast, although I didn't know it then, an answer of yes had the potential to set my life on a completely different course.

Taking a deep breath, I said, "Yes sir, I remember what Mrs. Parker said that day."

A low murmur went through the assembled slaves, perhaps believing that I had finally gone too far. No doubt, many felt that I had taken leave of my senses. My mother was still looking at the ground.

Mr. Fox shouted, "Dr. Parker, sir, let me take this boy out of here and teach him some manners. He's lying to your face and wasting our damned time." Glancing quickly at Mrs. Parker, he added, "Sorry, ma'am."

Dr. Parker held up his hand for silence, and he said in a voice shot through with menace, "Well then, Henry, what other verse did Mrs. Parker read that day?"

I was so frightened that I didn't know if, in fact, I would be able to recall the passage. I closed my eyes, tried hard to focus, and prayed that I would remember. Then, after what seemed an interminable delay, the words came rushing back to me. Without preamble, and with my eyes still tightly shut, I started speaking quickly:

> *Servants, be subject to your masters with all fear; not only to the good and gentle, but also to the fro . . . fro-ward.*
>
> *For this is thankworthy, if a man for conscience toward God endure grief, suffering wrongfully.*
>
> *For what glory is it, if, when ye be buffeted for your faults, ye shall take it patiently? But if, when ye do well, and suffer for it, ye take it patiently, this is acceptable with God.*
>
> *For even here . . . unto were ye called: because Christ also suffered for us, leaving us an example, that ye should follow his steps:*
>
> *Who did no sin, neither was guile found in his mouth:*
>
> *Who, when he was . . .*

The sound of Dr. Parker's booming voice broke my concentration. "Stop! That's enough, stop."

I opened my eyes and saw Dr. Parker and Mrs. Parker looking at me strangely. Mrs. Parker had one hand wrapped tightly around her belly while the other covered her mouth. Dr. Parker spoke with her briefly, and then said, "Nellie, you and Emaline get the boy cleaned up and bring him to my office after lunch. And see if you can find him some shoes." Without another word, he turned and went inside.

Mr. Fox released his grip on my arm and gave me a withering look before moving away. Although many of the slaves exchanged glances, or stole a brief look at me, no one spoke. Mrs. Parker, left alone on the porch by the abrupt departure of her husband, seemed unsure about how to proceed. Finally, she said, "That's all for today. You are dismissed." With that she turned and followed her husband into the house.

The slaves were talking and laughing as they started to drift away. This was the most excitement anyone had ever had at Mrs. Parker's Sunday service. As they left, I overheard some of them talking.

"Have you ever seen anything like that?"

"You see Mrs. Parker? She was white as a sheet."

My friend Marcie walked up to me and smiled. "You sure are something, Henry." She rubbed my hair before moving away with the others.

Only Nellie, my mother, and I were left in the yard, and Nellie didn't seem happy to be there. With a grimace she said, "Come on then, let's get you cleaned up as best we can." Momma and I trailed behind Nellie, kicking up small clouds of red clay dust as we went. A mottled brown chicken trotted across our path and disappeared into the shadows under the house. We walked around the side of the building, past the kitchen house, and covered the short distance to the barn in silence. "Emaline, pump some water into the trough while I get soap and some rags." Nellie gave me an appraising look and said, "I'll see if I can find you some clean clothes while I'm at it." Before leaving, she sighed softly and said, "Lordie, I never seen anything like that in all my life." She appeared to be on the verge of saying something more but, instead, simply turned and went back toward the house.

Though it was still early in the day, the cool air was beginning to dissipate, replaced by a pleasant warmth. Without saying a word, my mother started pumping water into the old wooden trough that stood outside the barn. She hadn't spoken to me since the service.

"You all right, Momma?" I ventured. She didn't look up but pumped even faster. Just by looking at her back, I could tell that she was mad.

"Momma, I'm sorry. I didn't mean to say anything."

She stopped pumping, her hands still tightly clenched around the rusted handle. She turned to me and said through clenched teeth, "Then why on earth did you say *anything*? You know better than to talk during Missus's Sunday service, and you promised me we would keep this to ourselves. Didn't I warn you there could be trouble if it came out?" Then, shaking her head, she hissed, "You must have lost your mind!"

I knew that I had made a serious mistake, but I couldn't do anything about it now. Suddenly overwhelmed by fear, I could feel tears start to roll down my cheeks. "I'm sorry Momma, I'm sorry. I didn't think they could hear me!"

With her jaw still clenched tightly, she said, "Well, they heard you, that's for sure."

I calmed myself as best I could and managed to ask the question that was weighing heavily on my mind. "Momma, what does Dr. Parker want with me?"

Nellie was on her way back, carrying a bucket in one hand and a bundle of clothes under the other arm. Momma made an unpleasant sound and said, "I don't know what that man wants with you, but whatever it is, I expect he's going to get it."

CHAPTER 4

PRELUDE

May 1843

They stripped off my clothes and gave me a good scrubbing. When they were done, I put on the clean wardrobe that Nellie had found. The shirt fit well enough, but the pants were too big, and Nellie cinched them at the waist with a length of rope from the barn. The clothing was not new, but it was much nicer than anything I had ever worn before. My old shirt and pants were threadbare and tattered, little more than rags. The pants had been pieced together from remnants of fabric, while the shirt, ripped and frayed, had hung loosely from my small frame. I felt uncomfortable in the new clothes and started to squirm. I wanted to take them off, but as

I looked at my discarded clothing lying on the ground, I knew that I didn't want to put those back on either.

The rest of the morning passed uneventfully. I accompanied my mother as she made her rounds, first to the slave hospital, then to several cabins in the quarters. My new wardrobe was a curiosity and drew quite a few stares and comments from the other slaves. My mother said little, and when we got back to our cabin, she told me to go inside. It was Sunday and I wanted to be with my friends, but she told me I needed to stay clean. She said that her and Nellie weren't about to wash me twice in one day. Momma sat outside the cabin, smoking from an old clay pipe, seemingly lost in thought. When she finally came in she got a fire going and fried two flour cakes in lard. We ate these in silence, washed down with some warm milk.

After lunch Momma said, "Well, I guess we better get you up to the house." There were so many questions I wanted to ask that my anxiety must have been plainly visible. Sensing my mood, she said softly, "Listen, Henry, I don't know what Dr. Parker wants with you, but you got yourself into this. Just do what he tells you, and let's pray that will be enough."

As we walked toward the main house, I felt a mixture of fear and excitement. Fear because Dr. Parker, who had never spoken to me until that morning, quite literally held my life in his hands. With a nod, or a snap of his fingers, he could turn me over to Mr. Fox, and that was a horror I dared not ponder. However, although frightened, I was also excited by the prospect of doing something different. Something, anything, that would disrupt the tedium of my day-to-day life. Until that day I had never been to the main house or worn such nice clothes. I had never been fretted over by Nellie or been the center of attention in the quarters. As a slave, one learned early on that there was safety in anonymity, and as a boy I had always tried to make myself as small and inconspicuous as possible. But in my heart, I longed for more, and I felt a child's pride that someone had taken notice of me. As I grappled with these conflicting emotions we emerged from the trees and walked across the broad lawn for my meeting with Dr. Parker.

* * *

We went to the back of the house and climbed the worn stairs. My mother pulled me into a brief but fierce hug. Her sudden embrace surprised me, as she wasn't inclined to give many hugs. In fact, I was so startled that I'm ashamed to say I didn't have a chance to hug her back. Nellie came out of the door accompanied by Sam, an old slave who had been with Dr. Parker for as long as anyone could remember. Sam had a kind face, close-cropped white hair, and walked with a pronounced limp. I didn't know much about Sam. He spent most of his time in Charlotte, but he always accompanied Dr. Parker on his visits to the plantation, and sometimes he would come to the slave quarters in the evening and play his fiddle, to the delight of all.

My mother held on to me for a moment longer before saying, "Henry, you go with Nellie and Sam now. They'll take you to Dr. Parker. I'll see you when you're done. Go on now." Reluctantly I followed them into the house, leaving my mother behind.

Once inside, Sam stopped and appraised me closely. When he spoke to Nellie, his voice was deep and unhurried. "I'll take the boy in to see Dr. Parker. You best keep working on Sunday dinner." Still looking at me, he continued, "I don't know what Dr. Parker plans to do this afternoon, but come four o'clock, I can guarantee he'll be ready for his supper." Nellie's only reply was a grunt, whereupon she went back to her work. Sam rubbed his chin thoughtfully and said, "Well, come on, Henry."

I followed him down a dimly lit corridor toward the front foyer. Just a few hours earlier I had been outside, standing on the lawn. I had often wondered what might be inside the big house, but now I was standing there. Sam stopped at a door on the right and knocked softly. I heard a muffled reply from the other side, and he turned to me and said, "Wait right here." After a pause he added, "I don't suppose I need to tell you more than once." He smiled down at me before opening the door and stepping inside.

While I was waiting, I had a moment to examine my surroundings more carefully. I was standing just inside the front door, and I was certain I had never seen anything so beautiful. The floor was made of wide, polished wood planks, covered by a large red-and-blue-fringed rug. On the left wall there was a small gray velvet settee, and on the opposite wall stood a wooden hutch with intricate inlaid designs. A broad oak staircase led to the second floor. There were several paintings on the walls, and somewhere in the background I could hear the soft ticking of a clock. I jumped at the sound of a voice behind me.

"Did you really remember all of those Bible passages?" I turned to see Mrs. Parker standing at the end of the hall. She moved closer and said, "More likely it was some type of trick, like a magician. Was that it?"

Before I could respond the door opened and Sam was standing beside me. "Oh, my apologies, Mrs. Parker. I didn't mean to interrupt. Dr. Parker is ready for the boy now."

Still looking at me she said coolly, "Well, go on then. Whatever it is you're hiding, I guarantee he'll get to the bottom of it."

Sam held the door open and upon entering the room I was immediately struck by a general sense of chaos.

Unlike the neat hallway in which I'd been standing, this room was a mess. Dr. Parker sat behind a large ornate desk, hunched over an open book. The windows were hung with dark curtains, which were partially open, allowing shafts of sunlight to spill into the room. There was a faded rug of indeterminate color covering the floor, and two well-worn armchairs faced the desk. Books, pamphlets, and papers were strewn everywhere. They sat in bookshelves, on overcrowded tables and chairs, and were stacked in uneven piles on the floor. Dr. Parker looked up, clearly annoyed. "Sam, where are his shoes?"

"I'm sorry, Dr. Parker," he replied in that preternaturally calm voice, "Nellie couldn't find any that would fit the boy."

Frowning, Dr. Parker waved his hand dismissively, briefly agitating the dust that hung in the air. "All right, that's all for now, Sam. I'll call for you when I'm done."

"Yes sir," Sam said, before quietly closing the door behind him.

Dr. Parker shut the book on his desk and snapped, "Well, don't just stand there gawking, come over here."

"Yes sir." I moved forward until I was standing a few feet from the desk.

He peered at me over the top of his spectacles. "Well, Henry, that was quite a performance you put on this morning. I checked with Mrs. Parker, and she confirmed that you recited those Bible verses word for word. She doesn't know how that was possible and, frankly, neither do I." He seemed to be waiting for a response.

I wasn't sure what to say, so I whispered, "Yes sir."

"You said that you can remember everything that you have heard. Is that right?"

I nodded. "Yes sir."

"I don't believe you," he said flatly. "I think that someone taught you those verses and that's how you know them. I told you this morning that I won't tolerate lying. Is that clear?"

My mouth had gone bone dry again, making it hard to speak. "Yes sir," I managed at last. "I'm not lying."

He drummed his fingers on the desk. "Well, I'll soon know the truth of it, and if it turns out that you have lied to me or wasted my time, I guarantee that you will live to regret it." With no further preamble, he picked up a book from his desk and started reading it aloud. He read perhaps two pages and then told me to repeat what I had heard. Many of the words were unfamiliar to me. In fact, I didn't understand the passage any more than those Mrs. Parker recited on Sundays. Nonetheless, I closed my eyes and did my best to repeat what I had just heard, stumbling over many of the words. No sooner had I finished than he turned to another section of the book and started reading again. This back-and-forth went on for quite some time, until I felt both mentally and physically drained. My head throbbed painfully, and

I desperately wanted to stop. But I knew that was not possible. As long as Dr. Parker kept going, I had to try to do the same. For what seemed an eternity I repeated passage after passage, no longer certain of the accuracy of my responses. Finally, just when I was sure I would not be able to continue, he stopped.

Looking toward the window, he took off his glasses and leaned back in the chair. After a moment he said, more to himself than to me, "Remarkable, simply remarkable. I have heard of this phenomenon, but . . ." He looked up sharply, as if he had just remembered I was still in the room. He stood and quickly moved toward the door, indicating that I should follow. We walked to the back of the house, where Sam was waiting. Dr. Parker turned to me and said, "You can go now. We'll talk again soon." Thrilled that my ordeal was finally over, I quickly left through the back door. Behind me, I heard Dr. Parker say, "Sam, go find Emaline and bring her to my office."

CHAPTER 5

CHANGE

May 1843

I bolted down the back stairs and ran across the wide lawn. I was anxious to tell my mother everything that had happened, but when I reached the cabin, she wasn't there. I searched the slave quarters, but I couldn't find her anywhere. She was not at the hospital with Old Tom, nor had anyone seen her recently. One of my mother's friends, a large man that worked the fields with us, was sitting in front of his shack, whittling.

"Toby, have you seen my mother?"

He took in my clothing and smiled before resuming his carving. "No, little master, I haven't seen her. I expect she is somewhere in those woods of hers."

She hadn't mentioned that she was going collecting that day, so I didn't think she had left the plantation. Perhaps Sam had already found her, and they had gone up to the house. I was disappointed. There were so many things I wanted to tell her about my time with Dr. Parker, and now I would have to wait. As I walked among the cabins, lost in thought, my friends saw me and started to gather round. They were anxious to hear what had happened and started to pepper me with questions.

It was good to see them, and my mood brightened immediately. We ran to the clearing behind our cabin, where I sat on an old stump. My best friends, Marcie and Ben, joined me there, and the others found places in the grass. I recounted my experiences of that afternoon, taking care not to omit a single detail. Like me, none of them had ever set foot in the house, and they wanted to know everything. The day had been difficult, but it was good to be with my friends again. Delighting in their company, I lost track of time. The sun had just dipped below the treetops when my mother found us there.

Hurriedly saying goodbye, I ran to her. "Momma, I've been looking for you."

She smiled and put an arm around my shoulder as we went into the cabin. Although I had just told the story to my friends, I didn't mind in the least repeating it to her. I was so excited that I spoke in a rush, scarcely taking a breath. She didn't interrupt and asked no questions.

Children can be very self-absorbed, so perhaps it's not surprising that, initially, I didn't notice my mother's somber mood. As I continued to talk, she slowly wiped her hands on her apron. I studied her profile in the fading light, and at that moment, she seemed much older than her twenty-five years.

"Are you okay, Momma?" I asked quietly.

She didn't answer, but I noticed she had started to twist the apron with her hands.

"Momma, what's wrong?"

She looked at me blankly, and though typically never at a loss for words, she seemed to be struggling for something to say. "Henry, you know that I have always wanted the best for you. You know that, don't you?"

"I know, Momma."

"Sometimes it's hard to know what's best. Sometimes the only thing you can do is put your faith in the Lord." She nodded vigorously, as if convinced of the truth of her own statement.

"What do you mean?"

Ignoring my question, she paced the room before continuing. "Maybe it's for the best. I just don't know, maybe it's for the best." She groaned and added angrily, "Hell, there isn't anything I can do about it anyway."

I interrupted her again, this time more forcefully. "Momma, what are you talking about?"

She sat at the table, and I did the same. After a moment, she took a long, ragged breath and said, "Dr. Parker says you have to go with him tomorrow. He's going to take you to live in Charlotte."

It took a moment for what she had said to register. Dr. Parker was taking me to Charlotte, away from the plantation? Why was he taking me away? "What about you, are you going too?"

She shook her head and managed a weak smile. "No, Henry, I'm not going. I've got to stay here and look after our folks. What would they do without me? Dr. Parker is taking you out of the fields and away from here. You're going to have a better life." Her voice faltering, she whispered, "It's what I always wanted for you."

I jumped up and ran to her, knocking over my chair in the process. "I don't want to leave you, Momma. Please don't make me go. I promise I won't ever say anything about being able to remember things. Please, Momma, don't let him take me!"

She held me tightly, comforting me as best she could, though by then her own tears were flowing freely. "I love you, Henry, you know that. You're my miracle boy and I will always love you. You'll get through this." She gently took my face in her hands. "Listen to me now. You're strong, and you're from a line of strong people. Don't ever forget that."

* * *

We lay together in her narrow bed that night, and she held me as I slept fitfully. I don't know if she slept at all. I was awakened just after dawn by the sound of birdsong outside our cabin. Without saying anything she got up, dressed quickly, and left. She came back a short time later with three brown eggs, which she cooked in a dollop of pork fat. She then mixed corn meal with water and fried a few corn cakes in the same pan. Eggs were a luxury for us and I didn't ask where, or how, she had obtained them. On any other occasion I would have savored such a treat, but on that morning, I seemed scarcely able to taste anything at all.

She emptied her collecting bag onto the table and started to fill it with a selection of dried plants and roots. As she placed each sample in the bag, she repeated its name and medicinal use. I expect that she knew this reminder was not necessary, and normally I would have told her so, but on that morning, I listened without comment. She wrapped up two corn cakes in a cloth for my trip and put them in the bag. There was nothing else to pack because I had no possessions to speak of. My most prized belonging was a small piece of black quartz that I had found one afternoon in the sweet potato field. However, when Momma prepared to place it in the bag, I told her I didn't want it. I said that she should keep it for me. I hoped that as long as she had my beautiful rock, we would stay connected, and I would see her again.

We walked toward the main house in silence, following the same path as the previous day. A shiny black carriage and a large wooden wagon were standing in front. Two horses were already harnessed to the carriage and wagon, while a third stood nearby. One of them turned his large head to watch our approach. A slave named Jackson was loading the wagon with baskets of fruit and vegetables from the plantation. He then climbed the front stairs and helped Sam carry down a large crate. As we approached, they lifted it into the the wagon. Jackson returned to the house while Sam wiped his brow with a rag that he pulled from his back pocket.

He took one look at my mother and said consolingly, "Don't fret, Emaline, I'll look after Henry. You have my word on that."

"Thank you, Sam. I would be in your debt. He didn't mean any harm—he's a good boy." She cast her gaze skyward, taking hold of the side of the wagon to steady herself. "Lord, Sam, I don't think I can do this. I prayed this day would never come. How can I go on without my boy?" She searched his face, as if looking for an answer, but Sam just shook his head and looked toward the house.

"We got to keep going, Emaline. You, me, Henry, we all got to keep going somehow." By then I was sobbing and clinging to my mother's arm. Sam ignored me and continued, "You know what happened to my boy. You tried to help him, and I appreciate everything you did, but . . ." He trailed off. "There is not a day that goes by when I don't think about him. But I had to go on. If I got myself sold off or killed, what good would that do? Your boy Henry is healthy and safe, and I promise I'll look out for him, like he was my own flesh and blood." Sensing movement from the house, he added hastily, "But right now, we got to get him in the wagon."

My mother nodded and roughly wiped her eyes. She bent down and held me tightly before allowing Sam to lift me into the back of the wagon. A moment later Jackson and Nellie emerged from the shadows covering the west side of the house. Jackson hoisted himself into the wagon's front seat and held out a hand for Nellie, who climbed in on the other side. After passing me the bag she had packed that morning, Momma held on to my hand. We were both crying now.

Dr. and Mrs. Parker came out of the house, followed by their son Matthew, his nanny Lucinda, and another Negro woman I did not recognize. The carriage had two upholstered bench seats, which faced each other. Lucinda settled into the forward seat, while Matthew and Mrs. Parker sat in the rear seat. Dr. Parker frowned when he saw my mother standing by the wagon.

"Emaline, we talked about this yesterday. Your being here isn't making this any easier for the boy. You best get on with your work now."

A dark look drifted across my mother's face, and for a moment it seemed that she might do, or say, something she would regret. In the end, however, she simply mumbled, "Yes sir," before moving away. The Negro woman clambered into the wagon and sat facing me. She was about the same age as my mother, but with a lighter complexion and curly brown hair. Although she said nothing, her face conveyed a great deal of sympathy.

Sam helped Dr. Parker onto his horse before he closed the carriage door and climbed into the driver's seat. Matthew leaned over the back seat, trying to get a better look at me. "Who is that and why is he crying?"

If there was a response, I didn't hear it, because at that moment Sam gave the reins a snap and the carriage started rolling. A moment later, Jackson got the wagon moving as well. I looked in the direction of the slave quarters, trying to locate my mother. I thought I saw someone standing at the edge of the trees, but it might have only been shadows.

We moved along the dirt track that ran from the house to the road. As we passed the cotton and sweet potato fields on our right, I could see that everyone was already hard at work. On any other day I would have been with them. As I turned to get a better look, several slaves stopped to watch our procession. I saw a girl that I thought was my friend Marcie, but from that distance I couldn't be certain. Mr. Fox rode into view on his large gray, and the field hands immediately returned to their work. Everything had happened so fast; there hadn't been time to accept my new reality. I felt like a great weight pressed on my chest, and my breathing became labored and shallow. I was being taken away from my mother and the life we shared. She had told me to be strong, and I wanted to be, but with rising panic I realized I didn't know how to do that without her.

As we left the plantation our procession turned north onto a narrow road hemmed in on both sides by thick green vegetation. The woman sharing the wagon with me said her name was Camille. She made several other attempts at conversation, but when I didn't reply she fell silent. We followed this route for more than an hour, passing several other large plantations and many small farms. One field bordered the road on which we traveled, and my heart lurched as I heard the field hands singing a familiar song.

This was the first time in my life that I had ever been so far from the Parker Plantation. I studied my surroundings closely, determined to remember every detail of the journey. If I ever got the opportunity, I wanted to be able to find my way back to my mother. Eventually we came to a much broader road that was clearly well traveled.

Camille said that this was the main road that led to town. Jackson turned the wagon west, and we headed toward Charlotte, and my new life.

CHAPTER 6

ARRIVAL

May 1843

After traveling along the road for some time, we crested a small rise and suddenly the town of Charlotte lay before us. Soon we were moving past numerous small homes and businesses. Buildings lined both sides of the road, more buildings than I had ever seen in one place. Many were emblazoned with colorful signs and placards:

Apothecary, Barber, Livery, Tannery, Dentist, Tailor, Cooper, Dry Goods, Boarding House, Solicitor, Cartage, General Store, Hardware, Millinery, Tavern, Wainwright

I didn't understand the writing, but still I made note of each one. I had grown up on a plantation, so while I did not recognize the words, many of the businesses we passed were familiar to me. I saw blacksmiths and carpenters, tanners, pigsties, and horse stables. There were colorfully painted structures with windows that displayed dresses and hats, and men's suits of clothing. Some buildings had tools, farm implements, or canvas bags filled with unknown goods stacked against their walls. Other establishments had no discernible purpose, but based on the sounds that spilled into the road, I imagined a raucous crowd within. In my short life I had never seen so many people or witnessed such a general commotion. As our small procession rolled on, a few people waved at the Parkers, but otherwise no one seemed to take note of our passage.

My senses were assaulted by a myriad of sounds and smells. Wagons rumbled by, horses trotted, pigs squealed, dogs barked, and blacksmiths' hammers pounded. Layered on all this was the constant clamor of people talking and shouting. Overwhelmed, I huddled deeper into the wagon. My distress must have been plainly evident, because the woman that had introduced herself as Camille moved to my side of the wagon and put an arm around me. Although I had just met this woman, I did not pull away.

With my eyes closed, I drifted back to memories of my mother with her plants, roots, and potions. I pictured her walking through the dappled sunlight of the woods. If I concentrated, I could see her face. I wished I were back on the plantation with her, instead of in this strange place.

After taking a right turn, we were soon in the very center of town, moving past larger and more elaborate structures, and a moment later, we passed an impressive brick building Camille said was the Presbyterian church. I had never seen anything like it, and I craned my neck to get a better look. Smooth stone steps led to a set of wide, polished double doors; there were tall stained-glass windows on either side of the doors and a much larger arched window directly above. Small towers rose from each corner, giving the structure a pleasing symmetry. But the most wonderful feature of the church was the tall, central steeple that rose high into the sky. It was designed to impress, and I marveled at how men had created such a magnificent building.

I thought that I would very much like to see the inside of the church and to examine the beautiful windows in more detail. This thought, however, was immediately supplanted by a sudden wave of guilt. It didn't seem right that I was able to see such wondrous sights without my mother. I hated Dr. Parker for taking me away from her, and I chided myself for momentarily losing sight of my anger.

The concept of having Sunday service inside was new to me. On the plantation, we had always received the Word from Mrs. Parker while standing on the lawn that fronted the main house. I wasn't sure why people needed to go inside to get their Scripture, but not having to endure the elements was certainly one advantage.

As we continued our journey, the sounds of the town gradually receded, and a short time later we were moving through a quiet neighborhood filled with tall trees and lush greenery. We passed several large residences, set amid carefully manicured lawns and gardens. I saw several Negro men tending the plantings, and I wondered if they had been born to this life or transported here against their will. In the end, I decided that how they got to Charlotte didn't matter. All of us were here now, and like them, I knew that I would have to make the best of it.

With Dr. Parker leading the way, Sam and Jackson turned the rigs smoothly into a circular drive that fronted a large home. I had thought the plantation house grand, but the structure that now loomed over us stole my breath away. The home sat well back from the street and was surrounded by mature trees, thick lawns, and lush, colorful plantings. The exterior was made of red brick, and a pair of dark green shutters framed each tall window. The front of the house had four windows on the first floor, two on either side of the door. The second floor also had four windows, directly above those on the lower floor, and one central window over the door. At its highest level, two imposing brick chimneys sprouted from the flat roof like horns. A broad set of stairs led to a shady porch, the roof of which was supported by tall white columns.

After bringing the carriage to a halt, Sam eased himself down from the driver's seat and helped Dr. Parker dismount before he opened the carriage door. Dr. Parker stretched his big frame and offered a hand to his wife. As if on cue, the front door swung open and a Negro woman emerged, wiping her hands with a rag. "Welcome home, Dr. Parker, Missus Parker. It's good to have you back."

Without a word Matthew jumped down from the carriage, bolted up the stairs, and ran into the house, with his nanny Lucinda in close pursuit.

Dr. Parker spoke to Sam. "Get the boy settled and let him know how things work around here. He can sleep out back with you and Jackson." He then turned his attention to me. "Your mother wants you to work hard and prove to me that I haven't made a mistake by bringing you here. Sam will show you around. Get your rest tonight; we'll start in the morning." He looked at Mrs. Parker expectantly, but she said nothing. Frowning slightly, he took her hand and together they climbed the stairs and disappeared into the house.

Camille, my traveling companion of the last two hours, gave me a quick smile before sliding from the wagon. She exchanged a brief look with the Negro woman standing by the door, who I noticed was peering at me curiously. Camille whispered something to her, whereupon her expression softened somewhat. They went into the house, quietly closing the door behind them.

Sam tied Dr. Parker's horse to the back of the carriage, then he and Jackson got the rigs moving again. We took a path that ran along the south side of the house and stopped in front of a sturdy wooden barn. The barn sat behind the main house and was situated in such a way that it was not visible from the street. It was flanked by several other small, neat buildings, one of which I deduced to be the kitchen house, based on its tall stone chimney.

Jackson helped Nellie down from the wagon. She looked back at me for a moment before heading in my direction. "Henry, you must be hungry. Come to the kitchen when you're ready and I'll get you something to eat." She smiled at me before walking away.

I was clutching the bag Momma had given me when Sam appeared next to the wagon. "Come on, Henry. Get down from there and come with me. We got to get these horses put away, then I'll show you where we sleep."

"You mean that boy is sleeping in our cabin," Jackson stammered. "There is barely enough room in there for you and me."

Sam had already started to unhitch the horses. "You heard Dr. Parker; Henry is sleeping with us. Where else you think he's going to sleep, with the women?" Fixing Jackson with a sidelong look, he added, "Besides, you don't always sleep here anyway."

Jackson colored visibly and snapped, "You best mind your own business, old man."

Sam chuckled. "You don't have to worry about me giving you away—you're doing a good enough job of that yourself."

Jackson scowled at me and spat in the dust. "The boy is cursed, and everybody knows it. That's what comes from being brought up by that hoodoo mother of his. What he did at the plantation wasn't natural and you know it. You can look after him if you want; just make sure you keep him away from me." With that, he hoisted one of the heavy baskets from the wagon and strode off.

Sam watched him go and said, "Don't pay any attention to him, Henry. His bark is worse than his bite. I told your mother I would look after you and that's what I plan to do. Now come on around here and let me introduce you to these two fine ladies. You like horses, don't you?" In fact, I had no experience with the animals, save for the huge gray Mr. Fox rode up and down the field rows, which was every bit as bad tempered as the overseer.

Curious, I climbed down from the wagon and approached Sam slowly. He was holding the reins of the large brown horse Dr. Parker had been riding. "This is Goldie, and the other two are Misty and Sally. Go on, you can touch her if you want. Just be slow and gentle." I hesitated, and Sam added, "Come on now, she won't bite." In a soothing tone he cooed, "Goldie, you're not going to bite Henry, are you?"

I took a tentative step forward and touched the big mare's neck, which was firm and well-muscled. She turned her head toward me and I moved back quickly. Sam laughed. "Don't be afraid. She's just showing that she likes you, that's all." I cautiously stroked her neck again. "That's it, I told you she liked you. Now come on, let's get these horses in the barn and make sure they're fed and watered. They worked hard today carrying all of us in this heat."

I hadn't said a word since leaving the plantation, but with one eye still on Goldie, I asked, "Why do the horses have names? Did Dr. Parker name them?"

Sam shook his head. "No, Dr. Parker doesn't pay much attention to the horses. To him, they're just something to ride, or pull his carriage." He bent down and lowered his voice confidingly. "I don't imagine that Dr. Parker even knows what their names are." He absently stroked the horse's neck and she leaned toward his touch. "Fact is, I take care of the horses and I named them. It makes it easier to tell them apart, and besides, I think they like having names. Seems better than just calling them 'horse.'" Sam chuckled at his own joke as he led Goldie into the barn, with me following a few steps behind.

The building had a large, open space with three stalls on each side. Sam showed me how to remove Goldie's bridle before leading her into the nearest stall. He went back outside and returned with Misty and Sally, whereupon he also took off their tack before leading them into stalls. As we were giving each animal water and oats, I noticed a much smaller horse, with a white stripe running down the center of its face, watching us.

"Which horse is that?" I asked.

"That's Master Matthew's new horse, Lightning. Dr. And Mrs. Parker gave it to him on his birthday."

"How old is he?"

"You mean Master Matthew or Lightning?"

I smiled. "How old is Master Matthew?"

"He just turned five last month."

"Did you name him Lightning?"

"No, that's the only horse here I haven't named. Master Matthew picked the name Lightning."

I had walked over to pet the pony when I heard someone yell, "What are you doing with my horse?" Shocked, I backed away from the stall.

Sam answered in his calm voice. "Ah, Master Matthew, this is Henry. He's going to be living here."

"I don't want him touching my horse," he whined.

"Well now, Master Matthew, we're going to have to feed and brush your horse sometimes, unless you've got a mind to start doing it yourself."

"You can do it, but not him," he said, pointing at me. "I don't ever want him touching Lightning."

And that was my first introduction to Master Matthew Parker.

CHAPTER 7

SETTLING IN

May 1843

The next morning a gentle rain was falling, drumming rhythmically against the thin roof of the cabin. Sam had made a straw pallet for me in the corner by his bed, and I spent my first night in Charlotte tossing fitfully. As I listened to the rain I drifted in and out of sleep, thinking about my mother. I wondered if she was also thinking of me, and I smiled inwardly, feeling certain that she was. Was she already awake? Had she also had trouble sleeping?

I thought after she got dressed and finished eating, she would probably visit Old Tom in the plantation hospital, if he was still alive. Also, two of the women were close to giving birth, and I imagined that my mother would be checking in on them as well. Vivid memories of her flooded me with fresh pain, and I felt my tears come again.

Somewhere in the distance a rooster crowed, the plaintive sound mingling with that of the rain. A short time later, I heard Sam stirring in his bed. Light was beginning to filter through the cabin's two windows, suffusing the room with a soft glow. I glanced toward Jackson's bed, but it was empty. He was already gone.

Sam slowly swung his feet to the floor and within seconds was seized by a hacking cough. What would my mother do? I thought she would probably give him some coral bean syrup, or maybe boneset, if he also had a fever. Unconsciously I fingered the bag of asafetida hanging round my neck, placed there by my mother to ward off illness.

When Sam spoke, his voice was still thick with sleep. "Wake up, Henry. Let's get up and get to it." We dressed in silence and I accompanied him to the barn, where he tended to the horses. He spoke soothingly as he gave each of them a measure of oats and some fresh water. Goldie, whose head hung over the stall gate, had been looking at me since I entered the barn. While Sam went about his work, I approached her cautiously and tentatively rubbed her neck. She seemed to enjoy it.

Sam had started shoveling out the stalls where the horses stayed. "Henry," he grunted, "you pay close attention to what I'm doing, because this is going to be your job one day." I could see that it was dirty work, but I didn't mind. I found that I liked being around the horses, and even at six years old, I was no stranger to hard labor.

After we finished our work in the barn, Sam and I went to the kitchen house for breakfast. The small building, constructed of irregularly sized red bricks, sat a short distance from the main house. The right side of the structure was dominated by a stone chimney, from which gray smoke drifted lazily into the cool morning air. When we walked in, I saw a lively fire burning in a wide, soot-covered fireplace. A heavy black pot hung over the flames, suspended from a thick iron bar, and firewood was piled high to the right of the hearth. Nellie was bending down, feeding a piece of wood into the belly of a squat black stove that sat against the wall to the left of the fireplace. Seeing us in the doorway, she shouted, "Make sure to take off those shoes. I don't want you tracking horse shit into my kitchen." Jackson and Roxanne, the woman that met us when we arrived, were already seated at a table in the middle of the room. They looked in our direction while they continued to eat. Sam pulled off his shoes and walked into the room. I still wasn't wearing any shoes, so I just stood in the doorway, unsure of what I should do. Nellie looked at me as she closed the stove door slowly. "Henry," she said gently, "come over here and sit down. I wasn't talking about you; I was talking about Sam with those big feet of his." Sam smiled as he poured himself a cup of coffee from the stove and joined Jackson and Roxanne at the table. Nellie put her hand on my shoulder and gently guided me to a smaller, narrow table along the far wall. "Sit right here and I'll bring you something to eat."

Sipping his coffee, Sam quipped, "Nellie, you going to bring me something to eat too?"

Nellie gave him a withering look and shot back, "I cook your food everyday, Sam. I'm not about to serve you too. I'm getting something for Henry. You can take care of yourself." I was initially startled at the tone of the exchange, but as they traded barbs, I could tell by their easy banter that all was said good-naturedly.

A moment later, Nellie brought over a bowl of corn porridge with pork fat and a thin slice of skillet bread. I hadn't taken Nellie up on her offer of the previous evening, opting instead to go to bed without supper. Now my stomach churned at the sight of the food.

"Thank you, ma'am," I said softly, as I attacked the meal with relish.

Nellie watched me eat, all the while cutting biscuits from dough that had been rolled out. She said to no one in particular, "This boy sure has a good appetite. Looks like we don't have to worry about him wasting away."

The previous evening Sam had explained to me the role of every slave living on the property. Nellie was the primary cook, and she prepared meals for the entire household, including the slaves. Roxanne was responsible for cleaning the main house, and also helped with the cooking if needed. She and Nellie slept in a room upstairs in the kitchen house. Camille, my traveling companion from the previous day, was Mrs. Parker's personal maid. As such, she slept in the main house, in a small room adjacent to Mrs. Parker's bedroom. Matthew's nanny Lucinda also slept in the main house. In addition to taking care of the horses, Sam served as Dr. Parker's driver and manservant. Finally, Jackson was a skilled carpenter who made furniture and maintained all the buildings on the property. Sam said that occasionally, if Dr. Parker felt he could be spared, he might also lease out Jackson's services to a friend or acquaintance. As I ate, it occurred to me that of everyone in the room, I was the only one whose role was unclear. I still didn't know why I had been brought there, and I imagined that all the others were curious about this as well.

From time to time my mother helped out in the plantation house, and she had told me that Dr. and Mrs. Parker ate a lot better than we did. However, until that morning in the kitchen house, I didn't know how much better. In addition to the biscuits Nellie was making, I could smell bread baking in the oven, while fat pork sausages sizzled in a pan. On a small table near the stove, two glass bowls were filled with boiled eggs and fried potatoes. There was also peach jam, honey, and fresh milk and coffee to wash it all down. Having been raised on slave fare, this abundance seemed to me more a feast than an everyday breakfast. Nellie followed my glance. "They eat good, don't they?" Then, looking directly at me she added, "Mrs. Parker keeps close tabs on all the food, and she makes sure I account for every scrap. If there is anything left over, she would rather save it for the hogs on the plantation than take a chance we might eat it. I guess she wants to make sure that none of us gets fat and lazy." Then, her face became grave, and she added seriously, "Besides, eating white folks' food will kill you, sure as any poison!" The shocked look on my face must have been comical, because soon they were all laughing. I smiled despite my mood, and then I too started to laugh. It felt good not to feel anxious or afraid, even if for just a moment. Outside, my fate, indeed my very life, was in Dr. Parker's hands. But at that moment in the kitchen house, in the company of these people, I felt safe.

* * *

After breakfast, Sam helped Nellie carry the food she had prepared to the main house. A short time later he came back and told me Dr. Parker had instructed him to make sure I had shoes before coming to his office. We were going into town. Sam showed me how to hitch Sally to the wagon. I started to get in the back again, but he stopped me.

"It's just the two of us, so you might as well ride up front with me." After we climbed in, he snapped the reins to get the horse moving. The rain had stopped, but thick gray clouds still hung low in the sky. As we left the house, I asked Sam if Dr. Parker had given us travel passes. He smiled and told me we wouldn't need them because most folks in town knew him, and that he worked for Dr. Parker.

Like the day before, the ride in the wagon was loud and jarring, but I was beginning to grow accustomed to its peculiar rhythm. Still, sitting on the front bench was a new experience for me, and I held on tightly to avoid being bounced into the street. Along the road we passed a few Negroes that Sam knew, and he greeted all with a word, or a nod. Once again, we passed the First Presbyterian Church, but this time instead of going straight, we turned right. As we rode along, Sam pointed out some of the sights.

"That's the county courthouse," he said, and a short time later, "and that's the U.S. Mint, where they make gold coins. They dig the gold out of the ground, not too far from where we are now." I looked at him blankly, so he added, "You've seen those shiny yellow teeth Mr.

Fox has, haven't you?" I nodded that I had. "Well, that's gold."

I didn't say anything, not wanting to seem ignorant, but for the life of me I couldn't imagine why anyone would go to so much trouble to make gold teeth for people like Mr. Fox.

We made another turn, and I soon detected a noxious odor. The smell was coming from a collection of low, soot-covered buildings. Black smoke curled into the sky from a couple of tall chimneys and the very air around the structures danced and shimmered with heat. Two men were standing outside, both so completely covered in soot and ash that it was impossible to determine whether they were white or Negro.

"That's the Mecklenburg Iron Works, where they make all kinds of things out of iron." I shuddered at the sight of such a foul place and hoped that I would never be forced to work there.

We soon pulled up to a ramshackle building surrounded by tall weeds. On the other side of the street a wizened old man sat in a rocker on the front porch. He watched us closely as we jumped down from the wagon and secured the horse. Sam lowered his eyes and said politely, "Good morning, sir." I mimicked Sam's actions and greeted the man as well. He didn't answer. In fact, his only response was to spit tobacco into a soiled cup he held in his hand. Sam opened the door of the building, over which hung a sign with a single word, *Cobbler*.

Upon entering, the first thing I noticed was the fragrant smell of leather permeating the entire space. Everywhere I looked there were shoes of all styles and sizes, seemingly in every stage of construction. A single window, set high in the wall, allowed only meager light into the room. In a far corner, a large black dog looked up when we entered, but soon returned to its nap.

A thin man with wiry gray hair sat behind a short counter piled high with shoes and bits of leather. He wore a faded brown leather apron over old clothes, which seemed to have been stained with every shade of black and brown dye. But to me, the most remarkable thing about him was that he wore a pair of small, silver-rimmed spectacles. Having never seen a Negro wearing eyeglasses before, I'll admit that I stared at him shamelessly.

Unlike the dog, he didn't look up as we entered. Instead, he directed all of his attention to the upturned shoe before him, where with a small hammer he drove even smaller nails into the shoe's sole. Sam cleared his throat.

"Good morning, Jacob. I brought you a new customer." After a few more taps of the hammer, the cobbler removed the fragile spectacles and gently massaged his temples before finally turning his gaze in our direction.

"Sam, it's always good to see you. How are Nellie and Roxanne?"

"They're doing just fine; I'll be sure to tell them that you asked about them."

He wiped his hands on a rag and smiled broadly. "Well now, who is this you brought with you, Sam?"

"Jacob, this is Henry. He's going to be living at the house for a while, and he needs some shoes. Henry, this is Jacob—a fine fellow, and a man in Charlotte that you need to know." The cobbler waved away Sam's compliment dismissively, but I could see he was pleased. Leaning over the counter, he looked at my feet for the first time, then looked back to Sam questioningly.

"This will be Henry's first pair of shoes, so give him some good ones. Otherwise, he may be disinclined to ever wear shoes again."

Jacob looked thoughtful as he ran his hand slowly back and forth across the top of his head.

"Well then, we had better find the right pair." He laughed. "In fact, I think I might have just the thing." He whistled as he stepped around the counter and began rummaging through a wooden crate filled with shoes Triumphantly, he waved a pair of black shoes in the air and then held them next to my feet. "Yes, I think these will do nicely. Sit down over here, young man."

As he fitted me with the shoes, I stared at the fragile eyeglasses that now protruded from his breast pocket. Eventually, my curiosity got the better of me.

"Mr. Jacob, where did you get your glasses? Did your master give them to you?"

The cobbler stopped what he was doing, an amused look spreading across his face.

"Henry, you don't need to call me Mr. Jacob. Just Jacob will do. That's what everybody else calls me." He tapped his pocket gently. "As for these glasses, I don't have a master—I'm a free man. I bought them myself, and this is my shop."

While I had heard that some Negroes were free, I had never actually met one before, certainly not on the plantation. "Were you always a free man, Mr. Jacob?"

He shook his head as he laced up the shoes. "No, I wasn't always free. I was once a slave just like you," he said, touching my chest with his finger.

I tried to make sense of what I was hearing. Jacob was once a slave, but now he was free. He even owned his own business. How could this be? By what alchemy could a slave become a free man? Not only had I never met a free Negro, but I didn't know of *any* slave from the Parker Plantation that had ever secured their freedom. Maybe Momma knew somebody that had gotten free, but if she did, she had never told me about it. I made note to ask her the next time I saw her.

I had seen slaves that tried to run away, but invariably they were dragged back to the plantation in shackles by the patrollers. The poor soul would be tied to a gnarled oak not far from the main house that everyone called the Whipping Tree. Before the spectacle began, usually in the morning, all the slaves were ordered to assemble on the lawn. The same lawn where Mrs. Parker held Sunday service. But on these days, it was Mr. Fox that did the preaching.

He called out to us between lashes. "This is what happens when you try to run." Crack. "We give you food, clothes, and a place to live, and this is how you repay us." Crack. "One way or another, you're all going to learn that you don't ever disobey your betters." Crack.

The bloody whipping went on and on until there were no more screams, and the slave, hanging motionless from their bonds, was either unconscious or dead.

My head spun with questions for Jacob, but before I could say more, he beamed and said, "There, all done. Stand up and walk around a bit; give them a try." I did as he directed, but as I took my first step I stumbled, and I likely would have fallen had Sam not caught me by the arm. I was embarrassed by my clumsiness, but Jacob didn't seem surprised. "They fit you well enough, but wearing shoes for the first time will feel strange. Just take it slow until you get the hang of it."

We thanked Jacob for the shoes and bade him goodbye. As we were leaving, I turned and asked if there were many other free Negroes in town. He considered the question for a moment before answering. "No, Henry, not many, not very many at all." We took our leave of him then, and when the door closed behind us, I again heard the soft tap, tap, tap of his hammer.

CHAPTER 8

THE ENTERPRISE

May–July 1843

After we returned from town, Sam took me to Dr. Parker's office, which was in the front right corner of the residence. We entered through the back door and walked down a quiet hallway. As we moved past open doorways, I saw intricately carved wooden furniture and sofas covered in plush fabrics, all resting on thick, multicolored carpets. Vibrant paintings adorned the walls, depicting elaborately dressed men and women, animals, and serene pastoral scenes. Everywhere brass doorknobs gleamed, crystal chandeliers sparkled, and polished oak floors shone. The house effortlessly conveyed that this was a family of wealth and privilege. Ironically, though I had neither, there I was.

Sam knocked softly on the heavy wood door, and upon hearing a muffled reply, we entered. The office was large and airy, with tall windows overlooking the home's front and side yards. The windows were hung with sheer curtains, which softened the light of the morning sun, suffusing the room with a warm glow. Opposite the door, Dr. Parker sat behind a large mahogany desk. Two upholstered chairs fronted the desk, while a seating arrangement consisting of a sofa, two chairs, and a low table occupied the right side of the room. A bookcase, covering the opposite wall, was filled with volumes of various shapes and sizes. A thick rug nearly covered the entire floor, and I wondered absently what it would feel like beneath my bare feet. Behind the desk hung a large painting, which dominated the room. The man in the portrait was dressed in an elaborate uniform of blue and white, the uniform of the Continental Army. I thought he bore more than a passing resemblance to Dr. Parker.

However, what fascinated me most about Dr. Parker's office were the curiosities and objets d'art that seemed strewn casually about the room. There were glass paperweights with intricate inclusions, colored rocks studded with crystalline projections, smooth marble sculptures, and small, delicately painted figurines. On one wall hung perhaps half a dozen small glass-fronted display cases, each holding an assortment of gaily colored insects. A box filled with white bleached bones sat in a corner, and animal skulls and skeletons seemed to occupy nearly every horizontal surface. The sight of so many unusual objects mesmerized me, and I knew that I could have spent many hours happily exploring the room. My reverie was broken by the sound of Dr. Parker's voice.

"Stop dawdling, boy. Come over here and sit down. Sam, that will be all for now."

Sam nodded. "Yes sir, Dr. Parker." He gave me a quick wink before quietly leaving the room.

I headed toward his desk, my new shoes causing me to stumble on the way. "Excuse me, Dr. Parker. Do you want me to sit in one of these chairs?"

"Of course I want you to sit in a chair. Where else would you sit?" I eased myself into one and waited.

He wore an unbuttoned gray vest over a white shirt, the sleeves pushed up over his forearms. He was writing in a thick leather journal that lay open before him. Having nothing else to do, I continued to scan the room. Eventually my gaze came to rest on a dull, pitted stone sitting atop a stack of papers on the desk.

"Do you know what that is?" I glanced up quickly and saw that he was no longer writing but had instead turned his attention to me. I looked back at the strange rock.

"No sir, I don't know what it is."

He picked up the stone and rotated it slowly between his thumb and forefinger. "This is raw gold," he explained, "just the way it comes out of the ground. This very nugget was taken from a mine just a few miles from here."

The only gold I had ever seen, like that in Mr. Fox's mouth, had been shiny and yellow. The stone that Dr. Parker held had a dull color. He was studying me, clearly waiting for an answer.

"That doesn't look much like gold," I ventured. "I thought gold was yellow and shiny."

Dr. Parker nodded slowly. "You're right, it doesn't look like gold now, but in the hands of a smith it would look like gold soon enough." He pulled out his pocket watch, holding it aloft briefly before slipping it back into his vest pocket. "In nature, things may begin life one way, but end up as something else entirely. There are many such examples. Chickens start off as eggs, tadpoles turn into frogs, and butterflies grow from caterpillars. This nugget doesn't look like gold now, but with a bit of time and effort it would look just like the gold in my watch. Do you understand what I'm saying?"

I of course knew what he meant; even at six years old I was familiar with the concept of change. Some mornings the sky would be clear and blue, but by afternoon it had turned gray and threatening. Yesterday I had been living on the plantation with my mother, but the next day I was in Charlotte with these people. Just that morning my feet had been free, but they were now imprisoned in stiff leather. In the end, I simply said, "Yes sir, I understand. It's like a seed that grows into a plant, and the plant makes flowers that turn into cotton."

He slapped his hand on the desk, indicating assent. "Yes, that's it exactly." He returned the gold to its original position and was silent for a moment before continuing. "Sam and Nellie tell me that you're settling in nicely. That's good, because I need you to be well rested and focused. You and I are going to be spending a lot of time together. Your memory is . . . unusual, and as a doctor, I want to study it, understand it. I have designed a few tests for you. From now on, unless I'm otherwise engaged, I will expect you to be here every morning after breakfast. Is that clear?"

I had suspected this was why he had brought me to Charlotte, but I didn't welcome the news. Our first meeting at the plantation house had been an unpleasant experience, one that left me drained. My work in the fields had acquainted me with physical exhaustion. But that afternoon in Dr. Parker's office on the plantation was the first time in my life I had ever been mentally exhausted. I couldn't imagine being subjected to that type of trial every day. But what choice did I have?

I hung my head and whispered, "Yes sir." Then, suddenly overwhelmed by my emotions, I blurted, "What about my mother?"

"What about your mother?" he said in a low voice. I didn't answer right away. I was very frightened of this man, and I knew I was taking a chance to speak to him so directly. "I asked you a question," he growled. "What about your mother?"

"She's alone, and she needs me," I cried. "When am I going to see her again?"

His eyes narrowed and a dark look crossed his face. "Your mother is fine; you have no need to worry about her. If I were you, I would worry about myself. Do you want to return to the fields? I'm sure Mr. Fox would be pleased to have you back. Or perhaps I should send you to another plantation altogether, one far away from here. Is that what you want?"

Alarmed, I shook my head vigorously. "No sir!"

"Well then, you need to stop all this nonsense. Your mother has her job to do, and you have yours. If you work hard and do well, you will see her again soon."

Fighting to regain control, I rubbed my eyes with the sleeve of my shirt.

"Yes sir, Dr. Parker, I'm sorry. I promise to work hard."

He opened a book that was lying on the desk, picked up his pen, and said lightly, "Excellent, now that we have that settled, let's begin."

* * *

And that was how our association started. Every day I would get up with the sun and help Sam tend to the horses. In time, I learned to love them all, but Goldie was my favorite. Somehow, she always sensed when I was coming, and every day she was waiting for me at the entrance to her stall. After the horses were fed and watered, I would take my morning meal in the kitchen house with the others. Then, after the Parker's had finished their breakfast, I would make my way to the office.

During those first weeks together, Dr. Parker and I would meet several hours each morning for what he called "memory testing." This he did in many ways. Sometimes he would recite long passages from a book, which I was instructed to repeat. As I did so, he traced his finger along the page, following my progress. Another test involved showing me a series of cards bearing pictures of common objects. I then had to recount the images I had seen, and the order in which I had seen them. At other times Dr. Parker would briefly display a complex shape or figure. I was then told to reproduce what I had seen on a chalk slate.

While these tests were certainly challenging, each also had several variations, some of which were much more difficult. For example, after reciting an extended book passage, Dr. Parker might repeat a single sentence or phrase. He would then ask that I continue the recitation from that point forward. Or he might ask me to repeat only every second or third word from the selection or say them in reverse order. Sometimes he would vary the amount of time I was exposed to an image before I was asked to reproduce it. The tests seemed endless, both in number and variation. It was tedious and exhausting work.

Other than to give me instructions regarding each session, we rarely spoke. During the tests he never displayed joy or anger, nor did he convey any information regarding my performance. I felt that I was doing well, and it seemed to me that the tests might actually be strengthening my memory. Still, I found his silence unnerving. After each test, Dr. Parker would document his observations in a thick leather journal that he kept in his desk. The process of recording his findings could take some time, but I was glad for the breaks and came to see them as a respite from the tedium of remembering.

During these intervals he would allow me to walk around the office, provided that I didn't touch anything. I occupied myself by memorizing every object in the room, and in time I knew the location of every book, bone, and bug. It was a game for me. I could even tell if something had been moved or disturbed since my last visit. One morning, during a break from testing, a hummingbird with a white body and black head hovered outside the office window: its wings moving impossibly fast. We were just inches apart, separated by only a thin pane of glass. I thought that it must be wonderful to be so free, to fly wherever you liked, whenever you chose, answerable to no one. Just then, as if to confirm my thoughts, it darted out of sight. I stood very still, hoping the little bird would return, but it was gone.

"What are you staring at out there?" Dr. Parker asked.

"There was a hummingbird outside the window."

"What about it? Haven't you ever seen one before?"

"Yes sir, I've seen them before. Their wings flap so fast I can hardly see them." I turned to look at him. "Excuse me, sir, may I ask you a question?"

"What is it?" he said with a touch of annoyance.

"Well, sir, I was wondering, if hummingbirds flapped their wings any faster, if they would disappear altogether?"

He sat back and gave me a long appraising look, as if he were seeing me for the first time.

* * *

Late that afternoon I left Dr. Parker's office, glad to be finished with our work for the day. I thought that I might look for Sam or go to the kitchen house and see if Nellie had something to eat. I didn't get very far. As I passed the entry to the parlor, I heard Mrs. Parker call my name.

"Henry, is that you?"

"Yes, Mrs. Parker, it's me." She was sitting in a high-backed chair next to an open window, fanning herself slowly. I was surprised she had called for me, because I hadn't spoken to her since my arrival in Charlotte.

"It's beastly hot today." She poured water from a pitcher into a tall glass before taking a long, unhurried drink. "Are you finished with Dr. Parker?"

"Yes ma'am, we're finished." She didn't reply. A thick leather-bound book inscribed with the word *Bible* rested on her lap. I stood in the doorway as she continued to fan herself, unsure about what I should do next.

After an awkward silence I asked, "Is there something I can do for you, Mrs. Parker?" She cocked her head, seeming to consider the question.

"Yes, there is something I would like you to do for me." She looked down at the book. "I have talked to Dr. Parker about you, and he says that your gift for mimicry is genuine." She looked out the window to the garden beyond. "My husband is a brilliant man, and I certainly trust his assessment. But it is . . . perplexing to me that

God would invest someone like you with such a talent." Her brow furrowed as she studied me. "Don't you find that odd?" she inquired.

Unsure of how to respond, I simply said, "Yes ma'am."

"So, you can see my dilemma. You may indeed have a God-given talent, or you might have been touched by Satan himself. After all, you do bear the mark of Cain." She seemed to be waiting for a response, but I didn't know what to say. I certainly wasn't going to say I had been touched by Satan.

She stood and walked to a nearby writing desk. Holding out a crucifix, she said, "Come here and take this."

I said, "Yes ma'am," as I took it from her hand. She watched me closely as I held the cross. After a moment, she picked up a glass and, without warning, threw the contents in my face. I was so startled that I took a step back, nearly dropping the cross in the process. Had Mrs. Parker gone mad? Should I call for Dr. Parker, or try to find Sam? I rubbed the liquid from my eyes and considered running from the room.

"Well, you're not one of Satan's minions," she said, taking the crucifix from me. "I told my minister that I thought one of our slaves might be touched by the devil. He said if you were of Satan, you wouldn't be able to hold a cross or tolerate holy water." She went back to her chair.

"So, I must assume that your talent is God-given. But it still doesn't make sense to me that you would have been given such a gift. After all, think of how much better use an . . . educated person would make of it?" She looked at me for a long moment. Finally, she shrugged. "But who am I to question the ways of the Lord."

"Yes ma'am." I blinked, water still dripping down my face.

She ran her hand reverently over the book's leather cover. "I have read this book nearly every day, starting when I was a girl, but can you believe that I've never read it from beginning to end. I have decided to do that now, and to have you listen to me. When we're finished you will know the entire Bible, something very few people can claim. And perhaps that is why God has brought you here. Do you understand?"

I felt lightheaded as I registered the meaning of her words: more memorization!

"Yes ma'am, I understand."

She seemed pleased and smiled for the first time since I entered the parlor. "Good, very good. We will begin tomorrow and read a few chapters every day. It will take quite some time to finish, but I know that you'll find it valuable." She looked at me expectantly, but I was too stunned to speak. "That's all. I will see you tomorrow."

* * *

As I left the house, I thought about what had transpired that day. Dr. Parker thought my gift was "remarkable." Mrs. Parker said it was "God-given." They might have been right, but at the time I didn't see how it mattered. What good was such a talent to me? It couldn't reunite me with my mother or set me free like Jacob. Still, if my talent was as special as they said, perhaps there was a way I could use it to my advantage.

Slaves were prohibited from learning how to read and write, but they couldn't stop me from memorizing what was in plain sight, could they? I decided that, from that day forward, I would memorize every word that I saw. Every single one. I wasn't yet sure how I would use them, but I had a strong sense they might prove useful someday.

I saw dozens of words every day. They were, quite literally, everywhere. They were printed on the covers of books and on the papers that littered Dr. Parker's desk, inscribed on clock faces, carved into furniture, or attached to tags that dangled from bones. Words were painted on the sides of buildings in town and on delivery wagons, stamped into milk bottles, and printed on bags of oats. I didn't understand the meaning of these words yet, but I knew they were important. I understood instinctively that they were the key to a hidden language that controlled access to knowledge, and to the power that flowed from that knowledge.

CHAPTER 9

MATTHEW

September 1843

A few months after my arrival in Charlotte, several of us were having breakfast in the kitchen house. Roxanne was regaling everyone with an impression of Mrs. Parker, including her habit of clasping and reclasping her hands together, causing all of us to laugh. Suddenly, a shaft of light spilled into the room, illuminating Roxanne. The poor woman froze in place, blinking rapidly at the unexpected brightness, her hands still knotted together. I looked toward the light's source, shocked to see the unmistakable silhouette of Dr. Parker filling the doorway. The laughter died away quickly. Since my arrival in Charlotte, this was the first time I had seen him in the kitchen house. Collectively we held our breath, not certain how much he had overheard.

Making no mention of Roxanne's performance, Dr. Parker motioned toward the two men. "Jackson, Sam, come outside. Let's have a look at that cabin." Without saying another word, he left as quickly as he had come. Sam briefly raised his eyebrows before he and Jackson grabbed their hats and headed for the door. After a moment, I followed them into the yard.

I found the three men standing in front of the small cabin I shared with Sam and Jackson. The simple structure sat just behind the main house, halfway between the barn and the kitchen house. It was very plain, consisting of little more than four walls, an exterior stone chimney for the fireplace, and a pitched roof. A single door and two small flanking windows cut into the front wall provided the cabin's only adornment.

Turning toward Jackson, Dr. Parker said, "Sam tells me that we need to expand the cabin to make room for the boy. I'm willing to consider it, but it would have to be done with a minimal investment of time and materials. What would you suggest?"

Jackson, who was widely recognized as a skilled carpenter, studied the cabin for some time before answering. Pointing to the right wall, he ventured, "Well, sir, if we brace the roof with two beams, this wall could be removed. The roof may not need the support, but I think it best to be on the safe side. After that I would add some new footings, lengthen the floor a few feet, frame out new walls, and extend the roof to cover the added space."

Absently swatting at a fly, Dr. Parker nodded slowly and asked, "How long would it take to complete the job?"

Removing his hat to rub his hand over his hair, Jackson considered the question before answering. "I expect that once all the lumber is here, and if I didn't have any other work to attend to, I could finish the job in four days, five at the outside."

"Very well. Get what you need from the lumberyard and get it done."

"Yes sir, I'll take care of it."

Turning to leave, Dr. Parker noticed me for the first time. When he saw my bare feet, he snapped, "For God's sake, go put your shoes on boy. You're not on the farm anymore."

Jackson started the job two days later, and after hurriedly completing my work, I rushed outside to watch the construction. By the time I arrived he had already taken down most of the right wall. Two thick lengths of wood were wedged under the exposed corners, one supporting each side of the roof. I sat on the large pile of wood that now dominated the yard, watching him work.

Then, from somewhere behind me I heard an urgent whisper. "Henry. Henry!" The voice sounded like

Matthew, but when I turned toward the house, I didn't see him. After a moment, I heard the voice again. "Henry, I'm over here." I looked back toward the house just in time to see a small hand waving at me from under the stairs. After checking to see that no one was watching, I ran to join him.

"Matthew, what are you doing?"

He shook his head vigorously. "Shhh, not so loud. She might hear you."

As I had suspected, Matthew was hiding from his nanny again. Lucinda was an older woman, perhaps fifty years of age, with thick legs and wide hips. She always moved slowly and carefully, as if her joints protested with every step she took. Unfortunately for her, Matthew was an active and mischievous child who would have posed a challenge even for a much younger and more agile guardian.

As we huddled together under the stairs, Lucinda came into view from the right side of the house. She stood for a moment looking around the yard, hands planted firmly on her hips.

"Matthew! Matthew, where are you? Wherever you're hiding, you can come out now. You played a good trick on Lucinda; I'll give you that. Come on out. I'm not mad at you."

It was an unseasonably warm day for late September. The sun, having already climbed up and over the main house, now hung low over the roof of the little cabin. Jackson, perched precariously on a weathered ladder, pulled a rag from his back pocket and wiped his brow.

After mumbling something unintelligible, Lucinda yelled, "Jackson, have you seen Master Matthew?"

Shaking his head, Jackson smirked. "No, I haven't seen the boy since this morning. Did you lose him again?"

Wagging a finger in his direction, Lucinda shot back good-naturedly, "Don't give me any of your lip, Jackson. I haven't *lost* him; the boy is just hiding somewhere. I must have looked after a dozen little lords and ladies in my time, and I have never lost anyone. Well, not for long anyway."

Lowering her voice, she added, "But that boy is a devil, that's true enough. I don't know why the good Lord saw fit to curse me with such a child." She grew quiet for a moment, appearing to reflect on something. "Have you seen Henry lately? I'll wager you that Matthew is with him. Those two are thick as thieves!"

Jackson fanned himself with his hat before looking toward the house. I froze, wondering if he had seen me crawl under the stairs, but he just shook his head. "No, I haven't seen Henry either."

Lucinda took another long look around the backyard before moving on to search the barn. After she left, Jackson looked directly at us and smiled before turning back to his work. Matthew tapped my arm and we bolted from our hiding place, up the stairs, and into the house. Once inside, we slowed down, quietly climbing the front stairs before heading to Matthew's room. Mrs. Parker was reading in the parlor. She did not approve of Matthew running in the house, and under the circumstances, we thought it best not to attract her attention.

Matthew was five years old, just two years younger than I, and we had become playmates shortly after my arrival in Charlotte. In those days, it was not unusual for a white child and a slave child to play together. Matthew had no siblings, and years later he would confide to me that our companionship was a carrot his father used to convince his mother to accept me into their home. I was also alone, having left my friends behind on the plantation, so I needed little prompting to embrace Matthew as a playmate.

I closed the door behind us, and we sat on the floor with our legs crossed at the foot of Matthew's bed. He had a spacious room, as large as the cabin I shared with Sam and Jackson. Two tall windows looked toward a massive oak on the left side of the house. Beyond that, other grand homes fronting North Tryon Street were just visible through the dense foliage. His bed, covered with a colorful quilt, sat against the wall opposite the windows, while a desk, chair, and bookcase completed the room.

Leaning toward Matthew, I whispered, "Why are you hiding from Lucinda again? You know your mother will be mad as a hornet if she finds out."

Making a sour face, Matthew whined, "I don't like her—she's old and fat. She said my tutor is coming soon and I need to get ready. I don't want to be stuck inside with him all day!" He picked up a small wooden horse, examining it briefly before hurling it toward the fireplace. I got up and retrieved the toy, which was undamaged, apart from a broken tail.

Sitting again, I placed the horse on the rug between us. Matthew looked at it and seemed to be deciding whether to throw it again. "Let's go to our fort and play," he said, brightening suddenly.

A dense grove of trees measuring several acres, not yet claimed by the town's growing appetite for lumber, was located perhaps two hundred feet behind the house. Matthew and I played there whenever we could, and our "fort" was a narrow valley between two great fallen oaks.

Matthew was often impetuous, even reckless, so though I'd just turned seven years old, it often fell to me to be the voice of reason. I also knew instinctively that if I was involved in one of his exploits, my punishment would likely be much more severe than his. "No, we better not go now. If you're gone too long everyone will be looking for you."

Matthew thought about what I had said, then nodded slowly, accepting my reasoning. "You're right. We don't want them to find our hiding place."

No, I certainly didn't want our secret discovered, and not simply because it was where we acted out our childhood fantasies of being cavalry soldiers or Indians. I didn't want our fort discovered because it was also where the book was hidden.

Two months earlier, during another of his unauthorized absences from Lucinda, Matthew had found a torn and weathered copy of *The American Primer* deep in an attic trunk. Since then, he had predictably moved on to other pursuits and forgotten about the book, but I knew it was still hidden under one of the logs.

By the time Matthew found the book, I had already committed many words to memory. For example, on many occasions I had seen the words *North Carolina*. However, I didn't know how to pronounce them, or what they meant. I only knew their shape. This is the same phenomenon experienced by people that are illiterate. If they see the word *Livery* painted on a building, based on their experience, and other visual and olfactory clues, they may begin to associate the word with a place that takes care of horses. My recognition of words worked in a similar way. I was not yet able to read, but even at seven years old I had already memorized the shapes of hundreds of words.

Using a similar primer to the one Matthew found, his tutor had begun to teach him to read, but after each lesson he was always careful to take the book with him. Huddled together in our fort, Matthew proudly read from *The American Primer* he'd discovered while I looked over his shoulder. Through Matthew I learned that words were not simply random shapes but were made of individual letters, each with its own distinct sound. More importantly, I realized that these letters could be strung together to construct the sound of any word, even those one had never seen before. This was the key I had been missing!

Armed with my newfound knowledge, I was able to decipher the sound of almost any word. For example, the words *North Carolina* were in fact pronounced *narth kar-uh-lah-nuh*, which I immediately recognized as the place where we lived! I would lie in bed at night assigning sounds to words I had seen. *Charlotte* was *char-lut*, *dictionary* was *dik-tun-air-ee*, *opium* was *o-pee-um*, and so forth. From that time forward, whenever I was in Dr. Parker's office or laboratory, I mentally deciphered the sounds of many other words. *Cathartic* was *ka-thar-tik*, *newspaper* was *nooz-pay-pur*, *physician* was *fi-zi-shun*, *property* was *prop-ur-tee*, and so on. I was surrounded by words, and they were no longer a mystery to me.

Matthew was completely unaware of the significance of what he had done, but I recognized that this was a dangerous endeavor. Though I practiced constantly, I was careful not to mention my newfound ability to anyone. I didn't say anything to Nellie or the other slaves, not even to Sam.

Suddenly the door opened, and Lucinda's voice filled the room: "There you are, Matthew. I have been looking everywhere for you!" She was standing just inside the doorway with her hands planted solidly on her hips. "Mr. Williams is waiting downstairs to begin your lessons."

Looking defeated, Matthew sighed, "I'll see you later, Henry," before trudging from the room.

As I was leaving, Lucinda stopped me with a hand on my shoulder. Bending low, she whispered, "Don't forget who you are. That boy is a Parker, and one day he's likely to be your master. I've seen it happen too many times. The sooner you realize he isn't your friend, the easier it will be for you."

As I left the house, I thought about what Lucinda had said and was suddenly gripped by fear. What if someone found the book? Would anyone believe me if I said Matthew had taken it? I slipped into the woods and tucked the copy of The American Primer under my shirt, nestled against my lower back. My plan was to burn it, but just as I came out of the trees, I heard Mrs. Parker's voice.

"Henry, what are you doing?" She was standing on the back porch, looking down at me curiously.

Thinking fast, I said, "Nothing, Mrs. Parker. I saw a fox and tried to catch it."

She frowned. "Well, I'm sure you have something better to do than chase animals. If you don't have enough work, I can certainly find some for you."

"Yes ma'am. I'm sorry, I have work to do."

"Well, get to it then."

I went into the barn and busied myself grooming the horses. I could feel the book pressing against my back like a hot coal. Sometime later, when I was certain she had gone, I ran to the kitchen house. Nellie was sitting at the table cutting a squash into small cubes. I walked past her without speaking and shoved the book deep into the fireplace. Using a poker, I pushed a log on top of it until I saw the book burning. I watched it for a few minutes until I was sure it was destroyed. When I turned to leave, I saw that Nellie was looking at me.

"What are you doing, Henry?" she asked sternly.

"Nothing."

Frowning, she pointed at me with the knife. "Don't lie to me. You're not doing nothing."

Looking back at the fireplace once more, I said, "Don't worry, Nellie. Everything is fine."

Nellie didn't say anything for a long moment. Finally, she shook her head and returned to her work. "Henry, I don't know what you put in the fire, but you better make sure it's burned up good, because I don't want any trouble and neither do you."

CHAPTER 10

WORK

November–December 1844

Many years earlier, Sam's son, Isaac, died from a fever. On occasion, Sam still spoke of him. He said that the thought of his son's death was painful, but with the passage of time, it had become less so. When Sam talked about his son, it was clear that his memories were becoming hazier and less distinct. Time had worn them down, leaving behind something more akin to dreams. My memories weren't like that.

I had been in Charlotte for more than a year, and during that time I had not been allowed to return to the plantation, or to see my mother again. I was six years old when we separated, but my memories of her were still vivid. When I thought of our time together, the past came back in brilliant detail. It was as if she were still in the room with me. I could see her face, her smile, her clothing. I heard her voice. I smelled her earthy scent. Unlike Sam, my memories had lost none of their potency. Time had not robbed them of their power to bring joy, or to inflict pain.

Sam did all he could to maintain the bond between my mother and me. Whenever he accompanied Dr. Parker to the plantation, he always found time to speak with her, even if only for a few moments. He would bring her up to date on my life in Charlotte and relay any messages I might have for her. Similarly, upon his return, I knew he would have news from my mother, along with a selection of the plants and roots she had collected recently.

Dr. Parker continued to meet with me, but after several months the testing became less and less frequent, eventually stopping altogether. However, even after his investigations were concluded, I was still required to come to the office every morning. There I would typically find him going through the newspaper, reading a medical journal, or poring over a thick book.

Adjacent to the office was a large room that served as his personal laboratory, accessible only through a locked door. The walls were covered with floor-to-ceiling shelving, which held a variety of chemicals, pieces of scientific equipment, and medical apparatuses. The room was dominated by two tall windows, which neatly framed the lush greenery of the side yard. Heavy curtains, capable of blocking all outside light when darkness was required, hung to the side of each window. A large square table sat in the center of the room, covered with a dense thicket of glassware, tubing, bottles, crucibles, and other experimental paraphernalia.

One morning, shortly after my testing had been concluded, I entered the office and without preamble Dr. Parker said, "Henry, bring me that thin black book, the one lying on the table." This surprised me for two reasons. First, he called me by my proper name, Henry, which he had rarely done. Second, he had previously told me not to touch anything in the office. So I was puzzled by the conflicting commands. Not certain how to proceed, I pointed to the book and asked hesitantly, "You want me to pick up this book?"

He looked over the top of his glasses and spoke slowly, as if I were a simpleton. "Of course I want you to pick it up. How else are you going to bring it to me?"

I did as he requested, and after completing that first simple task, over the ensuing months he started to use me more and more. I would bring him books or return them to their proper places on the shelves. Sometimes, he would read passages aloud and ask that I remember them for later recall. He found this particularly useful in the laboratory, where he no longer had to refer to a text to replicate a formula.

As he became more comfortable with my presence, Dr. Parker slowly, very slowly, allowed me to begin the process of straightening and organizing the office and laboratory.

Since my arrival in Charlotte, I had not seen anyone clean these rooms, not even Sam. Dr. Parker was uncomfortable with people, to use his words, "stumbling around" in his workspace. He feared that some of his valuable equipment or papers might be damaged or misplaced. The laboratory also contained a great many caustic and noxious chemicals, any of which could have been dangerous if spilled or mishandled. Consequently, both rooms were in a state of advanced disorder, or put more simply, they were a mess.

In the years that followed, I became his assistant in all but name. In addition to maintaining his rooms, I would assist with his experiments. He taught me how to dissect animals, and to recognize, collect, and preserve various organs. I also learned the proper way to boil bones in soda ash to clean them of all muscle and ligaments.

Many of the medicines he gave to patients were purchased from the local apothecary, and sometimes he would send me into town with a list of the supplies he wanted. However, there were instances in which Dr. Parker preferred to prepare the medicines he needed in his own laboratory, and in time I learned how to make all of these. I made laudanum by combining opium powder, alcohol, and cinnamon, and made paregoric, which in addition to opium also contained oil of anise, honey, camphor, and alcohol. Tinctures of cannabis, made by soaking the plant in an alcohol solution, were used for a variety of ailments.

Although it was critical that I knew the ingredients and their proportions for each medicine I prepared, Dr. Parker was always careful not to teach me numbers directly. Instead, rather than telling me that he needed so many grains of this, or so many parts of that, he would simply demonstrate how a particular formulation was made. He would then watch me closely, as I repeated the same steps. When I had learned the procedure, it would never be forgotten. Thereafter, Dr. Parker only had to say what he needed, and it would be done.

I think he believed I would learn to prepare the formulations much as a parrot learns to speak, by rote, with no understanding of the meaning behind my actions. Nonetheless, despite his precautions, I was beginning to gain an appreciation for various quantities, including weights and liquid measures. My mother had taught me how to count to twenty, so if Dr. Parker asked me to bring him two books, or five, or even twenty, I would have been able to comply.

One day while I was working in the laboratory, I had an insight that allowed me to begin unraveling the mystery of numbers. Dr. Parker put a weight marked with the number *5* on the left arm of the scale and told me to add salt to the right arm until the needle balanced in the middle. The weights were stored in a wooden box, arranged from small to large, each stamped with a different symbol. There were weights labeled *1, 2, 3, 5, 10, 20,* and so forth, up to *1000.* Though I didn't understand the symbols on each weight, based on their relative size I could surmise which numbers were larger. As I started to weigh the salt, Mrs. Parker came to the office and asked her husband for his assistance. When he left the room, instead of salt I quickly added other weights to the right arm of the scale.

In this way I found that the weight marked *5* could be exactly balanced by adding weights labeled *2* and *3* to the opposing side. I was thrilled by this early success, and thereafter whenever I was left alone in the lab for a few minutes, I continued to experiment.

Looking back, I'm not certain why Dr. Parker chose to train me as his assistant. One possibility is that, recognizing he needed help, he was more comfortable with me than anyone else. Practically speaking, he knew that he only needed to tell me once how he wanted something done and thereafter it would not be forgotten.

My mother never told me the identity of my father, so for a time I entertained the notion that I might be Dr. Parker's son. Ultimately, I rejected this idea. For one, I didn't think I resembled him in the least, or his son, Matthew. Also, at the time it seemed inconceivable to me that a man would treat his own son as chattel, relegating him to the fields. However, I would later learn that this happened all too often. Slave owners fathered a great many children with their female slaves, with most of those children remaining in bondage.

Eventually I embraced a different explanation. I came to believe that the reason Dr. Parker allowed me to become a fixture in his life was because my "gift" fascinated him. He had studied it at length, probed its boundaries, and tested its limits, but he was simply not ready to put it aside. In short, I think he enjoyed having me around, as one enjoys the company of a well-trained hound. As an avid collector and natural scientist, he was fascinated by my abilities. In the end, I believe I simply became another of his curiosities.

***

Late one afternoon I walked into the warmth of the kitchen house to visit with Nellie, as I often did. Though she was engaged in a vigorous discussion with Mrs. Parker's maid, Camille, she nonetheless graced me with a smile when I entered. "Henry, I hope you're not too hungry. Dinner won't be ready until later."

"That's all right, Nellie. I'm not hungry right now. I can wait." I headed for the table along the far wall, and by the time I sat down, they had resumed their discussion.

"A fancy dinner for ten people? Mrs. Parker must think there is somebody other than me doing the cooking out here. How am I supposed to make everything by myself? I would be working all day just on that one meal. What's everybody going to do for breakfast and lunch while I'm busy making a feast for all those white folks? They're not going to eat most of it anyway—the whole thing is just for show."

Sitting in the center of the room, Camille looked anxiously toward the main house before responding. "You're right, Nellie, but there is nothing to be gained by getting upset. The missus loves having guests, she always has. You didn't know her before she was married, when she was still Mary Higgins, but I've been with her since she was a young lady. There is nothing she likes more than having a house full of people, especially during the holidays." Chuckling to herself, she added, "Now, Dr. Parker on the other hand, I don't think he cares about dinner parties one way or the other."

Nellie, who had started to slice potatoes into a pot of water, made no comment. Motioning toward the window, Camille added, "They have that big house, full of beautiful things. Why shouldn't they show it off sometimes?" Nellie remained silent, the only sound in the kitchen being the plop of potatoes hitting the water. "Besides, didn't Mrs. Parker say that if you needed help, Roxanne could work with you in the kitchen that day."

Nellie's posture stiffened, and I braced instinctively for the inevitable eruption. After lifting the pot onto the stove, Nellie spun toward Camille and snapped, "Roxanne? She means to put Roxanne in the kitchen. She may do a fine job keeping the house clean, but she doesn't have the slightest idea how to cook a dinner like this. I would spend all my time telling her what to do, then watching to make sure she does it right! I can't believe Mrs. Parker suggested Roxanne." Nellie took two pieces of wood from the pile, threw them into the stove, and shut the door with a loud clang. "I would be better off doing everything myself."

"Cook everything yourself—are you sure, Nellie? That seems like too much for one person. Roxanne is a hard worker; wouldn't she be some help to you?"

Nellie wiped her hands on her apron before taking the chair next to Camille. "No, I think I better do the cooking myself, but I swear these parties are going to kill me. I'll talk to Mrs. Parker."

In the end it was decided that Nellie would do all the cooking, with Roxanne available to assist if needed. Breakfast that morning would consist of bread, fruit, and anything else that didn't involve preparation. For the evening menu, Mrs. Parker chose chicken consommé to start, followed by main courses of roast turkey, ham, and pheasant, accompanied by rice, kidney beans, mushrooms, pickles, sweetbreads, assorted vegetables, and freshly baked bread. For dessert, the guests would have their choice of apple fritters, molasses cake, or burnt cream.

Though the dinner was still a month away, Mrs. Parker, more animated than I had ever seen her, pressed everyone into service. Jackson repainted much of the home's exterior, including the shutters, porch railings, and balusters. Sam and I trimmed all the plantings around the house and carted in gravel from town to refresh the circular drive that fronted the property. With Camille's assistance, Roxanne gave the house a thorough cleaning, polishing the silverware, furniture, and floors, cleaning the glassware and china, and dusting the chandeliers and paintings. On the day before the party, I accompanied Sam into the nearby woods, where we cut fresh pine garlands for the windows and a small evergreen that we placed atop the round table in the parlor. Sam also took the carpets outside, hung them on a thick rope, and beat them clean.

As for all formal events, Sam would wear his livery, which consisted of a formal dark brown waistcoat with brass buttons on the chest and sleeves. The pants, which ended at his knees, were made from a lighter brown fabric. Tall cream-colored socks covered the lower half of his leg. His shirt was white cotton with a stiff collar, and dark brown shoes decorated with rectangular brass buckles completed the outfit. Though I didn't say so, I thought he looked ridiculous, and I wondered how anyone could be expected to work while wearing such clothes.

So, you can imagine my consternation when I learned that I was to assist Sam in the dining room and would be fitted for my own uniform. I had never worn anything so elaborate or restrictive, and I found the high-collared shirt and tight stockings particularly intolerable.

Roxanne laid out a couple of place settings in the dining room, which Sam used to demonstrate what would be expected of me. He would serve food from the left, while from the right side I would be responsible for filling and refilling the water and wine glasses. Sam demonstrated the proper method, keeping my left hand behind my back while pouring with my right hand. He then watched while I repeated his actions. After all the guests had been served, we would stand with our gloved hands crossed in front of us, each taking up a position on opposite ends of the heavy mahogany sideboard.

For the next few weeks, my training was reinforced at each evening meal, when I would help Sam serve dinner to the Parkers. Initially Mrs. Parker was not satisfied with my performance and constantly critiqued my posture and serving technique. After a few days, however, she concluded that I "would be adequate." Through all the training, Matthew looked on bemused, finding it difficult not to laugh at my plight. Wickedly, he drained two or three goblets of water during every meal, smiling broadly each time I was forced to refill his glass.

The evening's guest list, carefully crafted by Mrs. Parker, consisted of four of Charlotte's most prominent couples, Mr. and Mrs. Thomas J. Holton, Mr. and Mrs. John Irwin, Mr. and Mrs. William Phifer, and Mr. and Mrs. John H. Wheeler.

Thomas Holton was the owner and publisher of a local newspaper, The Charlotte Journal. John Irwin was a town commissioner and a Trustee of the First Presbyterian Church, of which the Parkers were members, the same church that had affected me so greatly during my initial arrival into town. Like Dr. Parker, William Phifer was a planter that also had a home on North Tryon Street. Finally, John Wheeler was the State Treasurer and had been the first Superintendent of the U.S. Mint on West Trade Street. The Mint took bullion, pulled from local mines like the Rudisill and St. Catherine, and converted it into shiny $1, $2.5 and $5 gold coins.

After dinner, as was the usual custom, Sam would entertain guests by playing his fiddle. I'd heard him a few times at the plantation, or in our cabin, but his best performances were usually reserved for the kitchen house.

Sometimes, after the evening meal, Nellie would ask Sam to play. At first, he would resist, feigning reluctance, but after a bit of encouragement he would get the instrument, tuck it under his chin, and start playing. He knew a great many songs and we would all stomp our feet to the music and clap. Invariably someone would get up and start dancing. Sometimes Nellie or Roxanne would pull me to my feet, yelling and clapping as I moved with the music.

In addition to Sam on the violin, Dr. Parker thought the guests would find it entertaining if I recited a selection from Shakespeare. He chose Henry V's speech to his troops before the Battle of Agincourt. A few days before the dinner he read the passage aloud slowly. He then asked that I repeat it, stopping me several times with instructions regarding where to pause for greater effect, or which words should be given emphasis. When he finally felt I was ready, he gave one final instruction before leaving the room.

"That's fine, Henry; you've memorized the selection perfectly. Now, there is just one more thing you need to do. When you give your speech after dinner, you will need to keep your eyes open."

For some reason the thought of this terrified me nearly as much as reciting Shakespeare to strangers. Since discovering my gift, whenever I wanted to recall what I'd memorized, I instinctively closed my eyes. Keeping my eyes closed had no effect on my recall; Dr. Parker had already tested for that variable. I simply felt more comfortable that way.

* * *

I was nervous when the evening of the dinner finally arrived. One after another the carriages rolled up to the house. I opened the front door as each couple reached the top of the freshly painted stairs. Sam served drinks in the parlor, while Nellie and Roxanne worked to finish the meal and transfer the first courses to serving dishes.

Soon Mrs. Parker announced, "Please, if everyone will join us in the dining room, dinner is ready." The group filed into the room, talking and laughing merrily as they went. As soon as they had taken their seats, Sam and I started serving dinner and drinks, standing silently by the sideboard between courses. The conversation was very animated, touching on topics as varied as the upcoming presidential election between James Polk and Henry Clay, the terrible flooding in the western territories, and the miracle of the first telegram sent from Washington to Baltimore. Conversation on local issues primarily focused on the price of cotton and how difficult it was to get it to market over the poor North Carolina roads. One of the men said that a group of investors had proposed building a railroad between Charlotte and Columbia, South Carolina, where the cotton could then be shipped on to the port at Charleston. Though I listened to the discussion intently, I stood rigidly with my eyes straight ahead. Sam had already told me that, although we would always be in the room, we could never appear to be listening to the conversation or be caught repeating what we had heard. He said that for people like Dr. and Mrs. Parker, a good servant was one that kept their eyes open, and their ears closed.

After dessert was served, Mrs. Parker announced that the evening's entertainment would consist of a selection on violin followed by a reading from Shakespeare. She never mentioned Sam or me by name. With a nod from Mrs. Parker, Sam tucked the violin under his chin and started playing. I was used to his fast ditties, tunes meant for relaxing, dancing, and celebration. The song he played that night was different from anything I had ever heard. It started subtly, a thin, impossibly long note hanging in the air before merging seamlessly into other notes, equally beautiful. As the plaintive sounds filled the room the guests listened raptly, some with their heads tilted back, others slowly swaying with the sound. I found myself greatly affected by the music, scarcely breathing as the notes tumbled one over the other, like waves crashing against a distant shore. Sam finished playing and the guests clapped politely, clearly appreciative of his mastery of the instrument. Forgetting my place for a moment, I smiled broadly, feeling very proud of him.

Then it was my turn. At a nod from Dr. Parker, I took a deep breath and stepped forward hesitantly.

This day is called the feast of Crispian. He that outlives this day, and comes safe home, will stand a tip-toe when this day is named, and rouse him at the name of Crispian. He that shall live this day, and see old age, will yearly on the vigil feast his neighbors, and say "Tomorrow is Saint Crispian." Then will he strip his sleeve and show his scars and say "These wounds I had on Crispin's day." Old men forget; yet all shall be forgot, but he'll remember, with advantages, what feats he did that day.

Then shall our names, familiar in his mouth as household words, Harry the King, Bedford and Exeter, Warwick and Talbot, Salisbury and Gloucester—be in their flowing cups freshly remembered. This story shall the good man teach his son; and Crispin Crispian shall ne'er go by, from this day to the ending of the world, but we in it shall be remembered—we few, we happy few, we band of brothers; for he today that sheds his blood with me shall be my brother; be he ne'er so vile, this day shall gentle his condition; and gentlemen in England now a-bed shall think themselves accursed they were not here, and hold their manhoods cheap whiles any speaks that fought with us upon Saint Crispin's day.

The guests were delighted with my speech, particularly coming from a boy of my age, and congratulated Dr. and Mrs. Parker on my performance. Dr. Parker accepted the praise with a slight bow of his head. Mrs. Parker waved away their flattery as if it was not important, but I could tell that she was also pleased.

A large man with wispy brown hair and a florid complexion slapped the table, shouting, "Robert, how in heaven did you teach the boy all of that! If I tried all day, I doubt I could get my niggers to remember more than two or three sentences!"

A thin woman wearing a dark green beaded dress said, "Seriously, Robert, he is very well trained." Turning to Mrs. Parker, she asked, "Mary, does he know any other passages?"

Before his wife could reply, Dr. Parker answered, "Not yet. We simply thought this would be a novelty that everyone might find amusing."

"Indeed, we did! In fact, if you would consider it, I would like to have him perform at our next dinner." Two other couples concurred, saying that they would be interested as well.

Dr. Parker, who exchanged a brief look with his wife, seemed to be thinking it over. "Well, we might be able to work something out, assuming you're willing to pay for his services. You have admitted yourself that his performance is . . . novel."

The woman in green smiled, opening her arms to encompass the group. "Of course, no one here would dream of depriving you of the use of your property without compensation. The last time Sam played for us, I believe we settled on a price of fifty cents. Would twenty-five cents be sufficient compensation for the boy's services?" Though Mrs. Parker appeared increasingly uncomfortable with the direction the conversation had taken, Dr. Parker nodded agreeably. "That's fine, Susan, very fair for a boy of his age."

* * *

After dinner was over and all the guests had departed, Sam and I left the house, heading toward the cabin we shared with Jackson. I had already started loosening the high collar of my uniform, anxious to free my neck from the stiff white restraint.

"Sam, I never heard that song before. When did you learn it?"

He thought for a moment. "I don't recall when I first heard the tune, but I liked the sound of it."

"Then how did you learn to play it?" I asked, genuinely curious.

"Didn't really have to learn. With a little practice, I can play most songs I've heard." Then changing the subject, he added, "You did a good job, Henry. I've been working for them a long time, so I could tell they were pleased with you." He paused for a moment before continuing. "If Dr. Parker hires you out for other people's dinner parties, what are you going to do with your money?"

I stopped tugging at my collar and looked up at him in surprise. "My money? I thought Dr. Parker would keep the money."

Even in the moonlight, I could see that he was smiling. "You're mostly right. If we're hired out, the money will be paid to Dr. Parker. I've heard that some owners don't give slaves any of what they earn. But Dr. Parker isn't like that. He always gives us some of what we make."

We started walking again, my mind racing with possibilities. "What do you do with your money, Sam?"

We had almost reached the cabin, but he stopped and spoke in a low voice. "I've been saving it, Henry, been saving it for years now. If you ever get any money, I suggest you do the same. I hope that I might have enough to buy my freedom one day. That is, assuming Dr. Parker would ever let me go." Perhaps sensing my rising panic, he said quickly, "But I don't have near enough money for that, not yet." Putting a hand on my shoulder, he added gently, "Besides, now that you're here, what would it look like for me to up and leave?"

* * *

Sam had been right; the Parkers were very pleased with how everything had turned out the previous evening. Even Mrs. Parker told me that I had done well. Though, of course, this was nice to hear, it couldn't compare to the excitement I felt when Dr. Parker said I would accompany the family on their next trip to the plantation. After more than a year, I would finally see my mother again.

We left Charlotte a few days after Christmas. When we arrived, I helped Sam get the horses settled in the barn before heading for the slave quarters. It was a cold, blustery afternoon, and I could see smoke rising from the chimney of nearly every cabin. I headed straight for the one I'd shared with my mother.

"Momma!" I yelled, throwing the door open. She was sitting at the cabin's only table and stood quickly when she saw me.

"Henry, I can't believe you're here!" She crossed the floor and enfolded me in a strong hug. Finally, holding me at arm's length, she said, "Look how you've grown. Toby, you remember my boy, don't you?"

Toby, who was also sitting at the table, smiled his big, easy smile. "Course I remember Henry."

"Come and sit down," my mother said, steering me to the chair she had been sitting in. "I'll get you something to eat." As she busied herself, I had a chance to look around the cabin. It looked mostly the same, but I could see there had been some changes since I left. For one thing, my mother's narrow bed had been replaced by a larger one. Also, the pallet I had once slept on was gone. I noticed that the pegs on the wall, though they still held my mother's clothes, now held men's as well. And though the cabin's shelves were still filled with her plants, they also held an assortment of small wooden carvings, the type that Toby was known to make.

Following my gaze, my mother said, "Toby and I are together now, have been since last year. I asked Sam not to tell you."

I looked at them both, trying to work through what she was saying. This was certainly not the homecoming I'd imagined. "Why didn't you want Sam to tell me?" I finally asked.

She sat on the edge of the bed. "I don't know," she sighed. "I suppose with everything you've been going through, I didn't want you to think you wouldn't have a place here. You must know, you're welcome here anytime."

But it didn't feel that way. In fact, it felt as if my memory had been erased from the cabin. Even the piece of black quartz I had left with her was nowhere in sight. I ate sullenly and said nothing.

"Don't be mad, Henry. Maybe I should have let Sam tell you before you got here, but I didn't think that was his place." She crossed to where Toby was sitting and put her hands on his broad shoulders. "Toby and I are happy together. You should be happy for us."

"I'm happy for you, Momma," I said with a forced smile. But I didn't feel happy. I had been living in Charlotte for more than a year, but I never thought of it as my home. My home had always been the small cabin I'd shared with my mother. But it didn't feel like home anymore. Even the place where I'd slept had been cleared away. But if this was no longer my home, where did I belong? The painful answer came to me suddenly—I didn't belong anywhere.

"Well, you sure don't seem happy," she said. "We'll put a bed in the same corner where you always slept. If we had known you were coming, it would have already been there. Isn't that right, Toby?"

"That's right," he said.

My emotions threatened to overwhelm me and I stood quickly. "That's all right, Momma, I'm supposed to sleep with Sam like I always do. I better get back before Dr. Parker starts looking for me."

As she studied my face, I sensed that she saw through the brave front I was trying to portray. Finally, she hugged me again and said, "It sure is good to see you, Henry. Come back whenever you have some time. We've got a lot to catch up on."

"I will Momma, I promise." I left the cabin quickly and started running toward the main house, thankful it was too dark for anyone to see my tears.

PART
2

CHAPTER 11

PURPOSE

January 1853

Most of my childhood passed tediously, one day shuffling after another in an unbroken line. I had been in Charlotte for nearly ten years. I was sixteen years old, closer then to a man than the boy I had been on my arrival. Though I was a child when I'd been taken to Charlotte, with God's protection and Nellie's cooking I had grown tall and strong.

I continued to work with Dr. Parker, who had become accustomed to, and even seemed to welcome my constant presence. In truth, though I'm certain he would never have admitted it, he had grown dependent on the vast repository of information I carried. Perhaps more importantly, he trusted its accuracy. After all, it was much easier to ask me to recall a formula, or recite a passage, than to look it up. I had become a living, breathing encyclopedia, and Dr. Parker took full advantage of my accumulated knowledge.

Years later I would learn that, shortly after my arrival in Charlotte, he had written a scientific article describing my abilities. In the text I was referred to only as Subject SB, possibly an abbreviation for Slave Boy. The article was published in 1845 in the Southern Medical and Surgical Journal. Dr. Parker's report was even cited in one of the local newspapers, and he received a modicum of recognition from his peers.

Remarkably, although by then I had recited passages from Shakespeare and other classical literature many times at Charlotte's finest dinner parties, no one suspected I was the subject of the article. I puzzled over how this was possible. How could my gift, so often displayed, go unrecognized? I have come to believe that this oversight was due to a fundamental aspect of human nature; namely, once formed it is very difficult for people to change their beliefs. And one such belief was that slaves were incapable of anything more than simple, menial tasks. The long passages I recited from literature were relegated to the realm of entertainment, little more than a parlor trick.

However, working for Dr. Parker gave me many opportunities to practice my reading, as his office was always filled with books and papers. Over the years I took advantage of my access by borrowing several books. However, this was a dangerous business, so I planned each episode carefully. First, I made certain that Jackson would be away. This was not difficult because Dr. Parker often hired him out. Next, I had to make sure there was a clear sky with a full moon. I found that if I turned my back to Sam, and was very quiet, I could read for a few hours without interruption. It also helped that he was a deep sleeper.

In addition to books, once each week two copies of a local newspaper, the *Western Democrat*, were delivered to the house. Dr. Parker kept a copy in his office, and the other was read in the parlor by Mrs. Parker, and sometimes Matthew. The next day, Sam would collect both copies and burn them. Dr. Parker had no reason to suspect that any of his slaves could read, but he was taking no chances. Consequently, he always kept his copy close at hand, and if he left his office, he usually took the paper with him. But on a few occasions, I saw the current edition of the *Western Democrat* lying invitingly on his desk.

The first few times this happened, I was wary. He was normally so careful with the newspaper, so why would he leave it unattended, and in plain sight? Was it possible that he was setting a trap for me? I had no legitimate reason to be hovering near his desk when he was away. And if I couldn't read, why would I be looking at a newspaper, or anything else on his desk for that matter? So, the first few times this temptation was laid before me, I took no action beyond watching and waiting. If it was a trap, I didn't intend to fall into it easily.

However, over time my curiosity proved stronger than my fear, and I decided to take a chance. When I was sure he had gone, I moved toward the desk quickly, listening carefully for any sound outside the door. I didn't touch the paper, but merely scanned the front page. The left side contained advertisements for hotels, commercial agents, music stores, shoemakers, and the like, but the right side of the paper was something else entirely. The first time I read the paper, I learned that Louis Napoleon Bonaparte had declared himself Emperor Napoleon III of France. An actual emperor. I heard footsteps in the hall and quickly returned to the lab, but it was too late—I was hooked! The newspaper provided a window into the wider world and, regardless of the danger, from that day forward I read it whenever I could.

I also continued to meet with Mrs. Parker, usually three or four days each week. After she had read the Bible to me in its entirety, a process that took almost a year, she asked me to recite it from the beginning. I did so while, with the book open on her lap, she traced my progress with her finger. By then my memory had been honed sharp by Dr. Parker and I made no mistakes.

Thereafter, the nature of our relationship changed. Whenever we were together, she would ask me to repeat a particular Bible verse, and when I was done, she would explain its meaning to me. Most interestingly for me, her Bible was richly illustrated and sometimes she would allow me to study the picture that accompanied a section. In time I came to almost enjoy our time together. Though the relationship was one-sided, it was a relationship, nonetheless.

* * *

On Sundays we attended service at the First Presbyterian Church. The main floor had a tall, steeply angled ceiling and was filled with row after row of smooth wooden pews. Though I don't know how it was determined, it was clear that the town's most prominent citizens always sat near the front of the church. The Parkers occupied the second pew on the left, next to the center aisle. I sat in the balcony with the other enslaved people.

There were perhaps forty or fifty of us sitting upstairs on any given Sunday, watched over by a solitary white man, Mr. Ambrose. He was a squat, thick man, clearly of mean circumstances, who sat on a stool in the back cradling a long, thin stick on his lap. His job was to keep an eye on us and make certain that we didn't speak to each other or disrupt the service in any way. Though he was at church every week, based on how he leered at the young Negro women, I don't believe he was a Godly man.

I will always recall the events of one Sunday. That morning, the sky was filled with sullen gray clouds that poured out a cold, steady rain. Christmas had been less than two weeks before and the minister, Reverend Cyrus Johnston, was preaching about the true meaning of the holiday. After listening to hundreds of sermons, it seemed to me they could be divided into three parts—a beginning, a middle, and an end. Reverend Johnston, who had already been speaking for more than thirty minutes, raised his voice to a crescendo that thundered through the church. He had clearly embarked on the third and final part of his message.

As he held the Bible aloft for emphasis, I allowed my eyes to roam over the other occupants of the balcony. I didn't move my head, for fear of attracting the attention of Mr. Ambrose; only my eyes moved as I surveyed the assembled. Though I recognized most of the people, my gaze soon fell on a beautiful young woman I had never seen before.

When the service ended, I stood and waited for her to turn in my direction so that I might see her more fully. She rose from the bench and joined a group of people slowly moving toward the stairs. Everyone in the balcony was on their feet, blocking my view, so that I still had not gotten a clear look at her. Keeping my eyes trained on her shawl, I also started moving, trying to time my arrival at the top of the stairwell to coincide with hers. My timing was good, and suddenly we were only inches apart. Her eyes had remained downcast as she walked, but for some reason she chose that moment to look up and I saw her at last. She had large, expressive brown eyes that rested comfortably on high, well-defined cheekbones. Perhaps it was my imagination, but I had the impression that when she saw me her full lips parted slightly. I do know that I stood stock-still, while my heart fluttered about uselessly in my chest like a caged bird. She looked at me for a heartbeat before beginning her descent down the narrow stairs. Rousing myself, I followed her down, but when I reached the main floor, she had disappeared into the crowd. I could only hope I might see her again someday.

My thoughts were interrupted when I felt someone slap the back of my head. "Henry, go and fetch the carriage. I'll not have my mother standing in the rain."

"Yes, Master Matthew, right away."

* * *

Though, as children, Matthew and I had been friends, over the years our relationship had greatly deteriorated. Lucinda had warned me that this was inevitable, and though I had known she was probably right, I suppose that I didn't want to believe her.

Unlike on the plantation, where I had many friends, Matthew and I had been the only children at the Parker home. While he was allowed, even encouraged, to interact with others of his age and social position, I had no such prospects. So, although there was a time when we had seen each other every day, over the years we interacted less and less, and even then, certainly not as friends.

Inexplicably, as he continued to drift away, initially I felt some measure of sympathy for him. I reasoned that our separation was through no fault of his own; he was simply becoming the person everyone wanted and expected him to be. However, with the passage of time, I realized it was also possible that he had always carried the seeds of hatred in his heart, and that they simply needed a receptive environment to take root and flourish.

The first rupture in our relationship occurred when Matthew was eight years old. It was a cold winter morning and, as usual, Dr. Parker and I were in his office. A fire was burning in the fireplace, providing more in the way of light than warmth. In preparation for an upcoming procedure, Dr. Parker was reading aloud from a book entitled *System of Surgery*. I was sitting silently in one of the chairs facing the desk, concentrating on absorbing his words, when Matthew burst in unannounced. Dr. Parker could focus intently on his work, often to the exclusion of everything else, and he loathed interruptions.

Clearly annoyed at his son's intrusion, he snapped, "Matthew, what is the meaning of this? You know better than to disturb me when I'm working."

I could tell by the look on his face that Matthew was crestfallen. I saw that he was holding something in his hand, perhaps intending to show it to his father. He quickly stuffed whatever he had in his pocket.

"Can I stay if I promise to be quiet," he said.

"No, you can't stay. I'm working now, and I can't have any interruptions. Do you understand?" Raising his voice, he yelled, "Lucinda!" Then more quietly, "Where the devil is that woman?"

Matthew looked at me, his face coloring visibly. "Henry is here. Why does he get to stay?"

Still holding the book open, Dr. Parker hardened his voice until each of his words landed like a blow. "Matthew, you need to go now. I won't tell you again."

As his son turned to leave, our eyes met, and for the first time I saw real hatred there. After he had gone, Dr. Parker resumed reading, but I found it hard to concentrate. Every time I closed my eyes, I saw Matthew staring back at me. I had seen that look before, and it triggered in me a primal instinct. *Watch out. Be careful. Matthew is dangerous. He will hurt you if he can.* It didn't take long for me to be proven right.

A few days later, Matthew and his father were preparing to go into town. I had saddled their horses and stood waiting for them outside the barn. When Dr. Parker started to ride away, Matthew waited for a few seconds and kicked me in the face with his boot. I landed on the ground hard, and he smiled as he rode away. "You need to be more careful, boy."

Though I couldn't have known it then, that was just the beginning of the many degradations, both small and large, that Matthew would inflict on me over the years.

CHAPTER 12

LOSS

May 1854

There are a great many experiences from my years in Charlotte that I could describe here, and undoubtedly some are worthy to be chronicled. However, to do so would consume far too much time. I could describe the closeness of my relationship with Nellie and Sam, particularly with Sam, who had become a father to me, the only one I had ever known. I might mention the completion of the Charlotte and South Carolina Railroad, and the mixture of fear and fascination I felt the first time I saw a train rumble into the station. It would certainly be worth noting the publication of *Uncle Tom's Cabin* in 1852, and the furious reaction it engendered among local slave owners and planters. I was present during many of those discussions, which often took place over lunch at the Parker home. But the event I remember most from those years was Sam's death.

As was my custom, I rose shortly after sunrise and went to the barn to care for the horses. The air was still cool and heavy, collecting as dew on the grass, and as fat droplets hanging precariously from the ends of green leaves. High, wispy clouds skittered quickly across the sky and I wondered, not for the first time, what animated their motion. Were they moving toward or away from something? Or perhaps they were nothing more than aerial nomads floating freely on the wind.

Soon after my arrival in Charlotte, Sam turned over the cleaning of the stables to me, as he had promised. I didn't mind. I enjoyed being around the horses, and soon I was also responsible for feeding, brushing, and washing them. Though Goldie was still my favorite, and I always made a point of stopping by her stall first, all the horses were special in their own way. Though not as friendly as Goldie, Sally never tired of being brushed down, and she was particularly fond of apples. Misty was a big, easygoing horse. She would wait in her stall patiently while I fed the others, somehow understanding that she would get her feed eventually. Matthew's horse, Lightning, had broken his leg and had to be put down. The replacement, Bessie, was the newest addition and the most bad-tempered. Even after so many years, whenever I entered the barn, she hung back in her stall, eyeing me warily, not inviting contact of any kind. I always approached Bessie slowly, cautiously, giving her a chance to get used to my presence.

Sam had also taught me how to harness the horses and hitch them to the carriage or wagon. Often when we rode through town, performing errands for the Parkers, Sam would let me take the reins. In time he joked that I was so good at handling the horses that he might give up driving altogether and become a man of leisure. Though he had said this in jest, I wished it were true. Over the years I had noted a significant deterioration in Sam's overall health and vigor. We still shared a cabin, and I could see clearly that each day had become a struggle for him. Even the smallest effort, such as walking up a flight of stairs, caused his breathing to become shallow and labored. On that morning, after I had finished feeding the horses and was on my way back to the cabin, Sam collapsed in the yard.

An hour later he was lying on his bed, ashen, struggling for each breath. Dr. Parker examined him briefly, shaking his head slowly before going back to the main house. Nellie and I were left alone with Sam in the cabin. She sat on the edge of his bed and gently took his hand in hers. She stayed for some time, just looking at Sam, before finally bending low and whispering something in his ear. When she stood, her cheeks were moist with tears. "I got to go and make lunch. You stay with him, Henry. I'll bring you something to eat later." She turned to take another look at Sam before quietly leaving the cabin.

I sat in a small chair near the wall and stayed with him all morning. During the day everyone in the household came and went. Mrs. Parker appeared after lunch with Matthew and started reading from her Bible. Matthew had rarely been in our cabin, and while his mother read, he appraised his surroundings, managing somehow to exhibit both boredom and disgust in equal measure.

Throughout the day, whenever their duties would allow, everyone came to the cabin to look in on Sam. Although they talked to him and sang to him, he remained silent, responding to no one. They also spoke to me in gentle, hushed tones, but like Sam, I remained mute, only nodding occasionally. As she had promised, Nellie brought a plate of food for me, which remained untouched beside my chair.

Jackson came in and looked at Sam a long time before putting a hand on my shoulder. "How are you holding up Henry?"

I looked up at the big man with tears in my eyes. "Sam's going to pull through Jackson; he has to."

Late that afternoon, the sun dipped below the trees that grew behind the house, bathing the sky in a rich orange glow. The temperature dropped quickly and, happy to have something to do, I started building a fire. Sam and I were alone. When the fire was well underway, I stood, brushing soot from my pants, only to discover that his eyes were open, and he was looking at me dreamily. For the first time that day he seemed alert. Delighted that he was awake at last, I moved toward the door and said, "Don't try to get up, Sam. I'll go and get help."

He shook his head, whispering, "No, don't leave, Henry, I want to talk to you."

Nodding I pulled my chair next to the bed and offered him a drink of water, which he accepted gratefully.

Clearing his throat, he continued in a weak, tremulous voice. "I'm sorry to leave you, Henry." Breathing heavily, he closed his eyes for a time before continuing. "I guess God has other plans for me. I know he has something big in store for you." The exertion of speaking seemed to tire him and again his eyes closed. I thought he might say nothing more, but soon he spoke again.

"Listen now. I want you to have the money I saved. It's wrapped in a piece of oilcloth . . . buried under one of those logs . . . where you and Matthew used to play."

I looked up, startled. I didn't think that Sam had ever known about our hiding place. Apparently reading the look on my face, he chuckled softly, the exertion triggering a fit of coughing.

"Don't look so surprised . . . I promised Emaline I would keep an eye on you . . . That's what I always tried to do."

Crying now, I shook my head and whispered, "You're going to be all right, Sam. You just need some rest. I don't want your money; I just want you to get better. You've been saving that money to buy your freedom. You told me so yourself."

Giving my hand a weak squeeze, he said, "Don't you worry about me, Henry . . . I don't need money now . . . not where I'm heading . . . I'm going to be with my boy again. I'll be free soon enough." Smiling, he closed his eyes and added, "Now hush and let me sleep for a spell."

After dinner, when Dr. Parker came to check on him again, Sam was gone.

* * *

We buried Sam in the Negro cemetery just west of town. As the rough wood box was lowered into the ground, I thought about the years we had spent together. On the day I left the plantation, Sam promised my mother that he would treat me as his own blood, and he had been true to his word. My initial time away from her was very hard. I missed her terribly, so much so that my heart could easily have become hardened with hatred and bitterness. Sam didn't let that happen. When I was angry, he listened, then helped me find ways to control my emotions. When I was depressed, he told me that there would be brighter days ahead. Sam always made time for me. He made sure I had everything I needed, even when he might not have enough for himself. I can't imagine what it would have been like to go through those years without him. He helped me to survive, but more than that, he taught me how to be a man. I loved him and now he was gone. Strangely though, I didn't feel grief. Instead I felt hollow inside, as if someone had reached in and scooped out everything that made me human.

The day after Sam's burial the household was already returning to normal and, as usual, I went to Dr. Parker's office after breakfast. Soon after my arrival he asked me to recite a reference from a text entitled *Asthma, Its Varieties and Complications*, by Dr. Francis Ramadge. However, for the first time since I became aware of my gift, my memory failed me. I tried, but I simply couldn't recall the passage from Ramadge's book, or for that matter, any passage from any book. I could tell that the memories were still there, but every time I tried to grab one, it remained maddeningly just out of reach.

My "amnesia" went on for several days, and in that time Dr. Parker's mood progressed from annoyance to anger. He threatened to have me punished if I didn't do as I was told, and I tried until I thought my head would split in two, but it was no good; the memories refused to come. One afternoon, as he was berating me, my grief, fear, and rage boiled over and for the first time in my life I yelled at him.

"Leave me alone, just leave me alone! Isn't it clear that I can't remember any of it."

Dr. Parker, clearly shocked, took my outburst as insubordination and sent Jackson to town to fetch someone that was known for his skill with a whip.

The man soon arrived carrying a long piece of plaited leather that he reflexively ran through his fingers. He spoke briefly with Dr. Parker before heading in my direction. Jackson was instructed to take off my shirt and tie my hands to a tree at the edge of the property. He did as he was told without saying a word, but before he left, he whispered, "I'm sorry, Henry."

With my face pressed against the rough bark I couldn't see what was happening, so the first lash sent a terrible shock through me, and I pulled myself against the tree, finding comfort in its unyielding form. The lashes continued to come, I'm not sure how many, and for a time I screamed after every stroke. The pain was unbearable, but I must have lost consciousness because soon I felt no more pain. The whipping might have continued, but my mind had become untethered from my body, and I was beyond caring. I had lost first my mother, then Sam, and I was alone. Sam had gone to be with his son, and part of me yearned to join them.

I don't know how long I lay in bed, drifting in and out of consciousness, but I was vaguely aware of someone, possibly Nellie, tending to my ruined back. In time I was able to sit upright, then to stand, and finally to walk again, every new exertion rewarded by searing pain.

Soon I was summoned to Dr. Parker's office. He made no mention of my whipping; in fact, he wanted to get back to work as if nothing had happened. But something had happened. In my grief following Sam's death I had committed the sin of raising my voice to my master, and I'd been whipped for it. Though I tried hard to project a calm demeanor like Sam, I hated this man with an intensity that was difficult to conceal. Dr. Parker might have wanted to put the past couple of weeks behind us and move on, but I wasn't ready to do that. Not yet anyway. So, when he said he wanted to "get back to work," even though I could feel that my memories had returned, in a fit of pique I told him I was still unable to recall anything. Enraged, Dr. Parker threw a book at me and yelled, "Get out! Get out of my sight until I decide what to do with you."

I waited in my cabin all that day, expecting at any minute to hear chains rattling and men coming to take me away. But no one came. That night I slept fitfully and, when the sun rose the next morning, I fed and watered the horses before joining Nellie, Jackson, and Roxanne for breakfast. The typically light mood of the kitchen house had turned somber. I could tell that everyone knew I was in peril. The blade had been raised, and we all held our collective breath, waiting for the final blow. We didn't have to wait long. Before I had finished eating breakfast, Dr. Parker walked into the cramped kitchen and without preamble announced, "Jackson, Henry, saddle our horses and hitch up the wagon. We're going to the plantation today."

CHAPTER 13

HEALING

May 1854

Later that morning we pulled away from the house on North Tryon. I was in the wagon with Jackson, while Dr. Parker and Matthew rode a few feet behind us. We passed through the now familiar streets of Charlotte, streets I had often traveled with Sam. I couldn't help wondering if this would be the last time I would ever pass this way.

Our caravan headed south until we came to the main east-west trade road, whereupon we turned left. We were traveling the same route that brought me to Charlotte ten years earlier. Jackson and I hadn't spoken since leaving the house, but he now asked quietly, "How are you doing, Henry?"

"I'll live," I said with a forced smile.

The wagon bounced through a small gully, and I winced at the sudden pain in my back. I wasn't sure what Dr. Parker had planned for me, but whatever it was, there was no escape now. In fact, I suspected they were riding behind us to prevent any possible escape. I had also noticed they were both armed.

I didn't think I was being sold, because if that were his plan it would have been easier to sell me in town. Charlotte had a thriving slave market. More likely, I was going back to work in the fields. Back to planting, tending and harvesting crops. Back to Mr. Fox.

As we passed a dogwood in full bloom, I thought of how my mother would make a bitter tea from the inner bark for headaches and tooth pain. She had taught me a great deal about plants and their medicinal uses, and I knew that if Dr. Parker had not taken me away, she would have taught me much more. Instead, her lessons had been interrupted and Dr. Parker had become my new teacher.

Because of our association I had learned how to formulate and prepare dozens of medicines. I also knew how he approached the treatment of many common ailments, having been at his side numerous times as he treated sick slaves, and having been present during many discussions he had with colleagues over lunch or dinner. I had gained a basic understanding of numbers, and of fractions such as one-half, one-third, and one-quarter. But most importantly of all, I had taught myself to read. Using clues gleaned from *The American Primer*, I had solved the puzzle. The book was of no importance to Matthew, and when it disappeared, he quickly moved on to other pursuits. In contrast, I never forgot its lessons, and as we moved through town on our way to the plantation, I silently pronounced many of the words we encountered along the way. *Ho-tel, mil-len-er, a-po-the-cary, hard-ware, sa-loon, un-der-ta-ker.*

Soon we were passing through the fertile farmland of the Piedmont. The deep, rich scent of the recently tilled earth intoxicated me. Most crops had been planted weeks ago, and recently sprouted corn, beans, sweet potatoes, and cotton stood in neat green rows, a colorful contrast against the dark soil. I knew this land, these plants, this life; it was part of my being, and despite the uncertainty of my situation, I felt my tension ease with each passing mile.

It was late morning when we pulled into the long drive leading to the Parker Plantation. There were fields on both sides of the road, and dozens of slaves were busy weeding the young crops. As we got closer, I recognized the work song they were singing and was immediately transported back in time.

I wait upon the Lord,
I wait upon the Lord,
I wait upon the Lord, my God,
Who takes away the sin of the world.
If you want to find Jesus,
Go in the wilderness,
Go in the wilderness,
Go in the wilderness,
Morning brother,
Go in the wilderness,
I wait upon the Lord.

We pulled up to the front of the plantation house. Jackson set the brake and I jumped down, relieved to stretch my back. I was looking at the tree line and the living quarters beyond when I heard Dr. Parker's voice.

"Henry!"

"Yes sir, Dr. Parker?"

"Get those horses put away and meet us behind the house."

"Yes sir."

I unbridled the animals and led them into the barn, making sure that they were fed and watered. After I exited the dark structure, it took a moment for my vision to adjust to the bright sunlight. Shielding my eyes against the glare, I saw Dr. Parker, Matthew, Mr. Fox, and a large Negro man I did not recognize standing on the bare red clay behind the house, perhaps thirty yards away. Everyone was looking in my direction and I froze, feeling the panic rise in me. Dr. Parker yelled, "Don't just stand there, boy, get over here."

In the few seconds it took for me to walk across the yard I became aware of several things simultaneously. I watched as Matthew put his hands on his hips, smirking. I saw a slow grin spread across Mr. Fox's face, and I noticed that the well-developed muscles of the slave standing behind him were taut, as if he expected some type of trouble. Only Dr. Parker remained impassive as he watched me cross the open space.

I forced myself to take a deep breath before speaking, willing my voice to remain calm. "Yes sir, Dr. Parker."

I could tell he was preparing to reply, but it was Mr. Fox that spoke first. "Well, look here, the little nigger is back. What's the matter, boy, did you miss your mama?" Then with a curl of his lip he added, "Don't you worry about her, she's doing just fine. I've been looking after her real good while you were gone." Though my face flushed red, I knew better than to respond to his provocation. The years had not been kind to Mr. Fox, and from the jaundiced pallor of his skin, it was clear his drinking had done its work. His death, when it came, was likely to be long, painful, and unpleasant. I wondered absently who would mourn for him.

When Dr. Parker spoke, his voice had an edge of annoyance. "All right, that's enough." He took out a white handkerchief and mopped his brow before turning his full attention to me. "Now listen to me. I'm only going to say this one time." Waving his hand toward the fields, he said, "Everyone here has got to work for their keep. Everyone." His eyes bored into me as he spoke. "Isn't that so, Mr. Fox?"

"That's right, Dr. Parker. Everybody works here, no exceptions."

Nodding, as if satisfied with the answer, he continued, "What I despise, what I won't tolerate, is any form of idleness or shirking. Do you understand?"

"Yes sir, I understand."

His voice rising, he continued, "I pay for the clothes on your back, the roof over your head, and the food you eat. Nothing in this world is free. Nothing!" Pulling the handkerchief from his back pocket he wiped his brow again. Closing on me quickly, he gripped my shoulder painfully and said, "Look at me now, because I want to make sure you understand me. Are you ready to get back to work?" He leaned forward, his face only inches from mine. "Are you ready to resume our work? Because if you're not, I'm sure Mr. Fox can find something here for you to do."

Matthew barked out an unpleasant laugh, which Dr. Parker either didn't hear or chose to ignore. "Well, what's it going to be?"

While I felt certain that my memory had returned, and that I could resume my duties, I had no wish to work for Dr. Parker again. I detested him for his casual cruelty and for everything he had done to me. Yet the alternative of being left on the plantation with Mr. Fox was also unappealing, even though I would likely be able to see my mother more often. There was also the very real possibility that I would be sold later and might never see her again. When I thought about what she and Sam would want me to do, my decision became clear.

"I want to work for you again."

"What did you say? Speak up."

I cleared my throat and said in a strong, clear voice, "I want to work for you again, Dr. Parker." I had become attuned to this man's shifting moods, having spent so much time with him over the years, and I saw a fleeting, but unmistakable, look of relief cross his face.

"Are you sure? Because if I give you another chance and you let me down again . . ." He trailed off, but his meaning was clear enough. "Do you understand me?"

I nodded. "Yes sir, I understand."

The midday sun bore down on us as he studied me carefully, weighing my fate. The open area between the house and barn where the five of us stood afforded no protection from the heat and I felt it acutely, perhaps more so because of the precariousness of my situation. I held myself still, waiting. It seemed as if this went on for a very long time, though in actuality it was less than a minute.

Finally, Dr. Parker said, "All right then. Come inside. We have work to do." Turning toward the overseer he said, "Thank you, Mr. Fox. It appears that I won't need your assistance today."

As Dr. Parker turned toward the house, Matthew, who was looking on incredulously, stammered, "Do you mean to take him back, even after what he did?"

Still walking, Dr. Parker said over his shoulder, "That's enough, Matthew. We can discuss this later."

But Matthew was far from being placated, and his voice took on an even more strident tone. "How can you forgive him after he showed such insolence?" Receiving no response from his father, he yelled, "Tom Wilson said we must take a firm hand with the slaves. If not, they will sense our weakness and take advantage of it."

Dr. Parker wheeled on his son and bellowed, "By God, Matthew, I said that's enough! When you're the master here you can run things as you please, but until then I make the decisions. Remember that before you speak again." He stared hard at his son until the younger man looked away. With that, Dr. Parker went up the stairs and into the house. As I left to follow him, Matthew grabbed my arm.

"You think you're smart don't you, telling him what he wants to hear to save your own skin? Well, you're not fooling me. My father may not see you for what you are, but I do." He released my arm and pushed me away roughly. "Now run along after your master."

I was two years older than Matthew, and at least a head taller, but I held my tongue. The boy that had once been my playmate had grown into someone unrecognizable. Matthew was Dr. and Mrs. Parker's only son, and I knew that one day he would likely inherit all their property, including me. But that was a future I preferred not to contemplate.

In the end I said nothing and simply climbed the rear stairs. As I reached the door, I caught a final glimpse of Matthew and Mr. Fox, huddled together in the dusty yard, deep in conversation.

* * *

It was late in the day when I was finally released from service. After peppering me with questions for more than an hour, Dr. Parker satisfied himself that my memories were intact. When I left the house, the sun was just visible above the western horizon, bathing the evening sky in a deep orange glow.

I walked through the trees that separated the main house from the slave quarters, keeping a lookout for Matthew or Mr. Fox. I had no wish to see them again that day. The hospital was on my right, and to my left stood the two rows of cabins, facing each other across a narrow dirt lane. It was suppertime and, after a long day of work, I suspected most of the inhabitants were having their evening meal. Only a few people sat outside enjoying a smoke or simply taking in the evening air. I felt sure that everyone knew of Sam's death and my shame at being whipped, but if they did, they said nothing. I had just reached the cabin my mother shared with Toby when I heard her voice.

"Henry, what a surprise. I didn't know you were coming. I'm getting ready to fix supper. Come on in."

I saw Toby heading toward us from the opposite direction carrying an armload of firewood. A rough bench stood by the cabin door surrounded by hundreds of curly wood shavings.

"How are you doing, Henry?" He smiled at my mother before following her inside and busying himself at the fireplace. There had been only one noticeable change in the cabin during the previous ten years; the addition of a third chair at the table. As usual, the shelves were filled to overflowing with an assortment of plants, roots, bark, and other oddments. Many of the items, such as alyssum, asafetida, boxwood, and phlox, had strong odors, and I closed my eyes, luxuriating in the rich memories triggered by their scents. I smiled inwardly, thinking there could be little doubt that this was indeed my mother's home.

"Did you hear about Sam," I asked.

My mother stopped what she was doing and looked at me. "No, we haven't heard anything. Is he all right?"

I shook my head. "No, he isn't. He died a couple of weeks ago."

She staggered slightly before sitting next to me. "Oh no, he was a good man. What happened?"

I struggled to tamp down the grief that still threatened to overwhelm me whenever I thought of Sam. "I'm not sure. For months he had been having trouble breathing, and one morning he just collapsed outside the barn. By the next day, he was gone."

She shook her head slowly as Toby sat down beside her. "I'm sorry, Henry. I know how much you liked him."

I nodded but said nothing. In fact, I had loved Sam.

She reached out and touched my hand. "How are you doing?" she asked softly.

I looked away, unable to meet her eyes. So much had happened since the last time I had seen her. I wanted to tell her everything, but I didn't know how to start. Time and circumstances had created an unnatural distance between us, and I feared there was no way to restore what had been lost. What would she think of me if she learned that, despite the pain and shame of being publicly whipped, I had nonetheless agreed to continue working with Dr. Parker. I sighed, knowing that I needed to tell her before she heard it from someone else.

She seemed to sense my inner turmoil. "I can tell that you've been through a lot, Henry. I wish I had been there with you."

At that, whatever tenuous hold I had on my emotions gave way completely. "They whipped me, Momma. Dr. Parker sent for a man from town and had me whipped."

She covered her mouth as if to stifle a scream, and I could see tears in her eyes. "Oh no, my poor boy." She got up and gazed into the fire. When she spoke again, her mood had turned serious. "Let me have a look at your back." Hesitantly I unbuttoned my shirt and let it fall from my shoulders. My mother didn't move at first, but after a moment she walked behind me, and she let out a low moan.

"Thank God it hasn't turned rotten," she said crisply. "Somebody must have salted it down good. Toby, put a pot of water over the fire. Dinner is going to have to wait. I need to look after Henry's back."

As I watched them work, I realized I was happy that my mother had found someone to share her life. I was glad she wasn't alone. During the next hour, as she gently ministered to my scarred back, my story flowed out slowly, like pus being coaxed from a wound.

CHAPTER 14

DUALITY

December 1854

From that time forward I resumed my work with Dr. Parker. In addition to looking after the horses, and my duties as his assistant, I also assumed Sam's role as driver and manservant. In the mornings I helped him dress for the day, and at night I laid out his bedclothes. Whenever he traveled to the plantation, I went along as well. At night I slept in a small alcove above the barn floor that was frigid in winter and sweltering in summer. This is where Sam had slept when he was at the plantation.

Every day when my work was done, no matter how late the hour, I would make my way to the cabin my mother shared with Toby. I might only stay for a few minutes, or for a few hours, but I never missed a day. Sometimes we talked until late into the night. If Toby fell asleep before we were done, which he often did, we would huddle together at the table, our voices low. Or, if the weather was agreeable, we might sit on the bench outside, our backs resting against the cabin wall. There was no way to replace the time that had been so casually taken from us, but we didn't dwell on what had been lost. My mother liked to say, "What's done is done," and on this matter, I agreed with her.

Though we saw each other every day, Dr. Parker never spoke of having me whipped. For him it was as if it had never happened. For me, however, the memories of that day were still vivid and raw. I hated him for everything he had done to me. But I knew that I had to bury my true feelings, bury them so deep they could never manage to push their way into the light. Showing my hatred would accomplish nothing. On the contrary, it had the potential to do a great deal of harm.

I dared not tempt fate twice. Those in power never tolerated anger, righteous or otherwise, from the powerless. Whenever I felt the bitterness inside me rising, threatening to spill over, I thought of Sam. Though I knew from our many conversations that he often felt as angry as I did, perhaps more so, outwardly he always appeared calm. I came to recognize that this was every bit as much a talent as playing the fiddle, Jackson's carpentry, or my memory. Indeed, it might be the most valuable talent of all, for until one mastered the skill of concealment, your very survival was uncertain.

Dr. Parker could be cruel, but he was far from the worst of the slaveholders. Even then I knew that some owners were capable of much greater evil. When I was eighteen years old, Mr. John Randolph, a man who had visited the Parker home on many occasions, was said to have caught one of his slaves, Tom, stealing food. As punishment for the theft, Mr. Randolph beat him so severely that he later succumbed of his injuries. Tom was perhaps a year older than me when he died.

Mr. Randolph had always seemed to me to be a pleasant man, with a quick wit and a ready smile. I found it disturbing that one person could possess qualities that were admirable and others that were abhorrent. I wondered if this duality of character was an aberration or was innate to man's nature. In the Bible, David, the slayer of Goliath, was considered a good king. However, the same man committed adultery with Uriah's wife, Bathsheba, lied about the affair, then had Uriah killed. Julius Caesar was a great general and a charismatic leader of men, but his ruthlessness and cruelty were well known. At a critical juncture his ambition drove him to cross the Rubicon River, in blatant defiance of the Roman Senate. During the American Revolution, Benedict Arnold, a general responsible for several decisive victories, turned against his compatriots and defected to the British Army before leading that army into battle against his previous comrades.

Even a cursory perusal of history reveals that many individuals revered for their courage, leadership, or ingenuity were also deeply flawed. Dr. Parker was no exception. I have already recounted the brutality and casual cruelty he visited upon slaves, both as punishment and as medical treatment. Though he was a physician, the suffering of slaves was of no concern to him. The Hippocratic admonition to "first, do no harm" seemed only to apply to his white patients.

In fact, I had heard Dr. Parker say on more than one occasion that Negros were mentally incapable of seeing to our own welfare and were fortunate if we enjoyed the guidance and protection of a white person. His views were not limited to slaves. He also believed that free men, such as Jacob the cobbler, suffered unnecessarily under the burden of their freedom. And that, in the long run, such individuals would be better off as chattel.

But at the same time, Dr. Parker was a man who clearly loved and cherished his family. He was a good friend who maintained many close relationships both within and outside Charlotte. When in town he faithfully attended church on Sundays, and overall was held in very high regard by the community. He was also a man of great intellect and learning, a voracious reader who constantly endeavored to stay abreast of the latest advances in natural science and medicine.

To remain current in his field, he engaged an agent in London and instructed the man to scour the Continent for the latest scientific books and journals. As a result, perhaps twice each year, a crate would arrive filled with the most recent offerings, which Dr. Parker would fall upon and devour like a starving man.

His scientific interests generally fit into two broad categories. The first focused on evidence that many common ailments were caused by foreign bodies too small to be seen by the human eye. This would later become known as the germ theory of disease, but at that time it was so new and revolutionary that it didn't yet have a name. Dr. Parker was an early follower of Ignaz Semmelweis's studies on the causes of puerperal fever, John Snow's investigation of a cholera outbreak in London, and the work of other similar, though less well recognized medical pioneers.

His other area of interest focused on the extraction of medically active compounds from natural sources, primarily plants. Through his studies, he had become familiar with the work of Dr. Withering, a Scottish physician that practiced in the late eighteenth century. Withering discovered that the dried extract of purple foxglove had a remarkably beneficial effect on patients with dropsy, or ailments of the heart. Unfortunately, the plant did not grow in the United States, as it might have helped Sam's condition.

Medical lore held that Dr. Withering learned how to use foxglove from an old woman that was traveling through his town. So, unlike many so-called learned men of the day, Dr. Parker did not immediately dismiss the plant-based remedies employed by my mother and other natural healers. Instead, he endeavored to understand which plants they used and for what purposes. He then sought to isolate, or extract, each plant's active agents. In this way he hoped to reproduce, or perhaps even enhance, their results.

His approach was not as far-fetched as it might seem. Already at that time, in addition to the discovery by Dr. Withering, morphine had been extracted from poppies, syrup of ipecac from the roots of *Carapichea ipecacuanha*, strychnine from plants of the genus *Strychnos*, quinine from the bark of cinchona trees, and so forth. Dr. Parker was aware of these and many other medicinal plants, and through his research he hoped to add to the known pharmacopoeia.

However, although his ideas had solid scientific underpinnings, this did not mean that they were readily accepted by his patients. The belief that illness was caused by an imbalance of the blood was firmly entrenched, and like most people of the time, the white patients that Dr. Parker treated expected to be bled or given an emetic or cathartic agent. From their perspective, unless there was clear evidence that the body was being purged in some way, how could they know the toxins responsible for their malady had been removed?

Conversely, his enslaved patients had no control over their bodies and therefore no power to refuse treatment, and Dr. Parker chose their therapy with no input from them. Therefore, it was ultimately the enslaved that bore the full weight of his experimentation.

CHAPTER 15

DISCORD

December 1858

O n a cold, sunny December afternoon, Dr. Parker invited three of his friends and fellow Freemasons to join him for lunch. The guests, Thomas Baldwin, Michael Harris, and David Mitchell were all well known to me from previous visits to the house. Matthew, now a young man of twenty, was also in attendance. I was told to wear my informal livery for the occasion, which consisted of black shoes, black pants, a white shirt, and a black silk vest with gold-colored buttons.

As usual, Nellie was responsible for preparing the food, but she no longer worked alone. Earlier that year the Parkers had purchased a young slave named Gloria to help Nellie in the kitchen house. Had she been consulted, Nellie certainly would have objected to the presence of another woman in "her kitchen," but she wasn't given the chance. One day Mrs. Parker simply introduced Gloria and informed Nellie that going forward she would be her assistant. I later heard from Roxanne that when Nellie was told, Gloria was already standing behind Mrs. Parker, appearing very uncomfortable with the situation.

Nellie was crestfallen. Did the Parker's no longer appreciate her cooking? Did they think that she was too old to run the kitchen house without help? Were they making plans to replace her with the younger woman? Roxanne, Jackson, and I did our best to offer reassurances, but really, how could we know what the Parker's had planned for her? How could we know what they had in store for any of us? The change was hard for Nellie, and she moped around the kitchen for several weeks.

Since my arrival in Charlotte, Nellie and I had always been close. After I was taken from my mother, she stepped in and helped to fill the void. But despite our relationship, nothing I said or did could rouse her. I mentioned my concerns to Dr. Parker, but he brushed them aside brusquely.

"The running of the household is Mrs. Parker's purview. I don't concern myself with those matters and neither should you."

Then slowly, ever so slowly, Nellie's mood started to brighten. I'm not certain what led to her improvement, but knowing her as I did, I think she just got tired of being sad all the time. She gradually accepted the presence of Gloria in her kitchen, and in time it appeared she even welcomed the companionship.

* * *

The first time I met Gloria was in the kitchen house shortly after she arrived. Word of her arrival had spread quickly through the house, but at the time I was at the apothecary in town picking up supplies for Dr. Parker. When I returned, I decided to say hello to Nellie before going to the main house. As soon as I walked into the kitchen, I knew that something was wrong. Nellie was talking to herself and chopping vegetables much more forcefully than necessary. I wanted to ask her what was wrong, but I couldn't speak. Indeed, for the moment, I was as pinned in place as surely as one of Dr. Parker's colorful butterfly specimens.

The source of my stupefaction stood on the other side of the room, well out of the reach of Nellie and her knife. It was the same young woman I had first seen several years earlier in the church balcony!

She wore a simple brown dress with a thin shawl draped over her arms and shoulders. Her posture was erect, and she seemed remarkably composed, despite

Nellie's angry display. Her thin, sculpted face was covered with dark, lustrous skin that seemed to glow, even in the poor light of the kitchen, and her short black hair was twisted into thick curls that ended at the nape of a long, slender neck. She looked on impassively as Nellie violently attacked another carrot, then she turned and looked at me for the first time. The effect was immediate. I felt my legs go weak, and it was only with the greatest effort that I managed not to look away. I wanted to say or do something, but I had been rendered mute. Though I'm sure I looked ridiculous, I decided then and there that she was the most beautiful woman I had ever seen.

"I'm Gloria. Mrs. Parker wants me to work in the kitchen with Nellie." She inclined her head slightly in Nellie's direction. "But it doesn't seem like she wants me here." Her melodic voice spilled into the room smooth and unhurried.

Nellie stopped her assault on the vegetables and pointed the knife at Gloria. "I've been taking care of this kitchen by myself since before you were born. I don't need any help now."

Gloria studied her for a minute before spreading her hands wide in deference. "I don't want to fight with you, Nellie. I don't have any more choice in this than you do. I know that you've been here a long time, and this is your kitchen. Just give me something to do and, I promise, I'll stay out of your way."

All the fight seemed to drain out of Nellie, and she leaned against the table, deflated. "Well, you could peel those potatoes in the bowl over there, as long as you don't throw out too much potato with the peel."

Gloria tied on an old apron but said nothing more. As she looked around the kitchen for a knife, I found my voice at last.

"The knives are over there in the corner. Pleased to meet you, Gloria. Folks around here call me Henry."

Nellie looked at me and snorted. "Well, why wouldn't we call you Henry? That's your name, isn't it? What's gotten into you?"

Gloria ignored Nellie's comment. She took a seat at the small table in the middle of the room and picked up a potato. "What do you do around here, Henry? That is, when you're not dawdling around in the kitchen."

I could feel the heat blooming across my face, but thankfully my voice was still working. "I'm Dr. Parker's valet and I take care of the horses. I also help him in the laboratory."

"Laboratory?" she asked, looking puzzled.

"Oh, sorry. It's the room next to Dr. Parker's office. I work there most days."

"Laboratory." She said the word slowly, like she was getting a feel for it. "I never heard of it. What kind of work do you do there?"

"All kinds really. I help him make tinctures, poultices, pills, ointments. Almost anything really." Then, as an afterthought I added, "I have a pretty good memory for things." Behind Gloria, I saw that Nellie smiled at that.

Reaching for another potato, Gloria looked at me and smiled for the first time. "Well, Henry, if ever I'm feeling poorly, I guess I'll know where to go for help." I stood awkwardly for a moment, struggling to think of something more to say.

"I don't know if you remember me, but I first met you in the balcony at church years ago. Well, I didn't really meet you, but we got to the stairs at the same time." Gloria seemed puzzled while Nellie looked amused. Yet remarkably, embarrassingly, I plowed ahead. "I know you're not always at church, but I look for you whenever we're there. I never knew your name but now I do. Gloria—that's a pretty name."

She smiled and covered her mouth with her hand. Was she trying to stifle a laugh?

"Henry," Nellie said softly, "I think you should let us get back to work." I nodded, and as I headed for the main house, I was chased by the sound of their laughter.

* * *

For the luncheon, Nellie and Gloria prepared ham, beef, mutton, Dutch salad, boiled potatoes, sweet onions, pickles, cornbread, and apple fritters. Gloria and I served the food, and when lunch was over, the men moved to the parlor for smoking and whiskey, the same room where Mrs. Parker and I studied the Bible. I served drinks, then stood just inside the door, ready to refill empty glasses or provide a lit match. As in the dining room earlier, no one took note of my presence, but that was by design. As Sam had told me once, "You got to make yourself invisible, Henry. They want to know you're there; they just don't want to see you."

After everyone was comfortably settled, the conversation quickly turned to politics.

"I think we need to take the threat seriously," said Mr. Mitchell. "If the abolitionists are successful, our entire way of life will be destroyed." He sipped his whiskey and looked around the room for support.

Dr. Parker said, "Don't you think 'threat' is too strong a word, David? Really, how are the Yankees a threat to us? I'll admit there are some that advocate doing away with slavery entirely, but they're a small, albeit vocal minority. During my medical studies I lived in Philadelphia for several years. I assure you that most men there believe, as we do, that Negros are an inferior race." There were murmurs of assent from the room. "But most importantly, I've heard no one from the North, no one in a position of authority, advocate eliminating slavery in those areas where it already exists. Not even that Black Republican, Lincoln."

"Well, I for one don't trust them," shot back Mr. Mitchell. "If Lincoln and the Republicans are so favorably disposed to the existence of slavery, why are they fighting so hard to keep it out of the new territories? You must agree that Kansas has been a bloody disaster. The atrocities committed there by the abolitionists will not go unanswered."

"I think you're making too much of the situation," Dr. Parker said, in his most reasonable voice. "I'll grant you that Kansas is a lawless territory now, but hasn't the march to statehood always been preceded by a period of instability? The situation in Texas was even worse before they joined the Union. Forgive me, but I really can't see how the current unrest in Kansas, more than a thousand miles away, imperils us here." He paused before adding, "What do you think, Thomas?"

Mr. Baldwin, who looked uncomfortable at being called out, spoke haltingly. "Well, I think you have both made excellent points. I'll grant you that the war for Texas was long and bloody, but it was not fought over the issue of slavery. I'm not certain it's an apt comparison." Addressing Dr. Parker directly, he said, "Robert, you have to admit that abolitionists are flooding into Kansas for the express purpose of ensuring that it enters the Union as a free state."

"And what's so wrong with that?" countered Dr. Parker, his voice rising slightly. "When the final vote is taken, if there are more men in Kansas that support slavery than oppose it, then they will carry the day. Isn't that how democracy is meant to work?"

Speaking for the first time since entering the parlor, Mr. Harris said, "I agree with much of what's been said, but with respect, gentlemen, I think we're avoiding the larger issue." He paused to make certain he had their full attention before continuing. "I know you would all agree that slavery is critical for our prosperity, indeed to our very way of life. It's not surprising then that we are determined to keep it in its present form. But make no mistake, my friends, there are elements in the North, powerful elements, that are equally determined to eliminate slavery everywhere it exists in these United States." He gestured to the room with the stem of his pipe. "I pray we are able to resolve our differences peacefully, but if the situation in Kansas is any guide, that's unlikely to happen."

"You sound pessimistic," said Mr. Baldwin.

"If you're asking if I'm uncertain that a peaceful resolution is possible, then yes, I am pessimistic." He lifted his pipe in my direction, and I moved forward silently to relight it. As I withdrew, he was already speaking again, more vigorously this time. "But I do feel certain about one thing. I believe that the best way, perhaps the only way, to avoid a conflict with the North is to prepare as if that conflict is inevitable." Someone started to speak but he talked over him. "I fought with many of them during the war against Mexico, good soldiers all. And like soldiers everywhere, they're less likely to become emboldened if they believe they will pay dearly for any aggression."

Sounding flustered, Dr. Parker said, "You speak as if war is inevitable, but surely that's not true?" Receiving no reply from Mr. Harris, he continued. "Unlike you, I have no military experience, but we're the same country. War with the North seems inconceivable to me. I realize that we don't agree on any number of issues, but even so, why in God's name would the North go to war with us?"

Mr. Harris didn't answer right away, the smoke from his pipe drifting slowly toward the ceiling. Finally, he said, "I'm sure you won't like it, but the simple answer is we're weak and they know it." Several of the men began to protest loudly, but Mr. Harris continued speaking as if he hadn't heard them. "Gentlemen, I love North Carolina as much as you do, but blind love can cloud your vision. You must try to think about this dispassionately. The North has more men, factories, railroads, ships and, well, more of just about everything else they need to make war."

All of the men were silent for a time as they registered the truth of his words. Finally, Mr. Baldwin said, "Michael, your points are well taken, but what would you have us do? You can't be suggesting that we capitulate without a fight?"

From the corner of my eye, I could see that Matthew was leaning forward in his chair, clearly agitated. No one else seemed to notice. Instead, everyone looked to Mr. Harris for a response.

"Well, the truth is, gentlemen, there is only so much we can do. The North has a clear superiority in terms of men and materials. We can't change that, certainly not in the short term. But as I said earlier, there are steps we can take to make ourselves a more difficult target."

"Such as?" asked Mr. Baldwin.

"Well, for years many of us have advocated for increased funds to strengthen our militias. The state legislature has finally agreed and that is a good first step. Also, as you know, just a few miles from here they have started construction of the North Carolina Military Institute. If war comes, the young men trained there will be instrumental to our defense. Volunteer militias are useful in a fight, no doubt about it, but they are no substitute for professionally trained soldiers."

Suddenly everyone seemed to be speaking at once, but it was Matthew's voice that cut through the clamor. "I can't believe what I'm hearing. You all act as if you're afraid of them. They insult us daily, but instead of defending our way of life, we sit here sipping whiskey and discussing all the ways we might lose!"

Everyone in the room fell into an uncomfortable silence, clearly taken aback by the harshness of Matthew's tone.

Embarrassed by his son's lack of decorum, Dr. Parker said, "Michael, I apologize for my son's rude behavior." He turned to look at Matthew directly. "I blame myself. He obviously isn't ready for the company of gentlemen."

Never taking his eyes off Matthew, Mr. Harris said tightly, "No apology necessary, my friend. I for one would like to hear the young man out."

Before Dr. Parker could reply, Matthew spoke again, more quietly this time. "I'm sorry if I offended anyone. In fact, I agree with much of what Mr. Harris has said. We ship our cotton north on railroads they control, using capital from banks they own, and then buy back the finished cloth at inflated prices."

Dr. Parker said, "All right, Matthew, you've made your point. Perhaps we should discuss this at another time." But Matthew would not be silenced.

"Have any of you read *De Bow's Review*? They lay out the issues very clearly. While the North insults our dignity and attacks our very way of life, we do nothing. Well, I for one will not allow a Yankee to dictate how I should live. I do not seek war with the North, but if it comes, we must be ready."

No one spoke for some time. Finally, Mr. Harris cleared his throat. His mood was somber. "Well, Matthew, if war comes, and I hope it doesn't, the South will need thousands of eager young men just like you."

* * *

After the guests had left, I was leaving the main house when I heard a commotion coming from the rear storage room. I opened the door, which was slightly ajar, and saw that Matthew had Gloria backed into a corner.

I wanted to pull him away from her, but I had been beaten before simply for raising my voice. In the end I just said, "Master Matthew, is everything all right?"

"Yes, everything is fine, get out of here," he hissed. But I met Gloria's eyes and could clearly see that everything was not fine.

"Yes sir, it's just that Gloria and I need to clear the dishes from lunch." This wasn't true, the dishes had already been put away, but it was all I could think of at that moment.

"I said get the hell out of here," he yelled.

I wasn't sure what else I could say or do, but I made up my mind then and there that I wasn't going to leave her. "Please, Master Matthew . . ."

He turned to face me, clearly furious now. "I told you to leave. Don't make me tell you again."

I was trying to decide what to do next when I heard Mrs. Parker's voice. "What's going on in here?" She was standing behind me and I backed away from the door to allow her to see into the room more clearly. "Matthew, what's going on in there?" When he didn't respond, she stared at him and frowned. "Gloria, you go on now. I'm sure you've got work to do."

"Yes ma'am," Gloria said, before stepping around Matthew and hurriedly leaving the storage room.

"You too, Henry."

"Yes ma'am, Mrs. Parker." I risked a last look at Matthew but averted my eyes from his murderous glare.

When I got to the kitchen house, Gloria was leaning on the table with her back to the door. "Gloria, are you all right?"

I thought she would be grateful, but when she turned to face me, I was surprised by the anger I saw there. "What did you think you were doing?" she seethed.

Her reaction stung me. I felt she had no cause to take that tone with me, and I could feel my own anger begin to flare. "What do you think I was doing? I was trying to save you from . . . whatever Matthew had in mind." Then with a sneer I added, "Unless you didn't want me to stop him."

"Oh, so that's it. You were trying to save me," she said, feigning surprise. "That's nice, but what about when you're not around? Did you ever think of that? What am I supposed to do the next time he comes sniffing around? Should I ask him to wait until you get there?"

I stepped toward her. "I can see you don't appreciate what I did, but don't worry, I won't ever do it again. You're on your own."

She glared at me for a moment, then shook her head and sat down, looking more dejected than I had ever seen her. I immediately regretted my harsh words. When she spoke again, there was no anger, only sadness. "Do you think this is the first time Matthew or somebody like him has put their hands on me? Do you? I'm glad you were there today, I really am, but maybe you or Mrs. Parker won't be there the next time. Like it or not, I've got to be able to look out for myself. I don't have any people here to watch out for me. The only thing you're going to do is get yourself killed, and I don't want to be the cause of something like that."

I was going to tell her that she wasn't alone and that, given the chance, I would do the same thing again. But we were interrupted by someone yelling outside.

"Henry, get out here!" It was Matthew. I looked at Gloria and sighed before turning to go out and meet him.

"Henry, wait!" Gloria was on her feet and grabbed my hand. "I appreciate what you did for me in the house, I really do." I nodded before going out to meet Matthew.

He was standing in front of the cabin I shared with Jackson. "Yes, Master Matthew, what can I do for you?"

"Ah, there you are. I should have known to look for you in the kitchen with the women. Saddle my horse, I'm going out."

"Yes sir."

"As I walked toward the barn, I could sense that he was right behind me. When we were inside, he said, "You may have my father fooled, but I see you for what you are, an uppity nigger that needs to be brought down a peg." I didn't respond to his provocation but continued to saddle his horse. Behind me, I could hear him gently slapping his riding crop against his leg.

When I was done, he snatched the reins from my hand and pushed the end of his riding crop into my chest. "Mark my words. One day, and it won't be long, you're going to regret ever setting yourself against me."

CHAPTER 16

GENERATIONS

October 1859–November 1860

O n October 16, 1859, John Brown and eighteen men attacked and captured the armory at Harpers Ferry, Virginia. The armory was quickly recaptured by state and federal troops, the latter led by a Colonel Robert E. Lee. Less than two weeks later, John Brown and six other men captured with him were sentenced to die. Though he was hanged on the second of December, the repercussions of his actions far outlived him. At the time, one newspaper wrote that "The Harpers Ferry invasion has advanced the cause of disunion more than any other event that has happened since the formation of the Government."

While many in the North viewed Brown as a martyr to the cause of freedom, most in the South saw him and his men as anarchists, determined to destroy their way of life by any means. Two free Negro men from North Carolina had taken part in the raid, and this only added to the sense of outrage and betrayal felt by many in the state. So, if the Haitian slave revolt of 1804 and Nat Turner's Rebellion in 1831 had made the South uneasy, John Brown's raid led to something more closely resembling panic. Many now believed that compromise with the North was impossible and calls for separation from the Union only grew louder.

Dr. Parker traveled around town frequently, and wherever he went there was talk of abolitionists, Abraham Lincoln, secession, and war. No one paid much attention to the slave standing behind him, and in that way, I was able to absorb much of the news of the day.

* * *

The following October, I was in the laboratory grinding milkweed seeds with a large mortar and pestle. Milkweed was known to be poisonous, but Dr. Parker hoped that the administration of small amounts might prove beneficial for the treatment of pain. He got the idea to try low doses of poisonous substances from the work of Paracelsus, a sixteenth-century Swiss physician. Paracelsus said that "Poison is in everything, and no thing is without poison. The dosage makes it either a poison or a remedy." Over the years Dr. Parker had experimented with various preparations of known toxins, with decidedly mixed results. Of course, as with all his unproven treatments, he intended to first test the milkweed extract on the enslaved.

Suddenly, I became aware of raised voices in the adjacent office. I had been so focused on my work that I hadn't heard anyone enter. Now alerted, I immediately stopped grinding the seeds and listened more closely. I recognized the voice of Matthew, and he and his father were clearly having a heated conversation.

"The school opened last year with forty cadets and D. H. Hill as the first superintendent. I'm sure you agree that it's a grand building." I knew that Matthew was speaking of the new North Carolina Military Institute in Charlotte.

Dr. Parker sounded tired, or perhaps just exasperated. "Yes, it's very grand. But Matthew, we've talked about this before. There is no reason to attend a military academy unless you plan to make a life in the army. Is that what you really want? Tensions are running high, and if war comes, as a cadet you would immediately be pulled into any conflict. Have you thought about that?"

"Of course I've thought about it," Matthew snapped. "I think about it all the time! You know that the abolitionists and Black Republicans want to destroy us. They have made their intentions clear. After they have freed our slaves, do you imagine that they will take pity on our weakened condition and cease hostilities? I don't believe that and I'm sure you don't either."

The door between the office and laboratory was open a few inches, and I saw Matthew point to the portrait hanging behind Dr. Parker's desk. "Your own grandfather fought against England in the war for independence. Now it's our time to fight."

Dr. Parker took off his glasses and slowly massaged his temples. When he spoke, he did so slowly and deliberately, as if lecturing an obstinate child. "My grandfather had no land or inheritance; hence his prospects were limited. This situation is very different. You're my son and sole heir and can't afford to risk your life needlessly."

Matthew barked out a short, harsh reply that I couldn't decipher.

His father continued, this time more gently. "Listen, Matthew, I know you're passionate about the cause, and I appreciate your enthusiasm, I really do. I'm not too old to remember what it was like to be young and care deeply about something." Then, as if rousing himself from a dream, Dr. Parker's voice became hard again. "But your life is too valuable to the future of this family. If war comes, and I agree it seems more likely every year, you cannot serve."

The look on Matthew's face was one of shock. "Do you mean to say that while others fight for North Carolina, you would have me hide at home like a coward!"

"I cannot speak to what others will do, but as our only son they cannot force you. We will hire someone to serve in your stead. There is no cowardice in protecting the interests of your family."

Matthew stood up abruptly, turning over his chair as he did so. His voice was choked with emotion. "Let me be clear, sir, for I want there to be no misunderstanding between us. If war does come, I'll be one of the first to enlist. I am twenty-two years old; you cannot stop me. With or without your blessing, I will be a part of this fight."

He started to leave, but then turned and added, "The only question you should ask yourself is this: Would you rather have me go to war as a trained soldier or as an untrained volunteer?"

With that he left the room, slamming the door behind him. When I looked back to Dr. Parker, he was staring out the window, seemingly lost in thought. I waited a respectable time before silently entering the office and righting the fallen chair.

Still facing the window, he said, "Henry, do you know about the life of Julius Caesar?"

My eyes closed in concentration as I searched my memories. "Only a little, sir, from the play by Shakespeare. Also, the name Caesar is mentioned in the Bible many times, specifically Augustus Caesar, Tiberius Caesar, and Claudius Caesar, but not Julius Caesar." I would have continued, but he turned to me and held up his hand.

"I'm sure you're right." He took a moment before picking up the topic again. "Julius Caesar was a general who later became the ruler of Rome. It was in his memory that other Roman emperors later took the name of Caesar." He looked tired, as though a great weariness had settled over him. "Even in Caesar's time, there must have been young men eager to squander their lives in war. Do you know how I know that?"

I shook my head. "No sir."

"I know there must have been such reckless young men because Caesar said, 'It is easier to find men who will volunteer to die than to find those who are willing to endure pain with patience.' Can you imagine that? Easier to find men who will die rather than endure with patience." He shook his head ruefully. "Caesar said that many, many years ago, but I believe it applies equally well to the current situation. Isn't that remarkable?"

This time I stayed silent, sensing that no reply was expected. Finally, he sighed and said, "That will be all for now, Henry."

"Yes sir, but I still need to finish the milkweed extract."

"Go on now. You can finish tomorrow."

"Yes sir, Dr. Parker."

As I left, I saw that he had already turned back to the window, and the darkening sky beyond.

On my way to the kitchen house, I thought about the milkweed extract, and all the other pills, powders, poultices, extracts, tinctures, and teas I had prepared for Dr. Parker over the years. Sometimes these preparations seemed to work, but many times they had no effect at all, or worse still, did real harm. Not for the first time, I wondered if helping him made me as guilty as he was. Was I an accomplice to his misdeeds?

The following week, during one of our trips to the plantation, I shared my misgivings with my mother. As usual, she didn't mince words.

"You're nothing like that man," she snapped. "Difference between you and him is he's got a choice, and you don't. He tells you what to make, then after you're done, he decides how to use it, and who to use it on." She lit her pipe, pointing the stem at me for emphasis. "The truth is, you're no more responsible for what he does than the man that makes ropes is responsible for a hanging."

When I mentioned my concerns to Nellie, her response was more circumspect. "I don't know, Henry; I can't see how you can be held to account for what he does. But I do know one thing: if you don't do what he wants, he'll just get somebody else to do it." We were the only ones in the kitchen house, and she stopped stirring whatever she was cooking long enough to look me in the eye. "And if that happens, where's that leave you?"

But circumstances didn't allow time for me to dwell on my work with Dr. Parker. Little more than a week later, on November 6, Abraham Lincoln was elected the sixteenth president of the United States, and almost immediately everything changed.

CHAPTER 17

DISUNION

November 1860–April 1861

The election of Lincoln fanned the flames of anger and resentment that had been smoldering for years. Once given life, the resulting conflagration engulfed the South, so much so that, by the time Lincoln was inaugurated on March 4, 1861, seven states had already seceded from the Union. South Carolina was the first on December 20, quickly followed by Mississippi, Florida, Alabama, Georgia, Louisiana, and Texas. By early June, Virginia, Arkansas, North Carolina, and Tennessee had also joined the Confederacy.

Everyone in the household could tell something was amiss, but as slaves our understanding of what was happening was, at best, incomplete. Still, in the regular course of our duties, we managed to gather snippets of information here and there. And of course, anything we learned was shared in the kitchen house.

"I heard Matthew tell Dr. Parker he thinks there will be war," Roxanne said.

"What did the old man say?" Nellie asked, carefully peeling the shell from a boiled egg.

"He didn't say anything, just kept eating. It seems like he and Matthew don't talk much anymore."

Nellie shook her head. "That boy has always been headstrong. Now it seems like he's champing at the bit to get into a fight."

"He's always fiddling with that pistol of his, like he can't wait to shoot somebody," Roxanne quipped.

Jackson laughed. "I wonder how brave he'll be when folks start shooting back."

Roxanne lowered her voice conspiratorially. "A couple of days ago I heard Matthew tell Mrs. Parker that, if war comes, he plans to be part of it. Said he doesn't think the whole affair will last more than two or three months."

"Why does he think that?" Gloria asked sharply.

"How would I know?" Roxanne said defensively. "I'm just telling you what he said." Turning toward me, she added, "Isn't that right, Henry?"

I dipped a piece of hoecake in some pork fat before taking a bite. "Roxanne's right. I heard it too. Matthew had some of his friends over last week, and they think that once the North knows the South is willing to fight, really fight, they'll let them go on their way."

"Now how would any of those boys know what the Yankees will do?" Nellie snorted. "It hasn't been that long since all of them were in short pants."

"Dr. Parker told Mrs. Parker that there was no way the North would let the South go," I continued. "He lived in Philadelphia for a few years, and he said the North will never give up the Union."

Gloria wiped her hands on her apron and frowned. "Well then, what does he think will happen?" she asked.

I ate the last piece of hoecake. "He thinks war is more likely than not but still hopes it will never happen." I looked around the room before continuing. "But if war comes, he thinks it will go on for years, and that in the end, the South is bound to lose." No one said anything more, as everyone digested this information in their own way.

* * *

Later that day, Dr. Parker poked his head into the laboratory and asked me to come to the parlor. When I arrived, I was surprised to see that Mrs. Parker and Matthew were already there. Dr. Parker took a seat near his wife, while I stood awkwardly just inside the room.

"Matthew and I met with Colonel Hill yesterday. The colonel has been asked to organize and lead a regiment from North Carolina. In fact, one of the companies is being recruited from right here in Mecklenburg County."

He paused, and not sure what else to do I said, "Yes sir."

"The initial deployment will only be for six months. I have provided funds to help supply the company, and in return they have agreed to appoint Matthew as a second lieutenant."

I glanced at Matthew, who was scarcely able to contain his excitement. It seemed he was getting his wish after all. In contrast to her son's ebullient mood, Mrs. Parker sat quietly looking at her hands.

"Congratulations, Master Matthew," I said with a smile. "I'm sure that you will make a fine officer."

"Thank you, Henry," he answered smoothly, taking a long sip of his drink.

And why wouldn't I smile? In my heart I was glad Matthew would be leaving, if only for a few months. But even as I had this pleasant thought, I could feel that something was amiss. Everyone in the household would find out about Matthew's deployment soon enough, so why had they brought me into the parlor to inform me personally?

Dr. Parker glanced at his wife, who was still studying her hands. "We feel confident that Matthew will make a success of it, but as an officer and a gentleman, he will require assistance. In fact, it will be expected."

I wasn't certain where the conversation was heading, but suddenly my stomach was clenched as tight as a fist, as if it already understood what I did not.

"In short, Henry, we think you are well suited to accompany Matthew to Raleigh and act as his body servant for the duration of his deployment."

I staggered slightly, as if his words had struck me physically. I looked around the room for support, but seeing none, I finally stammered, "But sir, my work here . . ."

"Will wait until you return," Dr. Parker said. "You are valuable to us, Henry. I'm sure you know that. If we didn't have faith in you, we wouldn't be sending you with Matthew. But as much as you may be needed here, his immediate need is greater."

Mrs. Parker spoke for the first time. "We want you to look after Matthew while he's away. He's known you since he was a boy, nearly his entire life. We can think of no one better to . . ." Her voice trailed off, before regaining its strength. "We can think of no one better to assist him while he's away."

I stood transfixed, unable to think of what I could say that would change their minds.

Matthew, who was studying me closely, said, "I can see that you're shaken by the news, and that's understandable—I'm sure it comes as a shock. But you need to collect yourself. We leave on the train for Raleigh with the rest of the company in two weeks. Do you understand?"

All of them were looking at me now. But my mind was still in such a state of agitation that I didn't answer immediately. I had often dreamed of leaving Charlotte to see more of the world, but not like this. I had no desire to follow Matthew anywhere; even the thought of it sickened me. I would be attached to an army that was fighting for the express purpose of maintaining my enslavement. What would be expected of me? How long would I be away? When would I see Gloria and my mother again?

A dark look passed across Matthew's face. "Henry, we leave in two weeks," he said slowly, taking time to enunciate each word. "Do you understand?"

Finally rousing myself, I said, "Yes sir, I understand."

Dr. Parker nodded, satisfied. "Very well, now that that's settled, you can go on back to your work."

"Yes sir, Dr. Parker."

Before I could leave Matthew added, "And Henry, in the future, when I ask something of you, I expect you to respond without delay. Don't ever make me repeat myself again."

Dr. Parker frowned but said nothing.

"Yes sir, Master Matthew. It won't happen again," I managed. I turned and left the parlor quickly, hoping that he hadn't seen my gathering rage.

I went back to the lab but found it impossible to concentrate on my work. I had known for some time that Matthew wanted to join the Confederate cause, but I certainly never thought I would be ordered to accompany him. And why should I be? His personal animus toward me must have been obvious, even to the Parkers. For my part, I thought him a shallow, self-centered, vainglorious popinjay, whom I'd spent the last few years trying to avoid whenever possible. I was certain they could have found someone better suited for the role. After all, I couldn't even cook. I was puzzling over why they had chosen me when Dr. Parker came back into his office and called for me to join him.

When I walked in, he started speaking without preamble. "You seemed displeased that we're sending you to accompany Matthew?"

"No sir," I mumbled.

"Speak up!"

"No sir," I said more loudly.

"You're lying," he snapped. "It's obvious that you have no wish to go." It wasn't a question, so I stayed sullenly silent.

"Speak up, damn you. I have neither the time nor patience for your nonsense."

The anger in me flared white hot and I stared at him directly, heedless of the consequences. "You're right. I have no wish to go."

"And why not?" he asked. "I would have thought you would jump at the chance to see some of the world outside of Charlotte." When I didn't respond he barked, "Well, was I wrong about you? You have my permission to speak frankly."

I could hear Sam's voice in my head telling me to be careful, but I ignored it. "See the world," I repeated slowly. "Of course I would like to see the world, but that's not what's being offered. You want me to accompany Matthew because he's foolhardy."

He colored visibly. "What did you say?"

"You told me to speak frankly," I said levelly. When he didn't respond I pushed ahead, having gone too far to turn back. "This is not about me seeing more of the world. You want me to go with Matthew because you hope that I might find a way to keep him alive."

Yes," he said, "we need him to come back safely."

"But you must know that I have little control of that. I can forage for food, cook his meals, and clean his uniform. If he falls ill, I can even try to bring him back to health, but I have no power to deflect a cannon shell or stop a bullet."

He glared at me, and I knew that our time of speaking together frankly was at an end. "Yes, you will do all that, and you will also do everything you can to keep him safe. That is your primary job. Have I made myself clear?"

"Yes sir."

"Good. And should you decide to get the idea to run, I will make certain that your mother, and Gloria, pay dearly for your actions." He must have seen my shock at the mention of Gloria's name because he smiled wickedly. "Yes, Matthew told me of your fondness for the girl. But don't concern yourself about her. She and your mother will be fine, that is, assuming you don't disappoint me."

* * *

Later that night, Gloria came to my cabin to see me. Dr. Parker had hired out Jackson to do some carpentry for a man in town, so we were alone. The night air was cool, and I shivered involuntarily. I'd been so dispirited after my meeting with the Parkers that I hadn't bothered to make a fire, and she did so without asking.

"We should leave, Gloria," I whispered. "There is nothing for us here. With everyone so wrapped up in war hysteria, we could slip away."

Shaking her head, she sat next to me and gently touched my hand. "Where would we go, Henry? Chances are we wouldn't even get out of North Carolina. And if they . . . no, *when* they caught us, we would be worse off than we are now. Even if we somehow managed to get away, what would happen to your mother? We couldn't leave her behind."

I looked away, but she reached out to turn my face back to her. "I understand why you're upset; you have a right to be. I'm upset too." She looked toward the main house and her mood darkened. "Nobody wants to get out of this place more than I do. But running isn't the answer."

"I know you're right. It's just that I've been pushed and pulled by these people my whole life. Henry, do this, Henry, do that. Go here, run there. My whole life I've been their puppet. They can starve us, beat us, sell us on a whim and there is nothing we can do about it." I tilted my head and bared my teeth in a skeletal grin. "The only thing we can do is keep smiling and say, 'Yes sir, Dr. Parker. Yes ma'am, Mrs. Parker. Anything else I can do for you?'"

"I know," she said softly.

"And now, after everything else they've done, they're sending me off to God knows where to babysit that dammed fool Matthew!"

"Henry, keep your voice down," she whispered urgently. "Matthew will be the master here one day."

I kept talking as if I hadn't heard her. "So, is this to be my life, Gloria? Living under their thumbs until I die an old man like Sam?" I shook my head slowly as my eyes welled with tears. "I just don't know if I can do this anymore."

She hung her head and didn't speak for some time. "I know it's hard, Henry, but I need you to keep going. I need you to do it for me because I don't know what I would do if something happened to you." There were tears in her eyes too, and instinctively, I put my arm around her.

I'm not sure how it started, but before I knew it, I was kissing her. All my anger, pain, and frustration fell away as I lost myself in her embrace. She pulled back slightly, and I could still feel the pressure of her mouth.

"Gloria, I . . ." She put a finger to my lips.

"Shh. You don't have to say anything. I feel the same way." We started to kiss again, more urgently this time. I wanted the moment to last forever, but soon she stood and walked to my bed. While I watched, entranced, she took off her dress and let it slide to the floor. I was beside her in an instant. I touched her warm skin while she slowly unbuttoned my shirt.

Soon we were lying next to each other in my narrow bed, touching, exploring, softly moaning. When we finally coupled, our bodies merged seamlessly. There was no awkwardness or fumbling. Being with Gloria felt as natural as breathing, and every bit as necessary. Everything that had been bothering me earlier had diminished in importance. My concerns would have to wait. Gloria and I were finally together, and that's all that mattered.

PART
3

CHAPTER 18

DEPLOYMENT

April-May 1861

Since I had been told two weeks earlier that I was leaving, Nellie and Gloria had tried their best to teach me all they could about cooking. I didn't seem to have an aptitude for it. In the end, Nellie said I had probably learned enough that I wouldn't poison anyone. Gloria just shook her head and laughed.

On the day of our departure, I was up before the sun. The early morning air was cool, but the clear sky promised a warmer day ahead. Jackson had returned from a job in Davidson the week before, and Dr. Parker told him that he would need to look after the horses during my absence. He wasn't happy about it. When he got back to the cabin, he threw down his hat and said that he didn't want to "be nursemaid to any damn horses." I could tell that he was serious, but I started laughing. There was no way to avoid it. Something about the idea of him being anyone's nursemaid just seemed hilarious. Jackson scowled at me, but in the end we both wound up laughing until tears streamed down our cheeks. What else could we do? The truth was he didn't have a choice any more than I did. Saying no wasn't a viable option. But Jackson's new duties wouldn't start until I was gone, and I hadn't left yet. So, on the morning of my departure, I headed to the barn alone, as I had done nearly every morning since Sam died. As usual, when I entered the horses were already alert, anticipating my arrival.

"Good morning. How's everyone doing today?" I asked soothingly. "Are you ready for your breakfast?"

I gave each of them fresh oats and water, then shoveled out their stalls and laid down fresh straw. I inspected Matthew's riding gear, including his saddle, halter, and other tack, making sure everything was clean and in good order. I got along much better with his horse, Bessie, ever since I'd discovered her love for carrots.

"Bessie, I'm going on a long trip today," I cooed, as she took the carrot from my hand. "I'll have to take a train to get there. That's right, I'm going on a train." She bumped me with her head—her way of asking for another carrot. I held up one, which she ate immediately.

"But don't worry, darlin', Jackson is going to take good care of you while I'm gone."

"Now I know why you never sweet-talk me—you're using it all up on the horses. Should I be jealous?"

Startled, I turned to see Gloria standing inside the barn door, a look of wry amusement on her face.

"Maybe you should be," I said, smiling. "She is very beautiful."

Gloria moved toward me languidly, never breaking eye contact. I could have watched her walk forever. Without saying a word, she put a hand on the back of my neck before pulling me into a long kiss.

"Um, that's nice," I said breathlessly. "I'm sure going to miss how you say good morning." Then, I added mischievously, "But what about Bessie?"

Gloria looked at the horse before turning back to me, her lips parted slightly. "She might be pretty, I'll give you that, but she doesn't care about you like I do."

After breakfast, Matthew and I said our goodbyes to Dr. and Mrs. Parker. I had already done the same with everyone in the kitchen house. Other than Gloria, we had all been together since I left the plantation nearly twenty years earlier. I was six years old when I was taken to the house in Charlotte, and if it hadn't been for Nellie, Camille, Jackson, Roxanne, and Sam, I don't know how I would have survived the experience. There had been no chance to see my mother before I left, but Nellie and

Camille promised they would tell her everything the next time they saw her.

Nellie hugged me tightly, then turned away quickly, swiping at something on her cheek.

"You're not crying are you, Nellie?" I asked good-naturedly.

"Crying, why would I be crying about you getting out of my kitchen for six months? It will give me a chance to get some work done without you being underfoot." I tried to hug her again, but she gently pushed me away.

"Go on now, Henry. You don't want to keep Matthew waiting."

I walked to Gloria, who was frying potatoes on the stove. Touching her arm gently, I said, "You take care of yourself. I'll be back as soon as I can."

She wiped her hand on her apron, embraced me quickly, and whispered, "Hurry back. I'll be right here waiting."

* * *

Jackson drove Matthew and me to the station, where we were meeting up with Captain Ross and the rest of Company C. Matthew sat in front, while I rode in the back with his baggage. He had two large saddlebags, a trunk, and all his riding gear. I had only a bedroll and a few other belongings in a canvas bag that was slung over my shoulder. Matthew had wanted to take Bessie, but the train from Charlotte to Raleigh had no accommodations for horses. He would need to secure another mount after we got to our destination.

Matthew was wearing a high-collar officer's uniform with two rows of brass buttons on the jacket. Dr. Parker had kept his promise to provide funds to outfit the company, and consequently, Matthew's official rank was second lieutenant, Company C, 1st North Carolina Volunteers.

Before we left, Matthew told me that in front of the men I should call him Lieutenant Parker instead of Master Matthew. My first thought was that addressing him as Lieutenant Parker was overly formal, but on further reflection, it was no more objectionable than calling him Master. I wasn't sure what a second lieutenant was supposed to do, but I didn't imagine that he knew much more about it than I did.

When we got to the station a large crowd was already there. A few officers were standing nearby, but most of the other men sat or lounged in the grass. What struck me most about these men was their age. Most of them looked to be no older than eighteen, or perhaps twenty. Matthew was only twenty-two, and at twenty-four I felt like one of the oldest people there. I wondered if the Union soldiers were as young as these men.

"Lieutenant Parker, you made it." I looked up to see three men in officer's uniforms standing by the wagon.

Matthew jumped down and saluted in a single fluid motion. "Captain Ross, it's good to see you, sir." Then facing the others, he added, "Gentlemen."

"Parker, I believe you know Lieutenant Davies."

"Yes sir. It's good to see you again, Davies."

"You too, Parker."

Captain Ross nodded, then pointing to the other officer he said, "And this fine specimen of manhood is Lieutenant Carter."

Matthew shook his hand warmly. "Yes sir, we've met on one or two occasions."

"Likely at the bar of the Mansion House, where he was unofficially stationed until signing on with Company C," Captain Ross quipped.

"I have indeed met Mr. Parker," intoned Lieutenant Carter, smiling broadly. Then he added with a wink, "Though I'm not at liberty to say where."

Jackson and I had already started unloading the wagon when Captain Ross turned his attention to us. "Parker, who are these niggers?"

Inclining his head in my direction, he said, "This is my boy, Henry. He'll be coming with us. The other one just drove us here."

"That's a pity," he said looking at Jackson. "We could always use a big nigger like that. What about the other boy, can he cook?"

Matthew considered the question and frowned. "No sir, I don't believe so. At least, not very well. We had a couple of girls that took care of the kitchen. He's a good hand with horses though."

Captain Ross looked me over appraisingly. "No matter, he looks stout enough. We'll find some work for him. Now come on, I want to introduce you to some of the other men."

Matthew turned to me and said, "Stay here with my gear. I'll be back presently."

"Yes, Master . . . sorry, I mean Lieutenant Parker."

Matthew frowned slightly but said nothing more as he walked away. Jackson watched them leave before saying in a low voice, "So, you got to call him Lieutenant Parker now?"

I shrugged. "Doesn't make any difference to me what I call him. 'Lieutenant' is just going to take some getting used to, that's all."

Jackson took another look at the assembled soldiers before spitting in the dirt. "You take care of yourself, Henry," he said seriously. "And if there's any shooting, get as close to the ground as you can manage."

For Jackson, who was usually stoic, this amounted to an emotional outburst. "I'll do that, Jackson. Thanks." With a nod he climbed back into the wagon, gave the reins a snap, and was gone. With a sudden ache in my chest, I realized that I was truly alone.

In the distance I heard the first shrill whistle of the approaching train. I looked in the direction of the sound but saw nothing. Perhaps a quarter of a mile away, the tracks curved and disappeared behind a stand of thick trees. I had seen and heard trains come and go many times, but of course I had never ridden one. I marveled at how such a huge machine, built almost entirely of iron and steel, could travel up to sixty miles an hour, reducing the travel time to Raleigh by at least five days. Having never traveled faster in my life than a horse-drawn wagon, I wondered how it would feel to move at such a speed? Would it be exhilarating, terrifying, or a bit of both? The rumble of the approaching train told me I would have my answer soon enough.

As some of the officers started to shout commands, the men stood slowly, stretched, and gathered up their gear. The train was closer now, and for the first time I could see a dark column of smoke drifting above the tree canopy. Another whistle sounded, much closer this time, causing a flock of sparrows to explode from the trees. A few seconds later the engine came into view, led by a grinning cowcatcher in front and a tall smokestack from which a ribbon of black smoke issued. As it got closer the brakes squealed, slowing the train and allowing it to slide neatly into the station. Everyone was on their feet now, and the platform, which had been quiet only a moment ago, hummed with activity.

Not wanting to miss the train, and unsure of what to do, I tried to find Matthew in the crowd. But with so many people standing and milling about, it was impossible. Then, with relief, I saw him, Lieutenant Carter, and an old Negro with a handcart heading my way. Lifting his saddlebags, he shouted, "I'll take these, you two get the rest of my gear on the train." He threw the bags over his shoulder, then he and Lieutenant Carter disappeared into the crowd.

I watched him go, then looked at the old man, who was already eyeing me expectantly. "Well, don't just stand there, give me a hand with all this," he said irritably. We hoisted the trunk, saddle, and the rest of Matthew's riding gear onto the cart. Afraid to lose sight of him, I followed closely as he expertly maneuvered through the crowd. We were heading past the passenger cars, toward the back of the train.

"Where are we going?" I asked.

"Where do you think, to the baggage car."

When we got there, a white man wearing a railroad uniform put up a hand for us to stop. "Whoa now, what's all this, then?"

Before I could respond, the old man said, using a decidedly more pleasant voice, "This is Lieutenant Parker's gear, from Company C. This is his boy. He's traveling with him to Raleigh."

"His boy, huh," he sneered. "Well, you got a ticket, boy?"

Ticket? I had forgotten about a ticket. I silently cursed Matthew for putting me in this position. "No sir," I said. "Lieutenant Parker, Matthew Parker, he must have my ticket."

He shook his head in disgust. "God sakes, this boy is so dumb he doesn't know he needs a ticket to ride the train," he shouted to another uniformed man standing nearby. "Well, hurry up and get that gear on the train. We're pulling out soon. You're sitting in there too. Find a place with the other niggers."

"Yes sir."

"Wait, what's your name?"

"Henry, sir."

He noted something on his clipboard. When he looked up, he seemed surprised to still find me there. "Well go on then, boy."

The old man and I loaded Matthew's baggage on the train. When we were done, he turned and left without saying another word. The sides of the baggage car had no windows, so the only light came from the gaps between the wood planks that made up the walls. I saw a few Negro men in the back of the car, sitting on sacks or crates. One of them waved me over.

"There's a spot here. You're welcome to it," he said. I moved to the back and settled across from him on a sack of flour. He reached out and we shook hands. "My name's Louis. I'm Captain Ross's man."

"I'm Henry. I'm here with Lieutenant Parker."

"Parker? Is that Dr. Parker's son?"

"Yes, do you know Dr. Parker?"

"Well, not personally," he chuckled. "But just about everybody around here knows Dr. Parker."

As my eyes adjusted to the dim light, I could see that there were two other men sitting directly across from us. One had his eyes closed and might have been sleeping. The other, who was studying Louis and me, seemed perfectly at ease resting against a wooden crate. He wore rough denim jeans and a cream-colored shirt with a bright red neckerchief knotted at his throat. On his feet he wore a pair of sturdy looking, but well worn, brogans. His brown felt hat had a wide brim with a colorful feather sticking from the band. I thought he might only be a few years older than me, perhaps thirty, but his pocked and weathered face made him appear older.

The man touched the brim of his hat in greeting. "I'm Gus, and that's my brother Joe," he said, pointing to the other man. "Where are you boys headed?"

"Right now, we're going to Raleigh, and after that I don't know. Guess we're heading wherever the soldiers are going," I said. "How about you?"

He nodded slowly, like he was trying to make sense of what I had just said. "So, your owners brought you here then?" Gus asked.

"That's right. Are you traveling with the soldiers too?" I asked.

The answer came from his brother Joe, who apparently was not sleeping after all. "We heard that there was going to be a fight and thought we might tag along. So, in a manner of speaking, I suppose we are traveling with the soldiers. We figured they might have a need for our services." He grinned.

Sensing my confusion, Gus added, "Joe and I make our living as hunters. Wherever men congregate, there's always a need for fresh meat."

"So, you're free men?" Louis asked.

"That's right, nobody owns us," Gus said proudly. "We're here because we want to be." Joe and I live in the mountains, a few miles outside a town called Asheville. You ever been in the mountains?" Louis and I both indicated that we hadn't.

He leaned forward, warming to his subject. "Well, it's the prettiest place you've ever seen. Forest as far as you can see, with plenty of fresh water, and game so thick you could shoot your dinner from the porch." Joe snorted, but Gus ignored him. "All I'm saying is a man can stretch his legs there without bumping into someone every couple of minutes. It's nothing like down here in the flatlands. Sometimes, Joe and I go for weeks without seeing another living soul. Isn't that right, Joe?"

"Sometimes longer," said Joe, who had already closed his eyes again.

I looked at Louis, but for the moment we had both been rendered speechless. Gus and Joe were free men who lived in the mountains and made their living hunting. I had so many questions I wanted to ask these men, but my thoughts were interrupted, because at that moment someone slid the outer door closed, thrusting the car into near total darkness. I squinted through a gap in the wall, trying to make sense of the world beyond. But it was like trying to decipher a painting from only a sliver of canvas.

A moment later the whistle sounded, and with a lurch, we started moving forward. The train picked up speed slowly, and in a few minutes, even the tiny slice of the world I could see through the wall became unrecognizable, the colors blurring together like I was looking through a kaleidoscope. There was a larger gap at the door, and I stood and made my way awkwardly there, hoping for a better view. At first, I saw only trees, but then the view resolved to a tableau of a long valley dotted with farmland and a river beyond. There was nothing to hold on to other than the door handle, and after almost falling twice, I slowly made my way back to where I'd been sitting.

"This your first time on a train, Henry?" asked Louis.

"Yes, my first time," I admitted. Then, after a pause I added, "It's not how I pictured it."

"What did you think it would be like?" he asked.

"I don't know exactly, but I suppose I thought we would be able to see more of the country we were passing through."

He smiled and settled himself more comfortably before also closing his eyes. "Well, I guess we'll see it soon enough."

CHAPTER 19

ENCAMPMENT

May 1861

O ur train arrived at Raleigh on the afternoon of May 5, having made several stops along the way. I stretched and walked to the door to get a sense of our surroundings. There were several buildings near the station, the largest with a sign labeled *McAvoy Cartage*, outside of which was a group of Negro men and several four-wheeled baggage carts. The ground was wet, but the sun shone brightly through scattered clouds, making everything glisten and sparkle.

A few moments later someone unlocked the door to our car, allowing the fresh air in, a welcome relief after so many hours of confinement. A railroad employee stood at the open door. "You boys come on out now. Stand over there until someone comes for you," he said, indicating a spot to his left.

I picked up my bag and bedroll, then Louis and I unloaded Captain Ross's and Matthew's baggage. The platform teemed with people, both soldiers and civilians, and the entire area was awash with noise. Everyone seemed to be talking or laughing or shouting at the same time. Though I couldn't see them, someone was making a speech, punctuated by sporadic clapping and cheers. Somewhere in the distance I heard a band playing.

"Have you ever seen so much confusion?" Louis shouted over the din. I indicated that I hadn't. This was the farthest I had ever been from Charlotte, or anything else I had known. It was disorienting and exciting to be so far from home, and I reveled in the experience.

Gus and Joe jumped down from the baggage car and joined us on the platform. I noticed that, in addition to their traveling bags, each of them was carrying a long, thin cloth-wrapped bundle. Following my gaze, Joe smiled and said, "I see you noticed my girl, Josie. Gus's lady friend is Mabel. Isn't that so, Gus?" In response, Gus gave his brother a lopsided grin. "Now Josie can be finicky sometimes, but once she settles down, she'll put a bullet through a squirrel's eye at fifty yards. Tools of the trade. Blacksmiths have their hammers, butchers got their knives, and Gus and I have Josie and Mabel."

On the train they had said they were hunters, but foolishly I hadn't thought they would have their rifles with them. In my defense, I had rarely seen a Negro carrying a gun, and never so openly. The thought of the armed mountain men walking through Raleigh made me smile. It felt good to be traveling with Gus and Joe, and I expect I stood a little taller in their company.

Matthew's gear was loaded into a waiting wagon along with that of Captain Ross and the other officers. At some unseen signal the soldiers crowding the platform started moving, and the railroad man indicated that we should follow them. I did as I was told, hoping that Matthew was part of the crowd ahead.

We left the station and were soon walking through the town of Raleigh. The streets were lined with people that cheered the Confederates as they passed. Many of the women waved and threw flowers. Louis, Gus, Joe, and I walked behind the soldiers, and the people lining the street stopped cheering when we came into view. Still, even though it was clear the adulation wasn't meant for me, I couldn't help feeling some excitement at the spectacle.

Raleigh was nearly twice as large as Charlotte, and as we walked, we passed many elegant homes and fine buildings. I was admiring a large brick house surrounded by a black wrought iron fence when we rounded a corner and the largest building I had ever seen came into view.

Built entirely of white stone, the three-story structure was fronted by four fluted columns and topped with a large dome. Louis bent toward me and said, "That's the state capitol. The governor has his office there." I looked at him quizzically and he added, "Before I was sold to Captain Ross, I used to work for a man that came to Raleigh a couple of times a year."

"I've never seen a building that big," I marveled. I tried to imagine how such a wonder had been constructed. Then, resuming the conversation, I asked, "Why did he sell you?"

"He didn't sell me. He died, and his widow sold me a couple of weeks later."

"Why did she do that?"

Louis gave a noncommittal shrug and said, "I don't know. For the money, I guess. I asked, but she never did tell me why." After a moment, he added, "She kept my wife and son though." Shocked, I looked at him and saw the pain etched on his face like an open wound.

"I'm sorry, Louis," I said solemnly. "I was taken from my mother when I was six, but I still see her from time to time. I hope you get to see your family again one day." He acknowledged my comment with a nod but said nothing more, surrendering himself to the memories.

Soon we were walking through a less affluent part of town, with poorly constructed buildings and narrow streets. A few yards away a group of several Negro men and women watched the procession impassively, displaying none of the enthusiasm we had seen earlier.

"Well, boys, it was nice to meet you," Joe shouted. "We'll say our goodbyes now. Gus and I are going to find some dinner and see what other diversions this town has to offer. I'm sure we'll see you again."

"But you don't know where we're heading," Louis said.

"I expect we'll find you easy enough." Gus laughed. "Even if they tried, it would be hard to hide this many men."

* * *

The walk to camp took another twenty minutes, the congestion of the town having been slowly replaced by farmland and open fields. The Company C encampment consisted of little more than a few tents for the officers and some abandoned buildings for the enlisted men. I could see that the meanness of the accommodations was clearly a disappointment to the men, particularly after such a splendid welcome from the townspeople. As we passed, I heard one of the soldiers complain loudly about the indignity of sleeping in a barn, particularly in his new uniform. Several other men agreed, each voice seemingly angrier than the one before. Finally, an older man said calmly, "At least we got a roof over our heads tonight. I suggest you enjoy it while you can. This being the army, there's no telling where we'll be bedding down tomorrow."

As the meaning of his words sunk in, I felt my mood plummet. If white men were being made to sleep in a barn, I had little hope for my sleeping arrangements. After some searching, I found Matthew standing by one of the tents, talking with a short, barrel-chested man.

"Ah, there you are. I thought we might need to send out a search party. Sergeant Bullock, this is my boy, Henry. He'll be my cook and valet for the duration of our deployment. When he's not otherwise engaged, feel free to put him to work."

With a cold smile that reminded me of Mr. Fox, Sergeant Bullock replied, "Yes sir, Lieutenant, I'll do that."

After he left, Matthew said, "Get my gear unpacked and squared away. Lieutenant Carter and I are sharing this tent, so keep all my things to one side. And get a fire started for coffee. I'll be back soon."

"Yes sir, I'll do that." Then, as he was turning to leave, I added, "Excuse me, sir, but where should I put my bedroll."

With a hint of annoyance he said, "Outside the tent, of course. Where do you think?" As I watched him walk away, I wanted to laugh at the bitter irony of my situation. Dr. Parker wanted me to accompany Matthew to help keep him safe, but in doing so, I'm sure they gave no consideration to my well-being. Matthew was their son and heir, whereas I was chattel, like furniture, or a cow. Clearly, Matthew's life had value, while mine did not.

I unpacked his belongings and arranged them as best I could on the right side of the tent. By the time he and Lieutenant Carter returned, I had a fresh pot of hot coffee on the fire. Later, when they'd turned in for the night, I unrolled my bedroll and tried to get some rest as well. After what felt like hours I finally fell into a fitful sleep. When I awoke early the next morning, I sensed that something wasn't right. Standing, I stretched and looked around, trying to find the source of my discomfort. Then, with a sudden realization, I started to search the area in earnest, becoming increasingly frantic with each passing minute. Finally, I gave up and slid to the ground, dejected. While I slept someone had stolen my only pair of shoes. I buried my head in my hands, trying to gain control of my emotions. Far from home, forced to sleep on the ground, and now shoeless, I felt like an ill-fated character from one of Shakespeare's plays. I could only hope it wasn't a tragedy. Taking a deep breath to clear my mind, I set about my work. This was only the second day of my journey, and I would have to be strong if I wanted to survive. By the time Matthew appeared at the door of the tent, I had almost finished cooking breakfast.

"Good morning, sir. I made some hoecakes and salt pork. Would you like to eat now or get dressed first?"

"I'll get dressed before breakfast, but I'll take a cup of coffee now." As I poured a cup, he looked at me and frowned. "Where are your shoes?"

"It would appear that someone stole my shoes while I was sleeping," I said, struggling to keep my voice under control.

Matthew looked confused. "Stole your shoes? You're saying that someone stole your shoes? Are you certain that you didn't misplace them?"

"No sir, I didn't misplace them," I said, as evenly as I could manage. "They were here when I went to sleep and when I woke up, they were gone."

"Is there anything else missing?" he said, looking around.

"No sir, just my shoes."

Lieutenant Carter came to the tent door, looking disheveled. "Good morning, Parker. What's all this?"

"Morning, Carter. My boy thinks that someone stole his shoes during the night."

"Well, they might have," he said, rubbing his chin thoughtfully. "I noticed yesterday that your boy had on a decent pair of shoes. I'm sure some of the men noticed it too." Then, turning to me, he said, "You won't need shoes for what you're doing. I'll take a cup of that coffee, though."

Lieutenant Carter took his cup into the tent. Matthew and I were left alone again. While I dished up his breakfast, he gave me what might have been a look of concern. For a moment he almost seemed like the old Matthew, the boy that had once been my friend. But just as quickly as it had appeared, it was gone, and he was once again Lieutenant Parker. "I'm sorry about the loss of your shoes. The men need footwear, that's true enough, but so do you. I'll see what I can do to get you another pair."

I handed him a plate and put my hands in my pockets to conceal their shaking. "Yes sir, I would be appreciative of anything you can do," I said, using the nonthreatening voice I had heard Sam use so many times.

CHAPTER 20

FIRST BLOOD

May–November 1861

T he North Carolina assembly voted to secede from the Union on May 20, and the regiment decamped from Raleigh and left for Virginia the very next day. We traveled first by train to West Point, and then down the York River by steamboat to Yorktown. During the first leg of the trip, we traveled on open railcars, so although I was tired, I dared not close my eyes. Earlier, a soldier that had been sleeping fell to his death from the train, and I had no wish to follow him.

The spring weather had been warm and wet, and everywhere we passed there was new, verdant life. I was able to recognize many of the same plants and trees I knew from Charlotte, including holly, oak, red cedar, magnolia, hornbeam, sumac, black cherry, laurel, hemlock, and dogwood. As we traveled farther north, I also saw a few plants I did not recognize. If I had an opportunity, I would gather some samples to show to my mother.

Traveling down the York River by steamer was both fascinating and frightening, as this was my first time aboard any type of watercraft. I marveled at how such a large ship, presumably weighing many thousands of pounds, was able to stay afloat. This triggered a vague memory of something Dr. Parker had once read to me. I searched my mind and soon found the reference. Thousands of years ago, a Greek inventor named Archimedes said, "A body at rest in a fluid is acted upon by a force pushing upward. According to his theory, the weight of the boat pushing down was offset by something he called "buoyant force" that pushed back up. What an amazing idea. As we moved downriver, I found myself smiling at what Archimedes had discovered so long ago, and I silently thanked him for keeping us afloat.

The journey thus far had been difficult, but if I were being honest, it was also exhilarating. In two weeks, I had seen more of the world than I had in my entire life up to that point. Nonetheless, I had been forced into the trip and still bridled at having no say in the matter. Ironically, *if* they had asked me, I might well have volunteered to make the journey. But asking wasn't something that often passed between masters and slaves. After all, if yes was the only possible answer, why bother to ask? Or, as Chief Justice Taney had written in the Dred Scott decision, a few years earlier, Negroes had no legal rights that a white man was bound to respect. Still, I was pleased to have had the chance to see some of the world beyond Charlotte, even if it had not been by choice.

* * *

It often seemed to me that bad news and good news traveled together. My experience in Yorktown was no exception. The good news was that, upon our arrival, everyone was issued a tent. Matthew and Lieutenant Carter's tent had four walls, a peaked roof, and a front flap that could be closed for privacy. Conversely, our tent was little more than a worn piece of canvas held up by two poles and staked to the ground on each side. But I was happy to have it and to once again have a roof over my head at night. I shared the tent with Louis. He was one of the only people I knew in camp, and I was very glad for his company.

The bad news was that, on the first morning after we arrived in Yorktown, Matthew told me to report to Sergeant Bullock for special duty. I found the sergeant and a few minutes later was walking with him and most of Company C toward the Yorktown Harbor. I asked

Louis, who had fallen in beside me, if he knew where we were going.

"I don't know for sure, but I heard some of the men grumbling about being expected to do nigger work. I imagine it has something to do with that."

Frowning, I lowered my voice and whispered, "What's nigger work?"

He smiled and said softly, taking care not to be overheard, "What do you think? It's any kind of work they don't want to do."

As we neared the water the distinctive sound of picks and shovels grew louder. Soon I could see that there were dozens of men, both white and Negro, engaged in digging a long, deep trench along a bluff that overlooked the harbor. More men had been sent to the woods to cut trees. The breastworks, as they were called, were three or four feet deep and built entirely of earth and wood. Yorktown was located at a bend in the river, just opposite a peninsula called Gloucester Point. This made it a natural place to position artillery to defend the harbor, and indeed some parts of the breastworks were already studded with a lethal array of cannons and mortars.

A burly Confederate dressed in slacks and a muddy undershirt spoke to Sergeant Bullock, who in turn began handing out assignments. When he got to Louis and me, he said, "You boys ever done any work with a pick and shovel?" Louis indicated that he had, but I shook my head no.

Making a guttural sound that might have been a laugh, he gave Louis a shovel before also thrusting one into my hands. "Well, I guess this is your lucky day. Find a spot over there and get to work. You'll get the hang of it soon enough."

We walked to the end of the line and started digging. None of the other men paid any attention to us. Everyone seemed to be in their own personal hell. It was dirty, difficult work and, after less than an hour, my back was stiff and my hands raw. I watched Louis and tried to match his steady rhythm. I don't think I did a very good job of it, but somehow, I managed to keep going.

To make matters worse, I still didn't have any shoes and was forced to work barefoot in the mud and muck. When I'd first arrived in Charlotte in 1842, the soles of my feet had been thick and tough from working in the fields. But twenty years of shoes had left my feet soft, and I acutely felt the pain of every rock and twig I stepped on.

By the end of the day, I was as tired as I'd ever been, and I scarcely had enough strength to walk back to camp. Matthew took one look at me and laughed. "I guess you did your first real work today. Get cleaned up and get my dinner started, I'm hungry."

"Yes sir," I managed, before slumping to the ground.

"Henry, what happened to you? You look worn to a frazzle."

I turned to see Gus standing over me, smiling. "I've been digging breastworks all day. Now I've got to make his dinner," I said, tipping my head toward Matthew's tent.

"Whew, you're sure a busy man. Well look here," he said, patting his game bag. "I've got two more rabbits left if you're interested. Get some water going and I'll skin them for you."

"Thanks Gus, how much are they?" I said, struggling to get to my feet. "I can ask him if he wants to buy them."

He pulled a large knife from the sheath on his belt. "Don't worry about it, Henry, you're a friend. The first time is on the house."

After dinner, I limped to a willow tree that was not far from the camp. I stripped some of the leaves and made a poultice for my sore feet. I slept soundly that night, but when I awoke in the morning, I was so stiff I had trouble even standing up straight. Yet somehow, I found the strength to return to the shovel detail that day and for the next two weeks. Over the years I've thought of Yorktown many times. I'm not certain how I was able to keep going. Was it strength of will, stubbornness, some manner of internal fortitude? Looking back on it now, I have to say I think it was pride. Many of the men, both Negro and white, were working on the breastworks and

I told myself that if they could bear it, then so could I. In fact, "If they can bear it so can I" became a mantra I repeated to myself over and over. Everyone was suffering, I could see that, but I simply wouldn't quit while Louis and the others still managed to dig. My pride wouldn't allow it.

* * *

The regiment saw its first real action in early June. Colonel Magruder, in command of all the Confederate troops, knew that the Union forces were dug in at Fort Monroe, about twenty-five miles south and east of our position. He directed his troops, including the North Carolina regiment commanded by Colonel Hill, to establish two forward positions at Big Bethel and Little Bethel, just outside Hampton, Virginia.

On June 6 we packed our belongings and made the twelve-mile march to Big Bethel. When we arrived, it was clear that the Union had already been there, as the church had been defaced with insults such as *Death to the Traitors*. This greatly angered the Confederates, and I could see they were spoiling for a fight. Colonel Hill positioned his troops on high ground overlooking the bridge across the Back River and straddling the Hampton–Yorktown Road. And much to my dismay, he immediately ordered us to again begin digging breastworks. But unlike at Yorktown, the mood in camp was buoyant. The North Carolina Volunteers had signed on to fight Yankees, and now it seemed they would finally get their chance. As I heard one of the Confederates say to another, "This is why we came boys."

The next evening after dinner, as I was helping Matthew pull off his boots, I asked him if he thought the Union would attack.

"I do," he said without hesitation. "Magruder has set a trap the Yankees won't be able to resist. The only problem is we're the bait." He laughed.

He was in a talkative mood, so I pressed ahead. "The bait, sir?"

"Yes, like worms on a hook," he said, wiggling his finger for emphasis. "We're camped within a few miles of their forward position. If they have any honor at all, which is highly questionable, they won't be able to ignore us."

Lieutenant Carter came into the tent and Matthew dismissed me with a wave of his hand. As I left, they were already discussing the coming battle in hushed tones. They didn't seem to be afraid. In fact, I think that they might have been excited. I thought of what Dr. Parker had said about young men and shook my head in disbelief. Why would anyone be animated by the prospect of a life-and-death struggle? Was this courage or just plain foolishness?

Matthew and I had our problems, and I certainly didn't look forward to him one day becoming my master, but what outcome did I hope for? If Matthew survived the war, he might send me back to the fields and Mr. Fox. Or I could be sold. If that happened, I would likely never see Gloria or my mother again. On the other hand, if Matthew died, the possessions of Dr. and Mrs. Parker would eventually be sold because they had no other heirs, and those possessions included me.

I had thought about it many times since we'd left Charlotte, and I always came to the same conclusion. It didn't matter whether Matthew lived or died. What mattered was who won the war. If the South won, nothing would change for us. Possibly, things might get even worse. But if the North won . . . then what? I didn't have an answer, but I knew that the South's defeat would bring changes, possibly for the better. The logic was inescapable. If we were to have any chance at a better life, any chance at all, the North had to win the war!

* * *

The Union attacked on the morning of June 10. Matthew and the rest of Company C were on the left flank, entrenched behind the newly constructed breastworks. Their position overlooked an open field and the river beyond. I had been told to stay behind the line and bring water to the men when they called for it. Of course, I was also expected to come to Matthew's assistance if he needed me. There was a grove of trees on the far left of the line, and I sheltered there with Louis and a few other men.

The battle lasted more than half a day, and during all of it, there was little respite from the awful roar of shot and shell, the air becoming thick with the smell of sulfur. At times, there were so many projectiles in the air, it seemed a miracle that more people weren't hit. I could see that Colonel Hill and the other officers were giving the men commands, but I couldn't make out what they were saying over the din. From my vantage point, it was impossible to tell how the fight was progressing, but I saw men fall on both sides. By that afternoon, two vultures had already started flying lazy circles above the battlefield.

I tried to keep an eye on Matthew, but it was nearly impossible in the smoke and dust. There was a lull in the fighting and Captain Ross signaled for water. Louis and I, each carrying two buckets, ran forward, staying as low as we could. As the men were drinking, I saw Matthew standing nearby. I dipped up a ladle of water and took it to him.

"Lieutenant, do you want some water?"

He wiped his brow with a handkerchief and lifted the ladle to his mouth. As he drank, I noticed that his hands were trembling.

"Are you all right, sir?"

"I'm fine," he said testily. "Why would you ask me something like that?"

"My apologies, sir, I didn't mean any harm. I was just inquiring . . ."

"You have no need to worry about me. See to the other men."

I did as he instructed, but I could tell that he wasn't himself. A few minutes later the shooting, which had been sporadic, started again in earnest. Louis and I ran toward the relative safety of the trees, and from the corner of my eye I saw him stumble and fall. I turned back to help, but he was already up and running again. Soon, we were each leaning against a thick bulwark of a tree.

"Louis, are you hurt?"

"I don't think so," he said, laughing nervously. "But I'm going to need another bucket." He held it up, and I could see that a musket ball had punched a ragged hole in the side.

I clapped him on the shoulder. "You're a lucky man," I shouted. "That ball didn't miss you by much."

I thought he hadn't heard me because he continued to stare at the bucket. Finally, he looked at me with the same pain on his face that I had seen in Raleigh. "Do you really think I'm lucky, Henry?"

I could see that he was waiting for a response, but what could I say? The musket ball could have ended his life. There would have been no more suffering. But death was final, erasing all your tomorrows and everything that might have been. I thought of something Gloria had told me before I left Charlotte and realized, with a rush of emotion, that she was right. Life was worth fighting for.

"I do think you're lucky, Louis. I don't know why God spared you, but he must not be done with you yet." Then, without thinking, I closed my eyes and said, "'Fear thou not, for I am with thee. Be not dismayed, for I am thy God. I will strengthen thee; yea, I will help thee; yea, I will uphold thee with the right hand of my righteousness.'"

When I opened my eyes, I watched a mixture of emotions play across his face. Surprise, fear, and awe all vied for supremacy, but in the end, I saw only determination.

"Thank you," he said earnestly.

* * *

Finally, sometime early in the afternoon, the fighting was over. For many hours my senses had been assaulted with so many sights, sounds, and smells that their sudden absence was disorienting.

When the fighting stopped, initially the Confederates had cheered. But as Matthew and the others surveyed their grim handiwork, there was only silence. For most of these young men, this had been their first taste of war.

Like me, they had not seen death on this scale, and it sobered them.

Matthew had a wild look in his eyes. "Arrogant Yankees! They said they would whip us with cornstalks. Now look at them," he yelled, sweeping his arm before him. But he couldn't fool me. I'd known him since he was four years old, and I could see that just beneath his thin veneer of bravado, fear held sway.

When we returned to camp I made a dinner of bread, salt pork, and coffee. After Matthew left to join some of the other officers for a drink, I washed his uniform in the creek. I had fallen asleep by the fire and was awakened by someone kicking my feet.

"Henry, wake up. These are for you. I hope they fit." Matthew, clearly inebriated, was holding a pair of shoes. They were not as well made as the pair I had brought from Charlotte, but they were certainly better than no shoes at all.

"Thank you," I said, meaning it. "I'm sure they'll do nicely." He waved absently as he made his way unsteadily to his tent. He never told me where he got the shoes and I never asked. There was no need. I already knew the likely source of his gift.

CHAPTER 21

OFFERING

November 1861

Word of the Confederate victory at Big Bethel spread quickly. The *Richmond Dispatch* wrote it was "one of the most extraordinary victories in the annals of war." Even the regiment commander, Colonel Hill, not usually one for hyperbole, said, "Does not the hand of God seem manifest in this thing?" Still, no matter the level of excitement generated by the victory, the volunteers from North Carolina had only enlisted for six months. That meant that in November, Matthew and the rest of the regiment's soldiers were released from service. We were going back to Charlotte.

But the war itself was far from over. Although the 1st North Carolina Volunteers weren't involved, there were several significant battles in the summer and fall of 1861, including First Manassas, Hatteras Inlet, Ball's Bluff, and Belmont. Each of these conflicts led to significant casualties, which only strengthened the resolve of both sides to fight on.

Our train pulled into Charlotte on a cold, blustery November day. Unlike the crowd that saw us off, the platform was largely deserted. I gathered my belongings and bade my friend goodbye.

"Take care of yourself, Louis. I hope to see you again someday."

"You too, preacher," he said. "I'll see you around."

After Big Bethel, as a jest, Louis had started calling me Preacher, and for some reason the name stuck. So much so that, by the time we left, the other Negroes in camp called me Preacher more than Henry. I'd never had a nickname before, but I didn't mind. In fact, I found that I rather liked it. I would miss Louis's companionship, which had made my time with the regiment more bearable.

When I got off the train, I saw that Jackson had come to meet us. He was already talking with Matthew when I joined them.

"It's good to have you back, Master Matthew. Dr. and Mrs. Parker are waiting for you at the house. I hope you don't mind that I brought Bessie along. I thought you might want to ride ahead."

Matthew was stroking the animal's neck contentedly. "No, I don't mind. It's good to see the old girl. I think I will ride ahead. Bring my belongings to the house straightaway." Saying nothing more, he unhitched Bessie from the wagon, swung up into the saddle and rode away.

Jackson gave me a long, appraising look. "Welcome back, Henry." He grinned. "It looks like the war hardened you up some."

I found myself smiling. "Good to see you, Jackson. I kept my head down like you told me. How is everybody?"

He stamped his feet against the cold. "They're all doing fine. Let's get these bags loaded and go to the house, then you can see for yourself. I'm about to freeze to death out here."

On the way he peppered me with questions about my time with the regiment. Though he was at least forty years old, like most of the Parker slaves he had never traveled more than a few miles from Charlotte. He asked about many things, but he was particularly curious about the train.

"What does it feel like to move that fast?" he asked. "Did it make you dizzy or sick to your stomach?"

"No, not really, but it takes some getting used to," I admitted. "After a while you don't really notice it anymore."

"Isn't that something," he said, shaking his head. We rode in silence for a while before he added, "I sure would like to ride one of those someday."

When we got to the house, Jackson steered the wagon to the side yard and stopped in front of the barn. A young Negro boy ran out and took hold of the horse's bridle.

"Henry, this is Nero. Dr. Parker brought him in to look after the horses while you were away. "Nero, this is Henry, fresh from the war." He must have seen my look of surprise because he added, "I'm no good with horses, Henry, you know that. But Dr. Parker told me to try. He said it would only be for the six months while you were gone."

I looked at the boy, who was watching Jackson and me talk. "So, what happened?"

"Well, lucky for me, they needed men to help build the new foundry buildings uptown. So he hired me out and brought in Nero to look after the animals. Better for me, and better for the horses I reckon," he said with a chuckle.

Nero had already unhitched Goldie from the wagon when I grabbed my bag and jumped down. "Nero, I'm Henry. It's nice to meet you."

"Hi," he replied, looking down, before he quickly led Goldie to the barn.

"Don't take it personally. He can talk, but he's mighty stingy with his words," Jackson mused. He saw me looking toward the kitchen house. "All that will have to wait. Dr. Parker said you were to come to the house as soon as you got here. Go on. I'll unload the wagon."

Taking a last look, I sighed and went through the back door into the main house. I heard voices coming from the parlor and headed that way. The door was open, and I knocked softly.

"Come in, Henry," Dr. Parker said. "Matthew was just regaling us with some of his adventures in the regiment. The papers are calling it the Bethel Regiment now. Isn't that right, Matthew?"

"Yes sir," Matthew said brightly. "The state legislature honored us with a proclamation and a ceremonial battle flag."

"Well, isn't that something. You must all be very proud." He beamed at his son, then he turned to me. "Well, Henry, what did you think of it all?"

How could I answer a question like that? Should I tell them of the general squalor of the camp, the bad food, the weeks of backbreaking labor digging breastworks, the stolen shoes? Should I tell them how I'd slept on the ground for six months with only a ragged piece of canvas for shelter? Would they want to hear about my friend Louis, and how he was torn from his family? In the end I simply said, "It was quite an experience, sir."

He nodded thoughtfully, and I had the feeling he understood some of the hidden meaning behind my words. "Matthew said that you did a good job of looking after him, and for that you have our gratitude," he said seriously.

Mrs. Parker, who was sitting next to Matthew looked at her husband. "It was God that protected Matthew. We can't lose sight of that?" she said. Dr. Parker didn't respond. "Matthew, did you read your Bible while you were away?"

"Yes ma'am, almost every day. Isn't that right, Henry?" he said with a half smile. I was caught completely off guard. In fact, in the six months we'd been away, I hadn't seen him open the Bible once. He had set a clever trap for me though. Either I would have to call him a liar or tell a lie myself. I chose my words carefully.

"I was working on the breastworks much of the time, Master Matthew, so I wasn't always around. But I'm sure it's just as you said." Matthew kept the smile on his face but his eyes flashed anger. Mrs. Parker smiled at Matthew and was preparing to say something more when Dr. Parker spoke again.

"Henry, we're going to talk for a bit more. Why don't you get cleaned up and have something to eat. Come to the office when you're finished."

* * *

Gloria and Nellie looked up at the same time when I opened the door to the kitchen house. Nellie spoke first. "Henry, you're back!" she yelled. Before I could respond, Gloria was on her feet and had pulled me into a tight embrace.

"Yes, Henry, you're back," she whispered.

"I missed you, Gloria," I said, stepping away to get a better look at her.

She smiled and stroked my cheek. "I sure hope you did."

"All right, that's enough of that," Nellie interrupted good-naturedly. "Henry, come over here and give me a hug." Giving Gloria a lingering look, I moved quickly to Nellie and kissed her loudly on the cheek.

"I missed you too, Nellie."

She hit me on the arm. "I said give me a hug," she laughed, "not whatever that was. Let me look at you." She was still sitting so I knelt in front of her. "Seems like you lost some weight. Did they give you enough to eat?"

"I got enough, Nellie, but it didn't compare to your cooking."

She waved away my compliment, but she smiled, nonetheless. "Well, sit down and we'll see if we can find something for you to eat. Gloria, don't we still have some of those biscuits from this morning?"

Gloria wiped her hands on her apron. "Sure do," she said, smiling. A moment later she brought a plate with two biscuits, apple butter, grits, and pork fat and sat down beside me. Unable to resist, I started eating immediately.

"How's my mother, Nellie?" I said between bites. "Have you seen her?"

"She's doing fine. I saw her the last time we went to the plantation. Maybe four or five weeks ago. She'll be glad to hear that you got back in one piece."

"And how are you doing?"

"Never better," she said. Gloria seemed unusually focused on the potatoes she was peeling. When I looked at Nellie, she turned away.

Frowning, I put down my fork. "What's going on? Is everything all right?"

"I'm doing fine. Why you keep asking? Did someone tell you something about me?" she said, shooting a dark look at Gloria.

I held up my hands. "Nobody told me anything, Nellie. I just got here. I was just asking how you're doing, that's all." Then I added gently, "Why, is there something to tell?"

Nellie had the look of someone that was struggling with a difficult decision. I waited, not wanting to rush her. Finally, she sighed. "I don't know, Henry. A few days ago, I woke up and I'd lost some feeling in my left leg, that's all."

"Are you able to walk?"

"Course I can walk," she snapped. Then, after a moment, she added quietly, "But when I do, my leg is subject to give out on me."

I glanced toward the house. "Do they know?" I asked, as evenly as I could manage.

"Not yet," she said, her voice cracking. "I'm sorry, Henry. I didn't want to put this on you on your first day back, but I'm afraid of what they might do when they find out."

Gloria had stopped peeling potatoes and was looking at the older woman sympathetically. I reached out and tried to take Nellie's hand, but she pulled away. "He's not going to do anything to you," I said. "They couldn't run this house without you."

She gave me a hard look. "You don't even believe that yourself. There is nobody here they can't do without."

Of course, I knew that she was right. If Dr. Parker found out about Nellie's leg, I wasn't sure what he might do. Bleeding, purging, and sweating were still widely accepted treatments, and though Dr. Parker used them from time to time, I wasn't sure how much he believed in their effectiveness. But beyond any therapy he might employ, I was most concerned about what would happen if Nellie's condition didn't improve. Having a cook whose leg might give out at any time was at best inconvenient, and at worst a hazard.

"Have you done anything yet to try and get the feeling back in your leg?"

"We've been wrapping it with warm compresses," Gloria said.

"Has it helped?"

"I don't know, maybe a little," Nellie answered, clearly agitated.

I reached for Nellie's hand again and this time she didn't pull away. "I'll get some peppermint oil from the lab that you can rub on your leg. But you'll have to do it at night, or the smell will give it away."

"And I can help you too, Nellie," Gloria said. "Just until your leg is better," she added quickly.

"Don't you fret about me. I'll be all right," she said with forced cheerfulness. Then, as if to prove her point, she stood and walked across the room. "Now, let me see if I can find that piece of apple pie I saved for you."

* * *

After lunch I washed and changed into clean clothes. I found Dr. Parker in his office reading a copy of the local newspaper, the *Western Democrat*. I noted that, in my absence, the office had reverted to the same disordered state in which I'd found it nearly twenty years earlier. Books, papers, and medical journals were strewn haphazardly about the room. He put the paper down when I came in, removed his reading glasses, and slowly massaged his temples.

"It's good to have you back, Henry."

"Yes sir. It's good to be back."

"I hope you're ready to get to work. We've got a lot to catch up on." I was standing in the middle of the room, perhaps six feet from his desk. Through the window I saw dead leaves covering the ground.

"Yes sir. What would you like for me to do?"

He pointed toward the far corner of the room. "Why don't you start by unloading the crate. It came in last week and I haven't had a chance to go through it yet." I looked in the direction he indicated and saw the type of small wooden crate his broker in London sent twice each year. Dr. Parker was always anxious to go through the materials, so it seemed odd that the crate was still unopened.

But instead of doing as he'd requested, I said, "Excuse me, Dr. Parker. Can I ask you something?"

"Yes, go ahead," he said warily. Though I had thought about this moment for several weeks, I suddenly found myself tongue-tied. "Well, what is it?"

I felt my heart beating rapidly, but not wanting to miss this opportunity, I pressed ahead in a rush. "Begging your pardon sir but . . . how do you think this war will end? I mean, the South has won some battles, that's true enough, but I saw the Union soldiers fight and die. Die by the dozens. I hope I'm not out of line, but it doesn't seem to me that they're disposed to give up anytime soon." He didn't say anything, so I kept going. "I've been thinking about it a lot since we left the regiment. You understand more of the world than I do. What do you believe is going to happen?"

Dr. Parker leaned back in his chair and appeared to be lost in thought. Finally, he said, "I don't have a crystal ball, so I can only tell you what I think. But you seem ready for some straight talk, and I guess we owe you that much." He indicated I should sit in one of the chairs facing his desk, and I did so, after removing several books that were already there. He glanced out the window before continuing. "Next spring, when the weather warms up, the war will start again. There are some that think it will be over soon, but I believe they're wrong. It's likely to go on for quite some time," he said, his voice trailing off. I had an empty feeling in the pit of my gut but said nothing, not wanting to interrupt him. "Matthew plans to go back, of course. We offered to pay a substitute to take his place, but he won't hear of it. He's determined to see it through."

I tried to discern the meaning behind his words, but my thoughts were like molasses. Eventually I managed to stammer, "I don't understand."

"Then let me make it plain," he said with a tinge of annoyance. "I'm trying to talk him out of it, but if

Matthew reenlists in the spring, he means to take you with him again."

"For how long," I asked weakly.

He didn't answer right away. When he spoke at last, his voice was barely audible. "All reenlistments will be for a minimum of three years." I stared at him dumbly, trying to make sense of what he'd said. Three years? Had I heard him correctly?

"Did you say three years?" He only response was a single nod. The room started to spin, and I grabbed the arms of the chair to steady myself. Six months with the regiment had been hell. How would I possibly survive for three years? When Matthew went back, I would have to go too, like a faithful dog trotting at his side. I yearned to jump across the desk and shake Dr. Parker out of his complacency. I wanted to pound my fists and scream at the unfairness of it all. Three long years. In the end, I just sat there, mute. Dr. Parker did the same. We faced each other across the broad desk for a long time, each lost in our own thoughts, while outside the window more dead leaves fluttered slowly to the ground.

CHAPTER 22

RETURN

Spring 1862

I went through the next few months in a haze, scarcely able to think of anything other than being forced to leave again. I didn't yet know the date of our departure, but I knew it drew closer every day. If Matthew wanted to risk his life fighting, he had every right to do so, but unlike him I had no rights. My entire life was controlled by the Parkers. When Matthew went to war again, I would be with him; what I wanted was irrelevant. Though I was twenty-five years old that spring, I didn't yet feel like a man. How could I if I wasn't free to decide where to live, where to work, or who to marry. And, if ever I was blessed with children, they would also belong to someone else. I was not a man, I was a simulacrum of a man, more akin to a favorite tool or implement. Something to be used and discarded.

One afternoon in March all my concerns were brought into sharp focus. I was in the office when there was a knock at the door. Dr. Parker was reading from an article entitled "Surgical Operations for the Relief of Defective Vision" published in *Transactions of the American Medical Association*. For my part, I was standing next to his desk, listening intently so that I might accurately capture the information. Clearly annoyed at being disturbed, he shouted, "Come in," much more loudly than was necessary.

After a short pause Matthew, his fiancée Sarah, and Mrs. Parker entered the office. Sarah frowned when she noticed me standing so closely to Dr. Parker. I acknowledged their presence with a nod before moving back from the desk. Matthew had known Sarah for many years but had not proposed until shortly after he'd returned from his first deployment. There is something about facing death that makes one focus more intently on living.

Matthew was wearing a crisp new uniform, and the ladies made it clear they thought he looked very handsome in his long frock coat with its high collar, decorated with golden buttons, belt, and trim. Mrs. Parker asked her husband, "Charles, doesn't Matthew look splendid?"

Dr. Parker's smile, when it came, seemed forced. "Yes, he does. It's certainly quite an impressive outfit." Matthew's cheeks colored at the implied reproach, but he said nothing.

Mrs. Parker, ignoring the tension in the room, said, "We're going to have refreshments in the parlor. Won't you take a break from your work and join us?"

Dr. Parker looked down at the open journal on his desk. "Thank you, Mary, but I really need to . . ."

Sensing his hesitation, she added quickly, "After all, Matthew will only be with us for a short time."

With a sigh Dr. Parker took one last look at the unfinished article and pushed himself up from the desk.

Mrs. Parker smiled graciously, perhaps knowing that the outcome was never really in question. "Henry," she said, "Nellie is in the kitchen getting everything ready, would you give her a hand."

"Yes ma'am, Mrs. Parker."

As everyone filed out of the office Sarah directed a cold stare in my direction, forcing me to look away.

Since our return I'd had very little contact with Sarah, and I'd certainly never done anything to offend her. But I knew I was being foolish. Innocence or guilt didn't matter; my future was written on her face as plainly as in one of Dr. Parker's books. When Sarah married Matthew, it was clear that my days in the Parker home would be numbered.

* * *

Later that month, we made our preparations to leave. The 1st North Carolina Volunteers, also known as the Bethel Regiment, had been disbanded, but Matthew and many of his fellow veterans had reenlisted in the newly formed 11th North Carolina Regiment. His previous commanding officer, Captain Egbert Ross, had been promoted to the rank of major, and Matthew was selected as one of his captains. The regiment was commanded by Colonel Collett Leventhorpe, an imposing former British Army officer that stood six and a half feet tall.

This time, instead of taking the train, we would travel overland to Raleigh, Matthew aboard his horse Bessie while I drove a wagon with our supplies. Matthew had learned a valuable lesson during his first deployment. Namely, the best assurance of having what you needed in the field was to bring it with you. This time we had spare clothes and shoes, extra blankets, cooking utensils, coffee, beans, grits, rice, and dried meat, along with many other items Matthew thought he could use.

Of course, since we might be away for three years, I made sure to pack all the medical supplies I could manage. From my mother I had bloodroot to stop bleeding, wormroot for worms, barberry to keep urine flowing, candle bush for stomach pain, horsemint for skin infections, cascara as a laxative, willow bark for fevers, white hellebore for pain, and dried elderberries and witch hazel for a myriad of uses. Anything I didn't have I would try to scavenge along the way.

From Dr. Parker I'd secured bandages, laudanum for sleep and dysentery, powdered opium for pain, Chlorodyne for coughs, coca leaves to calm nerves, and purgatives of varying strengths. Dr. Parker had also insisted that I take a bottle of chloroform. At that time, its use as an anesthetic had only recently become widespread and, in the unlikely event that Matthew needed surgery, Dr. Parker wasn't certain that the field surgeons would have any available.

Before we left I turned and took a long look at the house, not knowing when, or indeed if, I would ever see it again. Everyone had come out to say goodbye. It seemed that they were all trying hard to remain cheerful on what was, at its core, a very somber day.

Nellie, whose health had continued to deteriorate, gave me a long hug. "Take care of yourself, Henry. There's a lot of us depending on you to come back." I instinctively looked toward Gloria, who seemed lost in her own thoughts.

"You take care of yourself too, Nellie. When I get back, I'm going to be expecting some of your biscuits and gravy." We knew that there was a good chance we would never see each other again; nevertheless, we both smiled at this pleasant fiction.

Gloria and I hugged briefly and said goodbye. There was so much that I wanted to say to her, but this was not the time. I wanted us to be together and, if I made it back to Charlotte, I hoped we would be. I was sure she felt the same way, but we both knew that might never happen. There were simply too many unknowns.

Even if I returned safely, there was no certainty that Dr. Parker would allow Gloria and me to be together. Though this was my hope, I had never actually discussed it with him. What if Matthew became the master of the house and married Sarah? What if the Confederates won the war? What if one or both of us were sold? I could not even be certain that in three years Gloria would still feel the same way about me. By then she might have paired off with someone else. With sadness I realized that our dream to be together was little more than a fantasy spun of the finest gossamer, one that could be ripped apart at any time. The previous evening Gloria had put it more succinctly, as was her custom. "You get yourself back here first, Henry, then we'll see about all the rest."

We talked late into the night in the kitchen house, neither of us wanting to say goodbye. Then, just before I left to return to my cabin, I pressed a small package into her hands. "What's this?" she asked.

I looked around and lowered my voice. "Sam worked for years to buy his freedom, but he never had enough money. He said I was like a son to him, and when he was dying, he gave me everything he had. With what I earned over the years, there is more than two hundred and sixty dollars here. I need you to keep it safe until I come back." I paused before continuing. "And if I don't make it back, use it as you think best."

She shook her head emphatically. "I can't take your money, Henry."

"You're not taking it; you're just holding it for me until I get back. I'll rest easier knowing that it's somewhere safe. I can't take it with me. You remember what happened to my shoes?"

She looked at me for a long time, the only sound being the incessant buzz of insects outside the window. Finally, she grabbed both of my hands and squeezed hard. "I promise I'll keep it safe until you come back. But I need you to do whatever you have to do to stay alive. You hear me, Henry? You can't be out there worrying about me, your Momma, or anyone else back here." A tear slid silently down her cheek. "I want you to come back to me, but you've got to stay alive, that's the main thing. And if that means you need to run, then you run as far and fast as you can. You understand me, Henry? If you need to, you run and don't look back."

* * *

Matthew and I traveled at an easy pace with a party of more than thirty men from Charlotte and the surrounding area. The sky was overcast, making the weather cool, but the sun broke through from time to time, bathing everything in a pale light.

Matthew and the other officers rode horses, and there was one other wagon in addition to the one I drove. Those without horses took turns riding in the wagons, such that there was always someone on the seat beside me, while two or three others sat in the back with the baggage. Everyone else walked.

The regiment was scheduled to be mustered at the end of the month, and Matthew intended for us to get there a few days early. We saw many men on the road, most of them likely also making their way to Camp Mangum. A few Confederates were already in uniform but most, including Matthew, were not. I'm sure they felt they would be wearing them soon enough, so there was no need to rush things.

The road we traveled on was muddy and rutted from the passage of so many horses, wagons, and men. Most nights we found a suitable campsite just off the road. But a few times we found lodging in towns along the way like Albemarle, Asheboro, and Pittsboro. When we were in town Matthew and the other officers slept in a local house or inn, while the enlisted men slept in a barn or other building. There were three slaves in our party, Abraham, Isaac, and me, and as such we were expected to stay with the horses. It was our job to make sure they were fed, watered, and ready for the next day's journey.

* * *

When we finally caught sight of the camp, still some distance away, my first impression was of a field of hundreds of white tents stretching to the horizon. As we drew closer, I could see that the tents were larger than they'd first appeared, each one large enough to sleep six men. And there were men everywhere, more than I had ever seen in one place. It was impossible to estimate how many people were in camp, but I later heard that there were at least twelve thousand, four times as many as lived in Charlotte at that time. A sergeant pointed us toward the area where the 11th North Carolina Regiment was encamped, and we headed in that direction. After several wrong turns, and more shouted instructions, we finally found the regiment.

Dismounting, Matthew tied Bessie's reins to the back of the wagon. "Wait here, I'll be back soon."

"Yes sir, Captain Parker." As he walked away, I got down from the wagon, stretched, and took my first good look at the place. The camp was laid out as a large grid, with tents lined up back-to-back and the openings facing each other across narrow dirt roads. We had passed more than twenty such roads on our way here, and there were still more ahead.

A short distance away a few Confederates were sitting around a dying fire, and I noticed that they were looking in my direction. I inclined my head and touched the brim of my hat in greeting, but no one said anything or made a move. After a tense moment, I realized they were not looking at me, but at the contents of the wagon. Thinking back to the theft of my shoes the previous year, I knew we would need to stay vigilant to keep our supplies secure.

We had stopped at a sort of crossroads. There was a hand-painted sign on one corner that read *Camp Bethel*. I could see men all around me. Some moved about with purpose; most, however, were more relaxed and played cards or dominos, while others sat around cooking fires. Perhaps twenty feet away a man played a slow tune on the harmonica.

A nearby voice interrupted my thoughts. "Preacher, is that you?" I turned and saw Louis beaming at me. I was very glad to see him again and we embraced warmly.

"It's good to see you, Louis. I wasn't sure you would be back, but I hoped you would be." Then indicating the camp with a sweep of my arm, I asked, "And even if you were here, how could I hope to find you in such a place? Are you still with Captain . . . sorry, I mean Major Ross?"

Still smiling, Louis nodded. "Yes, I'm still his man. Guess I will be until the Lord calls one of us home. He's in the tent at the end, the one with the table and chairs out front." He looked over the contents of the wagon. "I see that Captain Parker came prepared this time."

I nodded. "I guess you heard about his promotion; seems like news travels fast."

"That it does. Truth is, there aren't many captains in the whole regiment. You'll get to know them all before long. Once I heard he'd re-upped, I thought you might be coming back too.

I lowered my voice to make sure that we wouldn't be overheard. "It's not like I had any say in the matter."

"None of us do," he chuckled, putting a hand on my shoulder, "but I'm still mighty glad to see you."

"What are you boys doing?" Startled, we turned quickly to face Matthew. I noted that Louis's hand was no longer on my shoulder.

"Nothing, Captain Parker. I was just waiting here like you said. Do you remember Major Ross's man, Louis?"

He nodded toward Louis but otherwise gave no indication whether he remembered him or not. "Follow me. I'll show you the lodgings I've been assigned."

When we got there, Louis helped me unload the wagon. "I best get going, Henry. If you need water, there's a creek about a half mile to the west. Just follow the path out of camp and you'll run right into it. I'll come see you later, after you're settled."

It had started to rain, and the camp looked even more squalid in the dim light. I shook my head and almost laughed at the absurdity of it. Settled? How could anyone ever feel settled in such a place?

CHAPTER 23

STAGNATION

1862

I n early 1862, a Union army commanded by General
Ambrose Burnside captured Roanoke Island, and New
Bern, North Carolina, in quick succession. New Bern, a
port city on the Neuse River, was a major stop on the
new Atlantic and North Carolina Railroad. Burnside's
victories threatened the entire Carolina coastal region
and put the Confederate supply lines in jeopardy. The
presence of Burnside's army also created an additional
problem. Whereas in previous years, runaway slaves had
been hunted down and returned to their masters, a new
law decreed that slaves would not be returned to their
owners but would instead be classified as "contraband

of war." Within weeks of Burnside's victory, hundreds of slaves had fled and joined the Union lines.

Though the governor implored the Confederate War Department for immediate assistance, none was sent. North Carolina would have to fend for itself. So, in early May, the 11th North Carolina Regiment was sent to Wilmington to see to the city's defenses, then a month later to Camp Wyatt, near the mouth of the Cape Fear River.

Only seven miles from Wilmington, Camp Wyatt was situated on a narrow strip of land between the Cape Fear River and the Atlantic Ocean. I had never seen the ocean before and was immediately in awe of its vastness and raw, elemental beauty. I knew that men routinely sailed the oceans of the world in wooden ships, but until I saw the Atlantic, I did not fully appreciate how remarkable a feat that was.

As we walked, frothy white waves crashed thunderously along the shore, saturating the air with a salty mist. Small crabs and insects scattered at our approach, while noisy seabirds wheeled and dived overhead. I had seen seashells in Dr. Parker's office, but not so many, or in such dazzling variety. I would have liked to stop and examine them all more closely, but sadly I had to keep moving. I did manage to pick up a beautiful Scotch bonnet, which I still have.

When we arrived, it quickly became apparent that there were two major issues with Camp Wyatt. The first was that there was no nearby source of fresh water. The water in the Cape Fear River, on which we were encamped, was brackish and therefore undrinkable, while water from a nearby well was brown, turbid, and unappealing. The second issue was that the entire camp was infested with fleas. Within a day, everyone was covered with dozens of angry red bite marks, particularly on their ankles and legs.

One evening I noticed Matthew was sitting on the edge of his cot, scratching furiously. My first thought was to abandon him to his discomfort. After all, he hadn't asked for my help, nor would he have been likely to do so, no matter how uncomfortable he might have been. His pride wouldn't allow it. But, in my own way, I was proud too.

"With your permission, sir, I have something that might help you with those bites." I held up a small brown bottle. "Wet a piece of cloth with this and dab each bite with it. It should give you some relief."

He took the bottle and studied it closely. "What is it?" he asked.

"It's a tincture of witch hazel," I answered without thinking.

He looked up at me and frowned. "What's a tincture?"

I saw the danger then and chided myself for being so careless. Any suggestion that I knew more about a subject than he did could earn me a beating, but lying was also not a good option.

"A tincture is a medicine made by soaking a plant in alcohol, sometimes for days or weeks." Then, after a pause, I added, "It's something that Dr. Parker taught me."

The range of emotions that played across his face were difficult to read. Was it surprise, confusion, jealousy, anger, or some combination of these? I had worked closely with his father for nearly twenty years, but it was as if, until that moment, he hadn't considered that I might have *learned* anything during that time. I thought I might have gone too far, but in the end, he simply said, "All right, I'll try it."

And the witch hazel did seem to help, because the next day his bites were not as red, and he seemed less troubled by them. I knew that the small bottle wouldn't last long, so I started thinking of ways to replenish my supply. But I didn't have to dwell on this problem for long because, only one week after arriving at Camp Wyatt, the regiment was ordered to move back to Wilmington. No battles had been fought or objectives won, so I couldn't help thinking that all the suffering of the past week had been unnecessary. But as we prepared to leave, I overheard no grumbling from the men about the futility of it all. Perhaps that would come later. At that moment, everyone's sole focus was on leaving Camp Wyatt, and the damnable fleas, far behind.

* * *

The greater war had been raging all that year, with the Confederate and Union armies fighting several major battles. I could tell that Matthew and his comrades were becoming increasing frustrated. While they were still in North Carolina, thousands of other Confederate soldiers were fighting and dying at places such as Shiloh, Seven Pines, Gaines' Mill, Malvern Hill, Manassas, and Antietam. After departing Camp Wyatt, they had expected to travel north to join up with General Lee's army. Instead, the regiment passed the summer guarding the Cape Fear District from a possible Union attack. This news came as a bitter disappointment. There wasn't much for the regiment to do, and Colonel Leventhorpe drilled his men constantly to maintain discipline.

Although the 11th didn't see any military action that summer, they had their share of casualties as many of the men suffered through bouts of dysentery, typhoid fever, typhus, and malaria. A great many of them died.

I did not become ill that summer, but many of the other Negros in camp did, including Louis who came down with a bout of typhoid. I tried to help him whenever I could, but frustratingly, there was little I could do. I brewed a batch of willow bark tea for his fever and added a few drops of laudanum to ease his discomfort. Though he was very weak, I managed to get him to drink some of the mixture for several consecutive days and, to my great relief, by the end of the week his fever had broken, and he started to feel better.

A couple of days later I saw him sitting with his back against a tall pine. "It's good to see you up and around," I said, smiling.

He smiled weakly. "Guess the Lord isn't ready for me yet."

"I can't say I'm surprised. At present you're a sorry-looking specimen." He tried to chuckle, but it sounded more like a rasp. Clearing his throat, he said, "I don't remember much of the last week, but I know that you helped me. For that I'm in your debt."

I was touched by his thanks, but I waved it away. "You owe me nothing. I'm just glad to see you getting back to yourself." Neither of us said anything more, and we sat together for some time in amiable silence.

When word got around that I'd helped Louis recover, some of the other Negro men started to come to me with their ailments. I always did what I could for them, as these men had few other options. They were far from home, separated from the people that might have helped them through an illness. The doctors in camp, indeed most Southern doctors, were reluctant to see Negro patients. Dr. Parker and others like him might treat a Negro, but they were an exception, and even then, one could never be certain of their motives.

The most serious illness that summer was yellow fever. Though endemic to Charleston, New Orleans, and other southern ports, Wilmington had not experienced an outbreak for more than forty years. The disease caused a high fever, nausea, chills, muscle pain, and in some cases, a foul-smelling black vomit. The skin and eyes of the sickest patients took on an unnatural yellow cast, and nearly half of those so affected ultimately perished.

Fear of the contagion drove everyone out of town or kept them confined to their homes. Within a short time, Wilmington had become virtually a ghost town. Even the new district commander, General Thomas Clingman, stayed away. In September, for the safety of his men, Colonel Leventhorpe moved the regiment from Wilmington to Camp Davis.

One afternoon in early October, just as the worst seemed behind us, I heard Matthew call to me. I put down the uniform I was mending and went to his tent. He was sitting at the camp desk cleaning his Griswold revolver. I saw immediately that he was in good spirits.

"Yes sir."

"Start getting everything packed up. We're pulling out tomorrow."

"Yes sir." Then after a pause, I added, "Begging the Captain's pardon, but can I ask where we're going now?"

He held the gun at eye level, carefully inspecting the barrel. He pushed the cylinder back in place and I heard several clicks as he pulled the trigger.

"We're heading north to join up with Lee's Army," he said distractedly, his focus still on the gun. "Looks like we're finally going to get into this fight. Now they'll see what this regiment can do." Momentarily lost in my own thoughts, I stayed silent. He turned to me impatiently and said, "Well, what are you standing around here for?"

"Yes sir, Captain. I'll get started on that right now."

I packed most of our belongings that night, and when I awoke the next morning, the sun was just beginning to appear, giving the sky a deep red glow. We ate a light breakfast, and I quickly packed the rest of our gear. The entire camp hummed with a nervous energy I hadn't seen in many months.

I saw Louis and asked, "Have you heard where we're heading?"

"I don't know for sure, but we're taking the north-bound train, so somewhere in Virginia I expect."

Though Louis worked for Major Ross, apparently I knew more about the situation than he did. This wasn't unusual. I wasn't necessarily exposed to more information than he was, but I was a much better listener. Also, my gift allowed me to reflect on the things I heard in my own time. And often, something that was initially confusing would become clearer upon further reflection.

So, by that morning, I already knew that Union forces had taken Suffolk, Virginia, and were threatening the rail line between Wilmington and Petersburg. I had also heard that the Wilmington to Petersburg line was critical to the success of the Confederate war effort. But even though we would soon be traveling on that very same line, I still found myself hoping that the Yankees would destroy it. I hoped they would destroy it so completely that it would be months, or possibly years, before another train could travel along the same tracks. I only prayed I wouldn't be on it when they did.

* * *

We disembarked at Belfield, Virginia, and were ordered to march thirty-five miles to Franklin, a small town on the Blackwater River. We set up camp and the very next day started digging breastworks on the west bank of the river. There were a great many fallen trees in the area, and we used these to reinforce the positions. We also built artillery emplacements, fortified with railroad ties, for guns with names like Long Tom and Laughing Charlie. In all, the defensive line extended for more than twenty miles. Many of the officers were openly skeptical that so much territory could be successfully defended with so few men. We didn't have long to wait, because a few weeks later scouts reported that several thousand Union soldiers had left their base at Suffolk and were heading in our direction.

Matthew's company had been assigned to guard one of the most likely crossing points, a bend in the river just south of Franklin. It had been raining on and off for days, leaving the ground sodden and muddy. The Blackwater wasn't a large river, like the York or the Neuse, and I could easily see the Union forces massing on the opposite bank. For a few minutes, the only sound was the sporadic crack of rifle fire. Then, as if responding to some unseen signal, the artillery on both sides of the river opened fire. Ignoring the mud, I dove for cover behind a fallen tree, perhaps thirty yards back from the front line. What at first seemed like a solid wall of noise soon resolved into distinct sounds. There were the deep booms of the cannons, the thumps of shells hitting soil, the cracking of splintered trees, and the pattering of dirt and debris as it rained back to earth. All these sounds were overlaid on the sharp retort of pistols and rifles and the muted shouts and screams of men.

The entire river valley was soon filled with a thick, sulfurous smoke that darkened the sky and clawed at my throat. Once, during a short lull in the firing, I looked for Matthew. His men were still there, taking cover just as I was, but I didn't see him. Almost immediately the cannons started firing again and I could see nothing more. This went on for what felt like an unimaginably long time, certainly more than an hour, but the smoke made it impossible to judge the time of day. Then, just as abruptly as the cannons had started, they stopped. I didn't move for several minutes, not trusting that the barrage was finally over. But after some minutes, I heard someone yell, "They're leaving, the Yankees are leaving!"

The men cheered and jeered loudly, and I finally stood on shaky legs to survey the scene before me. The ground around me was scoured of vegetation, and many of the trees were gone, but the breastworks had held. I saw a few bodies on the ground, but remarkably, most of the Confederates seemed unhurt. Then I saw Matthew, still wary of Union sharpshooters, move along the line in a crouch. I made my way to him.

"Captain Parker, is there anything you need?"

"No, no, I'm fine. You can head back to camp and get dinner started. I'll be along in a while."

He said all of this in a calm voice, and even tried to smile, but I could see that all was not well. For one thing, I noticed that there was a slight tremor in his right hand, which hadn't been there that morning. It wasn't much, but it was noticeable. Perhaps more importantly than that, the bravado that I had seen in his eyes the previous night was gone. I doubted that others would see the change, but I had known Matthew for a long time. I recognized the look in his eyes. He was afraid.

CHAPTER 24

PROCESSION

1863

As the year 1863 dawned, I noted that Matthew and many of his fellow Confederate officers appeared angry. At the time I didn't know why, and whenever I was nearby, they would either lower their voices or stop talking altogether. Something was clearly amiss. Then, one morning, as I was cooking breakfast, I overheard Matthew speaking with Major Ross.

"They know they can't defeat us on the battlefield, so now Lincoln and the Black Republicans are openly encouraging a slave rebellion," Matthew said.

"I agree. It's clear that any slaves that make it across the lines will be welcomed by the Yankees and protected."

There was a long pause before Matthew spoke again. "No doubt, it's a detestable document, but haven't there been deserters since the start of the war? I wonder if we're overreacting."

"Yes, of course you're right, but the numbers have been manageable. Now, because of this so-called Emancipation Proclamation, what had been a trickle will become a flood." From inside the tent, I heard papers rustling. "Listen to what he wrote. 'I do order and declare that all persons held as slaves within said designated States, and parts of States, are, and henceforward shall be free; and that the Executive government of the United States, including the military and naval authorities thereof, will recognize and maintain the freedom of said persons.' I don't think his intent could be any clearer."

Matthew said something I couldn't understand.

"And to make matters worse," Major Ross continued, "Colonel Leventhorpe believes that runaway slaves won't be the worst effect of Lincoln's proclamation."

"What could be worse?" asked Matthew.

"He believes that, because of this damnable document, England and other European countries will never recognize the Confederacy. By aligning the Union with antislavery, Lincoln has effectively isolated us. We'll get no help from Europe now."

What I'd overheard stunned me. President Lincoln had declared that the slaves were free, and that if we ran away, we would be protected. For years, with the assistance of the Union, runaway slaves had been hunted down and returned to their owners. But all that had changed. I was not surprised that Matthew was angry, and I smiled at the thought of it.

After so many years my freedom was within reach, as close as the nearest Union Army camp. Gloria had said that if I saw a chance to get free, I should take it and not look back. But I knew I couldn't do that. If I ran, it was her and my mother that would pay the price. Though I had no qualms about leaving Dr. Parker and Matthew, I was reluctant to abandon the women that had been so good to me. I would have to find another way.

* * *

Though the 11th North Carolina Regiment had seen some action at White Hall, New Bern, and Washington, until that time it had managed to avoid the largest and bloodiest battles of the war. That would soon change. In early June, the 11th North Carolina was absorbed into General Lee's Army of Northern Virginia. Still commanded by Colonel Leventhorpe, the 11th Regiment became attached to General Pettigrew's brigade, which was part of General Heth's division, which in turn, was a unit of General Hill's Third Corps. The Army of Northern Virginia had a total of three corps, the remaining two being led by Generals Longstreet and Ewell.

Though he had hated to do it, Matthew had been forced to leave his his horse, Bessie, in North Carolina. He soon secured another mount just outside Fredericksburg from a widow that had several horses. Her husband had recently died of consumption and, somehow hearing of this, the army commandeered the animals and paid her in Confederate scrip. I was one of the men sent into the barn to collect the horses. To say she was not pleased with the transaction would be an understatement, and as we left, she vigorously cursed us, General Lee, and Jefferson Davis for robbing her!

The weather that June was unseasonably warm, so each day we set out before sunrise to avoid the worst of the afternoon heat. When we arrived at Culpepper, General Heth ordered the division to dispose of everything that wasn't necessary. This meant that, in addition to his rifle and ammunition, each man could carry little more than a canteen, mess kit, and bedroll. There was a lot of grumbling from the men about having to leave their belongings behind, but they were heading into Union territory and would need to move quickly. Of course, it also meant that resupply was impossible. The army would need to forage for food and supplies as they went.

I could tell that something was bothering Matthew. As a young man, he had always been fond of distilled spirits, but that June he was drinking much more than usual. So much so that, some nights, I would have to help him undress and get to bed. I also noticed that, in more private moments, he appeared quieter and more introspective.

He had also become skittish. In fact, if I came into his tent unexpectedly, he would startle, then flush red with embarrassment. After this had happened several times, I started to make certain I made noise before I entered the tent.

I had no way to know what troubled his thoughts, and he certainly wouldn't have confided in me. Then one afternoon, I saw an unfinished letter on his field desk that he was writing to Sarah. Matthew had been called away for a moment, but I had time to glance at it quickly.

June 9, 1863

Dearest Sarah,

I hope this letter finds you well. It has been more than a year since I last saw your lovely face, and I think of you and home often. We are presently in Culpepper, Virginia, but are leaving here tomorrow. General Heth hasn't said much, but everyone has been told to pack light and bring at least three days' rations. I expect it will be some time before we get another decent meal. This war is a terrible business and there seems to be no end in sight. We are fighting for North

Carolina and our way of life, that much is clear, but I wonder what the Yankees fight for? After suffering so many defeats, I thought they would have given up by now, but they seem more determined than ever. They must know that we will never rejoin the Union.

The 11th is now part of General Lee's army and, as such, I'm sure we'll see our share of fighting. Some of these men have already fought at Manassas, Antietam, and Fredericksburg. After surviving such hardships, and seeing so many of their fellows die, it is difficult to ask them to fight on. But ask them we must.

You know that I was eager to join this campaign, and I am still proud to serve, but camp life has given me a lot of time to think, and I have finally come to a terrible realization. In this war, bravery doesn't matter. When death comes it is indiscriminate, with both heroes and cowards taken in equal measure. The only thing we can control is how we meet that death. It is the honor of my life to have been deemed worthy to lead these fine men, and I will always do my duty. I only pray it is enough to carry me safely back to you.

Suddenly, from the corner of my eye, I saw Matthew heading back toward the tent. Moving away might look suspicious, so I busied myself by rearranging a few items on his desk. I straightened up as he approached.

"Anything I can do for you, Captain?" He waved me away before sitting at the desk. I watched from outside the tent as he appeared to be studying the unfinished letter. Then, just when I thought he might take up his quill again, he tore the paper into several pieces, stood, and pitched them into the fire. Sarah would never learn of his uncertainty.

* * *

The next morning, we left Culpepper and headed north into the Shenandoah Valley. The land was lush and verdant and as beautiful as any I had ever seen. Louis and I were walking together. I'd already told him what I'd overheard from Matthew and Major Ross about Lincoln's Emancipation Proclamation. As we were walking, he leaned in close.

"If I ever get free, I would like to settle in a place like this," he confided. "Rich soil, fresh water, and a forest filled with timber. I'll wager you there is plenty of game too. My son Elijah loved to fish, and it looks like these rivers are full of them." Then, after a long pause, he added softly, "A man could do a lot worse." I voiced my agreement, but for some reason I found myself thinking of Gloria. I didn't know what my future held, but I knew that I wanted her to be a part of it.

"Do you think about your wife and boy much?" I asked.

He appeared taken aback by my question and gave me a sidelong glance. "Almost every day," he said slowly. "But after so many years, what's the point? My boy was only five when I was sold off. When I left, he only came up to my waist. He must have grown some since then," he said wistfully. "He probably wouldn't even remember me."

I wanted to say, *He remembers you, Louis*, or *You'll see them again one day*. But I didn't know if either was true, so I stayed silent.

The regiment moved steadily north, and by the second week everyone was tired and footsore. Neither Matthew nor any of the officers he served with seemed to know our destination, but most guessed we were heading into Pennsylvania, and then on to the capital of Harrisburg. Their suspicions were strengthened when we crossed the Potomac River on scows, entering the state of Pennsylvania a few days later. While I heard many of the Confederates express excitement at finally "taking the fight to the Yankees," at least an equal number seemed uncomfortable with being so far from home.

I overheard one solder say, "This isn't going to be easy—they'll be defending their land now."

"I just hope it isn't those damned Black Hats again," another man added. "Those Yankees know how to fight."

As we approached the town of Chambersburg, we passed a group of Negro men, women, and children on the road, being led south in chains. I exchanged glances with one of the men and will never forget the look of despair I saw in his eyes.

That evening, Matthew and some of the other officers were drinking whiskey they had confiscated from a local tavern. He came back to his tent later that night, clearly having had his fill, and I risked raising the subject.

"Excuse me, Captain, can I ask you a question?" He looked at me and nodded. "Well, sir, just before we got to town, I saw a group of Negroes in chains. I expect that the captain saw them too."

"I did," he said tightly.

"Well sir, I was just wondering if you knew who they were."

"Why do you care?" he asked suspiciously.

"No reason, sir," I said casually, "just curious."

He gave me a slow, lopsided grin. "Course I know who they were." He laughed. "They're niggers that thought they were free. They thought they were safe in Pennsylvania, but we got them now. They're going down south." I was horrified, and it must have shown on my face. "What's wrong with you?" he said, narrowing his eyes. "You aren't thinking of trying to run off, are you?"

I shook my head. "No sir, I'm not planning on running."

He took another sip of whiskey and stared hard at me for some time. "That's good, because if you did, when I caught you, and you *would* be caught, I would skin you alive."

I should have left it there, but the thought of those poor souls in chains irritated me, like a burr in my shoe. So later that night, as I helped him get ready for bed, I asked, "Begging the Captain's pardon, but about those Negroes. How do they know that some of them weren't free?"

"What do you mean?" he asked, clearly annoyed that I had brought the subject up again.

"What I mean is, sir, how do they know they're runaways and not free men?"

He looked at me directly and smiled luridly. "Well, it doesn't matter much now, does it? If they were free, they sure aren't free now."

As I bedded down that night, I couldn't stop thinking about the look on that man's face. Had he been a free man? Did that explain the despair I saw in his eyes? Since I was young, I'd heard folks talking and dreaming of their freedom. Before he died, Sam had talked about it too. In fact, he talked about it so often that I too started to believe it was possible. But that day, I saw the bitter truth. If they could put you in chains whenever it suited them, what did freedom really mean.

CHAPTER 25

CARNAGE

1863

At the end of June, instead of continuing to Harrisburg as expected, we turned east toward the town of Gettysburg. General Lee had brought the entire Army of Northern Virginia to the area, and though we hadn't yet seen them, there were rumors that a large Union force was shadowing us to the east. We set up camp near Cashtown on June 29, and the next morning General Pettigrew's brigade was ordered to move into Gettysburg to conduct reconnaissance and forage for food and supplies, particularly shoes, which were sorely needed.

As we walked the eight miles from Cashtown, we passed through a beautiful landscape of dark, inviting woods and green, rolling fields. When we reached the outskirts of Gettysburg, I was impressed with the sturdy stone houses, neat fence lines, and well-tended gardens, all surrounded by rich farmland. The largest building, which I later learned was a Lutheran seminary, sat atop a hill overlooking the town, and beyond that, larger hills loomed in the distance. My reverie was interrupted when the brigade suddenly slowed to a halt. We were near the rear of the column, still almost half a mile from town. Matthew pulled out a pair of field glasses and spoke to one of his men, an earnest young lieutenant named Davis.

"There are troopers on the ridge ahead, but from here I can't tell if they're local militia or Federals."

He handed the glasses to Davis, and after a moment the younger man said, "It's hard to say for certain, but there sure are a lot of them." Then, after a pause, he added, "And they already have the high ground."

Matthew nodded and mopped his brow with a handkerchief. Though still early, the day was already hot, and he had started to perspire. "Well, General Pettigrew is up ahead. I expect he'll have a better idea of who they are than we do." And perhaps he did, because a few minutes later word was passed down the line that the brigade had been ordered to pull back and rejoin the rest of the army near Cashtown.

The next morning, General Heth ordered both of his divisions, including Pettigrew's brigade, to move into Gettysburg along the Chambersburg Pike, the same road we had traveled the day before. When we were close to town, I could clearly see Union forces lined up on a ridge, behind a split-rail fence. Matthew called me forward and pointed to the woods on our left.

"Stay in the trees and, when the fighting subsides, offer assistance where you can. I might even need you later," he said with a forced smile.

"Yes sir."

For a moment it seemed that he wanted to say something more, but instead he spurred his horse forward. I moved into the woods and took cover behind a broad oak that offered a clear view of the field. As my eyes adjusted to the dim light, I looked around and saw that I wasn't alone. Louis and several other men were already there, along with an assortment of photographers, newspaper reporters, and other camp followers. Everyone was tense, and for good reason. Battles moved to and fro with a will of their own and, once the fighting started, only time would tell how safe our refuge would remain.

The Confederates left the Chambersburg Pike and formed a line on both sides of the road, opposite the Federals who were still quite a distance away. I could see Matthew waving his sword and shouting orders I could not hear. Though General Lee clearly had an advantage in terms of men, the Federals had cover and held the high ground. I could see that this would be a difficult battle, the outcome of which was far from certain.

Louis joined me and said in a low voice, "Looks like the Yankees are outnumbered."

I shook my head and frowned. "Maybe they are, but does it make sense that a couple of hundred men would pick a fight with a thousand?" His only response was a noncommittal shrug, so I continued. "The fact is, I don't think they would unless they knew they had backup. It might even be a trap."

Suddenly the Union started firing their rifles. The Confederates responded and, within minutes, the once peaceful field was filled with smoke and the shouts and screams of men. Everything had become chaos and, though I tried, I couldn't see Matthew anymore.

Soon the cannons joined in, and the fighting, the most vicious I had ever seen, continued all that morning. As more Confederates joined the battle, the Federals were forced to retreat toward Gettysburg, and they likely would have been overrun if the Union 1st Corps, including the Iron Brigade or Black Hats, hadn't arrived just in time.

As the fighting moved into town, Louis and I, as well as several other Negroes, emerged cautiously from the trees. We were directed by members of the Invalid Corps, Confederates that had lost limbs or had been so severely wounded that they were no longer able to fight. A one-armed sergeant oversaw the detail and ordered us to begin removing the wounded from the field. This we did reluctantly, as the battle was still very active, and none of us were eager to join the ranks of the fallen.

By this point, the ground was literally covered with bodies. Many of the wounded were conscious and, upon seeing us, begged for help. However, if their wounds were deemed too severe, the sergeant would simply shake his head, thereby indicating that we should leave them on the field. Seeing the look on their faces as we moved on was difficult, but I understood the grim calculus. There were just too many men to help.

The field hospital was perhaps half a mile behind the lines. Louis and I made eleven trips that day, alternating between carrying the front or back of the stretcher to give our muscles a rest. It was a thoroughly disagreeable duty, and at least two of the men we carried succumbed to their wounds en route.

The hospital itself was little improvement over the battlefield, as the ground was covered with dozens of men that had walked or been carried behind the lines, the wounded and the dead often lying side by side. Four open-air tents served as surgical theaters, and I detected the sharp scent of chloroform in the air.

As we prepared to make another trip, two wounded Confederates stumbled into the hospital and loudly announced, "The Yankees are on the run!" I closed my eyes for a moment and prayed they were mistaken. The Union had to win. If the Confederates won, they would be buoyed by their victory, and nothing would change. Not for the first time I thought about escape. We were already in Pennsylvania, a free state. Why would I willingly go South again? If I ran, I knew there was a chance that I might be caught and severely punished, perhaps even killed. But returning to Charlotte was certainly no guarantee of safety, and with an involuntary shudder I thought of Sarah, and the look she had given me in Dr. Parker's office.

When we were too far away from the hospital to be overheard, I whispered, "Louis, what do you think about what they just said? About the Union being on the run?"

"I don't know. I guess it wouldn't be the first time General Lee has whipped them," he said without looking up.

I looked around to make sure that we were alone before speaking again. "Do you *want* the Confederates to win?"

He gave me a hard look. "What does it matter what I want?" he hissed. "Since when has anybody cared about what we wanted?"

We walked along the dusty road in silence for a time, passing several other men heading in the direction of the hospital. Louis was my friend, but he was also

Major Ross's man. How much did I dare say to him? The distant sound of the cannons, which had never stopped, was closer now. Finally, making up my mind I said, "No matter what happens, I don't want to go back down south."

Though he made no reply, something changed in his bearing, and I could tell that he had heard me. As the silence stretched on, I wondered if I had made a mistake confiding in him. If he said something to Major Ross I would be put in chains, or worse. I was beginning to think I had said too much when, just before we came into view of the battlefield again, he said, "I don't want to go back either." Feeling an overwhelming sense of relief, I nodded but said nothing more. There would be time for us to talk later.

It was late in the afternoon and the fighting, which had started early that morning, seemed not to have decreased in intensity, but instead had moved into Gettysburg and the hills east of town. The one-armed sergeant was nowhere to be seen, but there was no shortage of injured men. Not wanting to stay any longer than necessary, Louis and I put the first wounded man we saw on a stretcher and started making our way down the hill. A few moments later we had to move aside for a wagon coming down the road. I was so surprised at seeing something so normal amid such destruction, I initially didn't notice what it was carrying. It was only when I heard Louis make a strange guttural sound that I took a better look. Major Ross was lying on his back in the bed of the wagon, clearly dead.

* * *

It was early evening before the fighting stopped. I didn't see Matthew until I got back to camp, where I found him sitting silently in his tent. His uniform was torn and dirty, but otherwise he appeared unharmed.

"Captain, are you well?" I asked softly. He gave no indication that he had heard me, so I spoke more loudly. "Captain Parker, it's me, Henry. Would you like some supper? Is there anything you require?"

He looked in my direction and I had the impression that he didn't immediately recognize me. Finally, in a voice completely devoid of emotion, he said, "Oh, Henry, there you are. Where have you been?"

"Yes sir, my apologies. I was waiting for you on the road." He frowned slightly, as if he were concentrating to translate what I had just said.

"Ah, I see, on the road," he said, turning away once again. Then he added in a tremulous voice, "Major Ross is dead?"

"Yes sir, I know. I saw him being carried from the field."

He nodded but said nothing.

"Can I get you some supper, sir? You must be hungry after such a long day." He didn't answer, so after a moment I turned to leave.

"Major Ross was a good man," he said. "He fought bravely today."

"Yes sir," I said softly.

"But when they put you in a meat grinder, courage isn't worth a hill of beans. Do you know that? It doesn't matter whether you're brave or not, you'll be chopped to pieces just the same."

* * *

Perhaps because they had fought a pitched battle the day before, General Heth's divisions were not put into action on the second day of the conflict. That meant that Matthew and his men had a day to rest. The Union had taken possession of the rocky hills east of town, and on the second day of the battle the Confederates tried to dislodge them. But even after many bloody attempts, and thousands of additional casualties, they didn't succeed, and when dusk fell the Union forces still held the high ground. That meant that there was certain to be more fighting the next day, and I could tell that knowledge cast a pall over the men's spirits.

That evening, Matthew sat in a clearing with some of his men. Though they should have slept, no one seemed in a hurry to meet the next morning. A young man, who looked little more than a boy, said, "I wish Sergeant Boyer was here. He always knew what to say." He looked at Matthew and added quickly, "No offense, Captain. I only meant that the sergeant could call up a passage from the Good Book when we needed it."

"No offense taken, private," Matthew said dryly. "Which verse did you have in mind?" Everyone looked toward the young man, and I could see that he was not at all comfortable with the attention.

"Begging the Captain's pardon," he stammered, "I never learned to read and don't know much about the Bible, but it was something about the Lord being my shepherd."

Matthew nodded slowly, lost in thought. "I know the passage you mean, but not well enough to recite it. My mother loves the Bible and reads it almost every day," he said wistfully. Then, after a pause, he inclined his head in my direction. "But I expect my boy knows it." Turning to me, he said, "Henry, do you know the passage he speaks of?"

"Yes sir, I know it."

"Well, go ahead then, let's hear it," he said impatiently.

The men were looking at me now but, unlike the young man, I wasn't nervous. In Charlotte I had recited many times for Dr. and Mrs. Parker and their guests. So, I stood up, cleared my throat, and started speaking in a firm, clear voice.

The Lord is my shepherd; I shall not want. He maketh me to lie down in green pastures; he leadeth me beside the still waters. He restoreth my soul; he leadeth me in the paths of righteousness for his name's sake.

Yea, though I walk through the valley of the shadow of death, I will fear no evil; for thou art with me; thy rod and thy staff they comfort me. Thou preparest a table before me in the presence of mine enemies; thou annointest my head with oil; my cup runneth over. Surely goodness and mercy shall follow me all the days of my life; and I will dwell in the house of the Lord forever.

For a moment, no one said anything. Then the young man spoke, his voice soft, but thick with emotion. "Yes, that's it. Could you say it again?"

When I was done, several of the men asked me to recite some of their favorite passages from Deuteronomy, Isaiah, and Philippians. Other men drifted over to listen, and I had to admit that the overall mood of the company seemed somewhat improved. I glanced toward Matthew, and though he was looking in my general direction, he seemed focused on something behind me. I turned to look, but saw nothing there.

* * *

The next day, General Pettigrew's division, which included Matthew and all his remaining men, were ordered to join General Pickett for an assault on the

Union center. To get there, they would have to cross almost a mile of open ground. Though the men accepted the news stoically, I could see that they were troubled by it. I overheard one Confederate say to his comrades, "The Yankees are dug into those hills like ticks. We'll be sitting ducks out there."

After a light breakfast, Matthew wrote letters to each of his parents and to his fiancée, Sarah. By late morning the three divisions, more than twelve thousand men, had assembled in the woods just west of town. Remarkably, for such a large assemblage, all was quiet except for the shrill song of a finch, somewhere high in the trees. Almost one hundred and fifty cannons were pointed at the Union lines, and early that afternoon, the Confederates opened fire. The barrage, the largest I had ever seen or heard, was clearly intended to weaken the Union defenses. Of course, the Union began firing their cannons as well.

The cannonade went on for an interminably long time, so long that it seemed as if the sound of cannons firing and shells exploding were the only sounds in the world. At some point the Union cannons stopped, but the Confederates continued for a full two hours. Finally, after all the cannons had fallen silent, the men prepared to move out, hoping that the Union defenses had been weakened.

"Why don't you see what you can round up for dinner," Matthew said to me in a voice loud enough for others to hear. "When I get back, I expect I'm going to be mighty hungry."

"Yes sir, I'll see what I can find." He gave me a quick nod and our eyes met for an instant. To my surprise, even after Major Ross's death, his eyes didn't convey fear or despair, only resignation. I watched as he and the other Confederates left the protection of the trees and assembled on the field in neat ranks. Soon they began moving toward the distant Union lines. For some time, nothing happened. Then, without warning, the Union cannons began firing again, to terrible effect. I tried to follow the progress of the battle, but there was simply too much smoke and the men were too far away to see anything clearly. Not far from me, I saw General Longstreet and his staff looking out over the field and I couldn't help wondering what he was thinking.

CHAPTER 26

CLOSURE

1863

As the last light of the day faded, two of Matthew's men brought him back to camp. He was unconscious, with severe wounds to his chest and abdomen. I could see that he would not survive his injuries. Apparently, the attack on the Union line had not been successful and thousands of Confederate soldiers had been killed or wounded in the attempt. A few of Matthew's comrades came to the tent to check on him, but when they saw his condition, none stayed for more than a few minutes.

That evening, as a heavy downpour beat against the roof of the tent, I sat by his bedside and waited. It was almost an hour before he regained consciousness. He tried to say something, but initially, no sound came out. I dipped a handkerchief into a basin of cool water and allowed some drops to fall between his lips. I did this several times until he was finally able to speak. His voice was little more than a whisper, and his words were slow and halting, but I was able to understand him.

"Henry, what happened?" he managed, wincing from the exertion. "Did we win?"

I was sitting in a chair near his bed and leaned in close. "No sir, the Union line held. You were wounded during the battle and they brought you back here."

He looked around the tent, perhaps realizing for the first time where he was. It took him a moment to gather himself, then he asked, "Why didn't they take me to the hospital?"

"They did," I answered simply. He looked at me, and I could tell that he was trying to decipher what I had said.

"Ah, I see," he said finally, looking away. "They sent me off to die." I didn't respond, and for several minutes the only sound was the rain and his ragged breathing. Finally, he said, "I guess you want me dead too?"

I thought about his question as I watched the water stream past the tent opening. "No, I have no wish to see you dead. You haven't always treated me well, but no, I don't want your death."

He was sweating profusely, and I suspected that he had a fever. "May I touch you to check if you have a fever?" I could tell that he didn't much like the thought of it, but he nodded yes.

"You're very hot. If you'd like, I can give you a willow bark tea for the fever and some laudanum for the pain." He shook his head no and waved me away before closing his eyes.

Sometime later, when he opened his eyes again, he spoke languidly, as if in a dream. "Henry, you're still here."

"Yes, Matthew, I'm here," I said, dripping more water between his lips.

"When I'm gone, will you bury me?"

"Yes, I'll bury you."

"On that little hill, just west of camp?"

Yes, if that's what you want."

"And tell my father where to find me?"

"I'll tell him."

"Tell him . . ." He hesitated for a long time. "Tell him he was right. I shouldn't have come." I nodded but said nothing.

He looked at me through rheumy eyes. "I'm sorry I treated you so badly."

"It doesn't matter now."

"I had no cause . . . no cause to treat you, or the girl that way."

I stiffened at the offhand mention of Gloria and almost laughed at the absurdity of it. Was this his idea of an apology? Was he looking to me for absolution? Finally, I leaned in close and asked, "Then why did you?"

He didn't say anything for a long time, so long that I thought he had drifted off. And indeed, if he were to answer honestly, what might he say? I mistreated you because you were a slave, and it was expected of me? I belittled and humiliated you because I liked the feeling it gave me? I shook my head and chided myself for being foolish. If I got any response from Matthew at all, it wouldn't matter what he said because I already knew the simple truth. He did it because he could.

I was startled when he spoke again. "Truth is, I was angry with you. You spent more time with my father than I did."

"That was not by choice," I protested. "Being taken to Charlotte, following you here, none of this has been my choice."

"I know," he said weakly.

"I was taken from my mother when I was only six years old."

"I know," he repeated.

I got up and stood at the opening of the tent, looking out at the rain. Matthew didn't start life hateful; he had only done as he had seen others do. His father had been the true author of my suffering.

"Henry."

I turned to see that he was looking at me, and I sat next to the bed again. "I'm here, Matthew."

"What will you do when I'm gone?" he asked.

I thought about his question. What would I do when he was gone? I certainly had no allegiance to the Confederate cause, never had. After a moment, I simply said, "I don't know."

He nodded. "Bring me some paper and ink—I want to say goodbye."

I did as he asked, and with difficulty, he managed to write a few lines to Sarah and each of his parents. Then he wrote out a final note. "This is for you. It's your manumission. You're a free man now."

Confused, I took the paper from him. "Thank you, Matthew, and no offense, but isn't Dr. Parker the only one that can free me?"

He tried to laugh, but the sound that came out was more of a wheeze. "He gave you to me. You've been my property since we left Charlotte last spring."

I looked at the paper in wonder. How could something so desirable and elusive as a man's freedom be granted with only a few hastily scribbled words. I folded the paper carefully and put it deep in my breast pocket. I wanted to ask Matthew why his father had given me to him, and why he had freed me. But I never had the chance because, when I looked up, he had drifted off again.

I sat with him until morning, but he never spoke again. Although he woke once more during the night, he was feverish and only mumbled incoherently. Then, just before dawn, he took his last breath.

As the army was preparing to leave, I rounded up Louis and two other Negro men and we hurriedly dug a grave. We made quick work of it, as the rain had made the ground soft. Two armed soldiers watched impassively as we worked.

There was no time to bury most of the dead, but Matthew had been a captain and, as such, was accorded the respect of a proper burial. We laid him to rest just off the Chambersburg Pike, on a small hill overlooking Willoughby Run.

Matthew had asked what I would do when he was gone, and I had given the question a good deal of thought while I sat with him. I didn't have an answer when he'd asked the question, but by morning my path was clear. Whatever plans the Confederates had for me, I had no intention of going back across the Mason-Dixon Line with them. I also suspected that they would likely not accept Matthew's deathbed manumission. I would have to make my own way.

We started to move South with the remnants of Lee's Army, a ragged line of men and wagons that stretched for many miles. It was still raining, and the muddy roads made for slow travel. I walked with Louis and at least twenty other Negro laborers, most of whom I recognized. We were less than a day's march from the Maryland border, so if we were going to escape it would have to be soon. But running without a plan was foolhardy. I had seen enough men brought back in chains to know how that ended.

Then, just as I was pondering our next move, fate intervened when a detachment of Union cavalry attacked without warning. Suddenly, all was chaos. Louis and I scrambled for shelter behind an overturned wagon that had been carrying wounded men, now lying one atop another like cordwood. There was a stand of trees not more than twenty yards to our left, and strangely, in the heat of the battle, I thought of a quote from Shakespeare's play, Cymbeline: "Boldness be my friend." I tugged on Louis's shirt, and without waiting for a reply, sprinted for the safety of the trees. Louis was right behind me, and we kept running until the sounds of the skirmish faded away. I expected at any minute to hear shouted commands from our pursuers, or the crack of a rifle shot. But when we finally stopped to catch our breath, it was clear that no one had followed us. The date was July 4, Independence Day.

We found a depression on the bank of a stream, partially covered by tree roots, and lay there for the rest of the day, listening for any pursuit. Finally, driven by hunger, we crept from our hiding place to look for food. There wasn't much available, but we were able to find a few handfuls of dewberries and some chickweed. I also located a few edible mushrooms. Following my lead, Louis tried to pick a few more, and he would have eaten them if I hadn't grabbed his arm.

"You can't eat those—they're poisonous. They'll make you sick, could even kill you."

He frowned. "They look like the ones you picked." I tried to show him the difference, but he just shook his head. "Still look the same to me," he grumbled. "I guess I had best leave the mushroom picking to you."

* * *

The next day, wet, hungry, and covered in mud, we made our way back to the Fairfield Road. We stayed hidden for nearly an hour, listening for sounds of the retreating army, but heard nothing. We finally emerged from the woods and started to retrace our steps to Gettysburg. I knew there was a risk we might encounter Union troops, but reasoned they held far less danger for us than the Confederates. Also, though we didn't know the location of Lee's Army, it seemed unlikely that they would have returned to Gettysburg. So it was that early on the morning of July 5, after we had been walking on the road for less than a quarter of an hour, we were surrounded by four armed Union soldiers. Two blocked the road ahead and two more were behind us. There wasn't anything we could do other than raise our hands.

One of the men, a squat, thick-necked sergeant, said, "So where do you boys think you're going?"

With my hands still raised I said, "We're heading to Gettysburg, sir."

"Well, are you now. And why would the likes of you two be wanting to go to Gettysburg?" he asked, smiling crookedly.

"We were being held by the Confederates, but escaped yesterday," Louis answered.

He took in the dried mud on our clothes and wrinkled his nose. "Looks like you two escaped from a pigsty," he quipped, prompting a snicker from one of the other men. Then indicating that we should lower our hands, he said, "You boys aren't going anywhere looking like that. I think you best come with us."

We followed him through the woods for about a quarter of a mile until we came to a clearing with several hundred Union soldiers, all of whom seemed to be looking at us. Then we continued through the camp until we arrived at an area where several Negro men were sitting. One of them rose at our approach.

"These men are runaways like you. Show them where they can find some soap and water to get cleaned up, then get them something to eat. I'm sure the captain will want to talk to them." The man watched the sergeant walk away before turning his attention to us.

"Well now," he drawled, running his hand over his beard, "where did you two come from?"

"Don't know where they came from, but it looks like they crawled through a swamp to get here," one man observed.

"You shouldn't talk, Ham," the man said. "You didn't look much better than they did when you first got here," he continued with a chuckle. He was large and powerfully built, with smooth, dark skin, inquisitive eyes, and an easy smile. I assumed he was their leader, as all the others seemed to defer to him. "They call me Mack. What names do you go by?" We told him our names. "Well, Henry and Louis, pleased to meet you. This is Ham," he said, pointing to the man at his side. "That's James over there, and . . . I don't see Shep, but you'll meet him later. Come on, let's get you cleaned up."

He carried two buckets to a rain-swollen stream and filled both. "Strip off those clothes and wash up as best you can. When the water is too dirty, dump it out and fill up the bucket again with clean water. It would be faster to wash in the stream, but these men won't drink water we've been washing in. Understand?" We nodded that we did. "And don't put those clothes back on, they've had it. I'll find you something to wear."

As we started to take off our sodden clothing, he asked, "Where are you from?"

"North Carolina," I answered, feeling good to be free of my mud-stiffened shirt, but careful to retrieve my manumission.

Mack said, "I'm from Virginia. Grew up on a plantation near Fredericksburg. The Union came through last month and I figured I would never have a better chance to get free. They're organizing regiments of colored troops in Philadelphia, and me and some of the boys are planning to get there and join."

Louis looked up. "Colored troops—where did you hear that?"

"Heard it from the Union soldiers," Mack said. "We're going to give them a little taste of what they been giving us all these years. You interested?"

To my surprise, I heard Louis say, "I might be."

"Well, that's fine. I don't imagine they will turn any of us away."

* * *

Later that day, after we had gotten cleaned up and had something to eat, the sergeant returned and took us to a large, open tent. Inside was a lanky Union officer sitting at a table that held a battered field desk.

"Begging the Captain's pardon, but these boys have run ran away from the rebs."

He looked at us for a few seconds before returning to his papers. "What did you men do there?" he asked indifferently.

"We worked for Major Ross and Captain Parker of the Eleventh North Carolina," Louis said.

"They were attached to General Pettigrew's brigade," I added.

He put away the paper he was reading. "That so," he said. He pulled out a small, dark cigar and looked us over while he took his time lighting it. "And you just up and left them?" he asked.

"They're dead," I said. "They both died at Gettysburg."

He nodded slowly. "A lot of men died these last few days, on both sides, but you're welcome here." He leaned forward before continuing, "Let me ask you something: Do either of you fellas have any information about Lee's Army that I might be able to use?"

Louis and I looked at each other. "What kind of information?" I asked.

"Anything at all," he said, waving his cigar in the air. "You might be surprised at what you know. How is the army organized? Who are the commanders? That sort of thing. We likely already know all this information, of course, but it's always good to double-check." Louis told him what he knew, and the captain just listened and nodded. Then he turned to me. "You got anything to add?" he asked.

During my time with the Confederates, I had never revealed my gift, not even to Louis. The only person that knew of my abilities was Matthew, and other than having me recite a few Bible verses on the night before the last battle, he had certainly not given anything away.

But in just a few days, everything had changed. On Friday I was a slave in a Confederate Army camp, had buried Matthew, and escaped on Saturday, the fourth of July. Now, on Sunday I was with the Union Army in Pennsylvania and a free man. There seemed to be no reason to continue hiding my gift.

So, I told the captain what I knew of General Lee's army and the commanders of the Third Corps, as well as all the division, brigade, and regiment commanders. I let him know the number of cannons the Confederates had used before Pickett's charge (I had counted them), and that they had expended their entire supply of shells during the cannonade. I told him that the army was nearly out of food and were now eating whatever they could forage. I also let him know what other supplies were running low, and what I had seen in the wagons heading south. I would have said more if he hadn't interrupted me.

"Hold on. How is it that you know all of this?" he asked.

I shrugged. "I've always had a good memory."

He stopped smoking and looked at me suspiciously. "You have a good memory, is that what you're telling me?" he asked.

The look on Louis's face told me that he was also confused. "Yes sir, I remember everything," I said flatly.

The captain laughed and started smoking his cigar again. "Well, that must get awfully tiring," he said with a chuckle.

I could tell that he didn't believe me, and after all that we had been through, I found this infuriating. I took a deep breath and started telling him what I had seen in and around his camp since being stopped on the road earlier that day by the sergeant and his men. I described each man in detail, as well as their uniforms, which ones needed mending, and what they wore on their belts. I told him how many Negro men were camped by the stream and what their names were. Then I told him how many tents were between the Negro camp and his tent, six on the right and eight on the left, the locations of the cooking fires and musket stacks, and the number of horses in the enclosure at the end of the field. Then for good measure, I started to recount, word for word, everything that had been said, and by who, since the sergeant had brought us to his tent.

He had stopped smoking again and stood up abruptly, nearly knocking over his chair. "All right, that's enough of that. Sergeant, watch these boys until I get back." He left the tent without saying another word, heading in the direction of the Negro camp.

The sergeant, with a hand on his pistol, was glaring at me. He was only a few feet away, so although Louis looked at me questioningly, he said nothing. A few minutes later the captain returned and relit his cigar. Pointing to Louis, he said, "Sergeant, escort that man back to the contraband camp." Then, turning to me, he said, "What's your name, son?"

"Henry, sir."

"Well Henry, my name is Captain Jenkins. Why don't you and I talk for a few minutes."

CHAPTER 27

CONVERGENCE

1863

After meeting with Captain Jenkins, I returned to the far end of the camp. No one said anything, but their furtive glances suggested they had been talking about me. I saw Louis sitting at the edge of the clearing, and I made my way over to him. He raised a hand at my approach.

"Hey there, Henry. You been with the captain all this time?" Though he asked the question casually, I could tell by his voice that something had shifted in him, and possibly also in our relationship.

"Yes, I just got back."

"What did he want to talk to you about?" Several nearby men looked away, working hard to give the impression that they weren't listening to our conversation.

"Nothing really, just asked me some questions about General Lee and the Confederates, and if I knew anything about where they might be heading."

"What did you tell him?" he asked, frowning slightly.

I'm not sure why, but I took umbrage at the tone of his question, which struck me as accusatory. "I told him everything I knew. Why wouldn't I?" I said tightly. "The Confederates are no friends of mine . . . or yours."

He stood up slowly and stretched his back. "You're right about that. I got no use for any of them," he said, spitting in the dirt for emphasis. I could see that he had more to say, so I leaned against a pine tree and waited. A moment later he said, "Tell me something, Henry—how did you know all those things? You told him there were . . . how many cannons did you say?"

"Almost one hundred and fifty."

"One hundred fifty," he repeated slowly. "When I was growing up, an old lady on the farm taught me to use my fingers to count to ten," he mused. "I don't know how much one hundred fifty is, but I know it's higher than I can count. When did you learn your numbers?" he asked seriously." Then, before I could respond he added, "Can you read and write too?"

Suddenly I understood his accusatory tone and felt a sudden wave of guilt. His pride was wounded because he believed I'd been hiding things from him, and he was right, I had been. But how should I answer? How could I tell him that I'd taught myself to count? Even if I did, I doubted he would believe me. I had kept my secret for so long that I was reluctant to let it go. We were in Pennsylvania, where educating Negroes was not a crime, so I had no reason to be fearful. But fear learned over a lifetime did not die easily. "Yes, I can read and write," I said. "I learned when I was in Charlotte."

"Did Captain Parker know?"

I shook my head. "No, no one knew. If anyone had found out it would have been dangerous."

He lowered his voice conspiratorially. "So, who taught you then?"

I had known this moment was coming and there was no way to avoid it; I would have to tell Louis a lie. I just wasn't prepared for the questions that would come if I told him the truth; namely that I had taught myself. "An old slave named Sam taught me. I don't know how he learned."

He nodded, and then he said timidly, "Can you show me how to write my name?"

I picked up a nearby twig and wrote *L-O-U-I-S* in the dirt, sounding out each letter. "Now you try," I said.

He took the stick and, kneeling on one leg, copied the word I had written. *LOUIS, LOUIS. LOUIS.*

A few minutes later I used my hand to clear away everything. "Now, can you write your name again?"

I noticed that other men were crowding around us now. Louis hesitated before writing *L-O-U-I-S*, this time without a guide word to follow. Smiling, he looked at me and said, proudly, "That's my name, Louis." I found that I was smiling too. Before the sun set, I had also showed the other men how to write their names, and for the first time in my life, I felt truly useful.

* * *

The next day the Union Army decamped and started the pursuit of the Confederates. Mack, Ham, and the other men had already decided to stay with them, and that morning, as we made ready to leave, Louis told me he was going too.

"I have to do it, Henry," he said as he gathered his few belongings. "I don't know where my wife and boy are, or if I'll ever see them again. But if I do, I want to be able to say that I fought to get them free."

I tried not to show my disappointment. "I understand, Louis. I know you'll make a good soldier. In fact, I pity the rebs that cross paths with you," I said, as brightly as I could manage.

"Why don't you come too?" he asked seriously. "After all we've been through, it won't be the same without you."

"No, I don't think so," I said, shaking my head. "I really want to see Philadelphia. And the truth is, I've only been free for a few days. I'm not ready to surrender my liberty to the Union, or anyone else, so soon." But even as I said it, I knew these weren't the only reasons.

"What are you going to do when you get to Philadelphia?" he asked.

I shrugged. "I'm not sure. Find work I hope."

For a moment, the only sound was the quick tap, tap, tap, tap, tap of a woodpecker somewhere high in the trees. Finally, with a look of finality, Louis said, "Well, you take care of yourself, Henry."

"You too, Louis," I said, embracing him warmly. "I hope to see you again someday." We walked together until we got to the road. Louis and I shook hands, and I bade goodbye to the other men. I watched for a moment as they headed south toward Emmitsburg before I turned north.

Less than two weeks later, the Union and Confederate armies fought again near Williamsport, Maryland, at a place called Falling Waters. I pray that Louis made it through the war safely and was reunited with his family, but sadly, I never saw or heard of him again.

* * *

As I walked, I nervously scanned the trees on both sides of the road for any sign of the Confederates. It seemed unlikely that they were still in the area, but anything was possible. I had witnessed firsthand how zealously they had rounded up any Negro men they found, and I had no wish to become one of their captives. Then, just as I was thinking it might be safer to stay off the road, I heard the unmistakable sound of a wagon approaching.

I ran into the woods and hid myself in the under-brush. A moment later the wagon came into view. It was being driven by a plump, ruddy-faced man in well-worn work clothes. A sturdy-looking woman in a flower-print dress sat beside him on the bench. They pulled the wagon to a halt directly across from where I was hiding. After setting the brake, the man pulled out a handkerchief and wiped his brow.

"Hello, you there, we saw you on the road. Come on out, we won't hurt you."

I cursed myself for being so careless, and though they looked harmless enough, I stayed silent.

"Please come out," the woman said.

They clearly knew where I was, so there seemed little reason to stay hidden. After looking around to make certain they were alone, I came out slowly.

The man smiled broadly. "Well, there you are," he said. "There's no need to hide. Best we can tell, the rebels have all cleared out."

Keeping my distance in case I needed to run again, I said, "Can't be too careful."

He laughed and bobbed his head in agreement. "That's true, that's true; I probably would have done the same in your place." Then, as if remembering something important, he added, "I apologize. My name is David Stearns, and this is my wife, Helen."

"Pleased to meet you," she said.

After an awkward pause, Mr. Stearns continued. "If you don't mind me asking, where are you heading?"

There didn't seem to be any harm in telling him, so I said, "Philadelphia."

He made a whistling sound. "Well, that's quite a way from here. Gettysburg is maybe five or six miles farther down this road, then it's another forty or so to Harrisburg. From there you'll have to make your way to Philadelphia, and unless the rules have changed, the Pennsylvania Railroad doesn't allow Negroes on the train."

I nodded but said nothing.

"Philadelphia is a mighty big place, full of all kinds of people. Helen and I went there once, but we didn't care for it much. Always been country folks, I guess." He looked at his wife and smiled. "What's your name, if you don't mind me asking?"

"Henry."

"Pleased to meet you, Henry," he said. "Listen, I don't mean to pry, but if you don't have any immediate plans in Philadelphia, I have a proposition for you."

"What kind of proposition?" I asked.

He slapped his leg. "Right down to business, I like that. Well, Henry, we have a farm not far from here. We were heading back home when we saw you. Anyway, we grow some of the best apples you've ever tasted. Isn't that so, Helen?"

"They really are good," she said, beaming.

"Well, these last couple of years, because of the war, we've been having trouble getting help. Then, if that wasn't bad enough, now they say they're going to draft men into the army. Force them to join whether they want to or not. We only had two farmhands left, but once they heard about the draft, one of them took off a couple of weeks ago." I must have looked confused because he quickly continued. "Sorry, I'm running off at the mouth. The point is, the apples are starting to ripen, and we could really use some help to get them picked. The job comes with fifty cents a day, food, and a place to sleep."

I didn't want to appear too anxious, but I desperately needed everything he was offering. I didn't have any money and nothing to eat other than some Johnny cake and weevil-infested hardtack. I had been planning to look for work in Gettysburg, but in truth I had no desire to return to the place where so many men had died, and likely still littered the ground. Digging more graves did not appeal to me.

"How many trees do you have?" I asked.

"About four hundred. Have you picked apples before?"

"No, but I used to work on a farm."

"What a blessing to run into you," he said cheerfully. "We sure could use your help. Helen is a good cook, as you can see," he said, patting his belly. "Like I said, Philadelphia is a big place. I'm not prying but, if you don't have any money, it will be hard for you there."

I had no doubt that he was right, and I was already salivating at the thought of a home-cooked meal. It had been a long time.

"I'll do it, but not for fifty cents a day. I'll need a dollar."

Mr. Stearns's face reddened. "A dollar a day is too much," he said, waving a hand in the air. "Experienced hands don't get that much."

"Then I thank you for your offer, sir, but I'll take my chances down the road."

He started yelling at me, but I noted that he didn't leave, so I stood my ground. With so many apples ready to be picked, I reasoned that he needed me more than I needed him. After some spirited back-and-forth, we agreed on seventy-five cents a day, and I was soon bumping along the road in the back of their wagon. We turned onto a narrow dirt lane, and I saw a neat brick farmhouse sitting atop a low rise. There was a barn and several smaller buildings set off from the house. To the left there were hundreds of apple trees.

Their only remaining farmhand was named Jim, and when I arrived, I could see that he was not pleased. I couldn't hear what was being said, but I could see that he and Mr. Stearns were arguing about something.

A few minutes later, looking somewhat embarrassed, Mr. Stearns told me that there was no room in the bunkhouse, and I would have to sleep in the barn. I found out later that Jim had shared a large room with the other farmhand but had refused to bunk with me.

"That will be fine," I said. "I've been sleeping in a tent for the last two years, so having a solid roof over my head will be an improvement."

He smiled, clearly relieved. "Well, that's settled then. Let me show you where you'll be sleeping."

"Thank you, Mr. Stearns, but can I ask you for one more thing? I need a pen and some paper. I've got to write a letter to someone to let them know that their son was killed at Gettysburg. I can pay you for the ink and paper from my earnings."

He looked troubled and shook his head slowly. "There's no need for that, you don't have to pay me back. Come with me."

I followed him into the house, which was neat and well ordered. He told me to sit at a table in the parlor and he returned with a bottle of ink and a dip pen.

"Thank you, Mr. Stearns."

"You're very welcome, and when you're done, I'll mail it for you in town if you like."

I stared at the empty sheet of paper for a few minutes. For years, I had pictured words in my mind, and had surreptitiously practiced writing them in dirt, dust, or even in the air. But though I had seen it done many times, I had no experience writing on paper. I only hoped Dr. Parker would be able to understand what I would write. Taking a steadying breath, I dipped the nib in the ink and carefully started writing.

Dr. Parker,

I am sorry to have to tell you that your son, Matthew, died at Gettysburg on July 3rd. After an artillery barrage that lasted for nearly two hours, Matthew and more than ten thousand Confederates were ordered to attack the Union center. In order to get there, they had to cross a mile of open field, then a fence that ran along the road, and finally a stone wall. It was an impossible task. Almost from the start, they came under unrelenting fire from Union cannons, and those that made it to the fence were then in musket range. I don't know on which part of the field Matthew fell, but he was carried back to camp that evening with grave wounds to his chest and abdomen. They had taken him to the field hospital, but the doctor there said there was nothing that could be done.

I sat with him all that night, while he moved in and out of consciousness. He told me to tell Sarah, his mother, and you that he loved you all, and to let you know that you were right, he shouldn't have gone to war. He was able to write a note to each of you, which should now be in the hands of Colonel Leventhorpe, along with the rest of Matthew's possessions. Matthew passed early on the morning of July 4th, and we buried him properly.

Before he died, he told me that you had given me to him before we left Charlotte, and he freed me. I don't know why he did this, but I believe, as his life was ending, he might have felt remorse for some of his actions. Nevertheless, regardless of his reasoning, I'm glad that my period of servitude is at an end.

When this war is over, should you one day wish to return his body to Charlotte, I vow that I will lead you to his grave. I only ask that, in the

interim, you keep my mother and Gloria safe.
They are both precious to me.
   Yours respectfully,
   Henry

* * *

As promised, Mrs. Stearns was a wonderful cook. A typical breakfast might include apple butter, baked apples, waffles, boiled eggs, biscuits, and ham or bacon. Dinner could be chicken soup with wide, flat noodles, meatballs, dumplings with pork or chicken, potato casserole, or sausage and sauerkraut. Dessert was usually a slice of apple pie, and though I would never admit it to Nellie or Gloria, Mrs. Stearns's pie was the best I'd ever eaten.

One night, when he was out smoking his pipe, Mr. Stearns found me standing in the yard looking up at the stars. "Ah, Henry, I see you're a stargazer like me."

"Yes sir, I do like to look at them."

"Do you know the constellations?" he asked. I told him that I didn't.

He looked at the night sky. "See there, that's the Big Dipper," he said, pointing to a group of bright stars. And that's Sagittarius. I've heard people say it looks like a teapot," he said, squinting, "but I never thought so." He pointed out a few other constellations before adding,

"Some people think the stars are angels, sent to watch over us. Have you ever heard that."

"No sir."

"I don't know if it's true, but it sure is a comforting thought."

As he bade me good night and resumed his walk, I looked at the sky again. Though it was entertaining to imagine what shapes they most resembled, or that they might be benevolent angels, my interest was in the stars themselves. I had learned from one of Dr. Parker's books that astronomers believed all stars were like our sun; fiery balls of gas, albeit much more distant. I had always been amazed that there were so many of them, more than I could possibly count. I also puzzled over how they moved through the sky, moved so much that some were only visible at certain times of the year. But because I knew the earth moved around the sun, it seemed likely that the stars were fixed and only appeared to change their positions, and in fact it was us that were moving through the sky. So, instead of dwelling on angels, or celestial teapots, I closed my eyes and pictured myself standing on the earth as it traveled around the sun. Only an infinitesimal part of a vast clockwork universe.

PART
4

CHAPTER 28

ODYSSEY

1863

I worked for Mr. Stearns until early September, weeding the orchard, pruning and topping trees, and picking apples. I would have stayed longer, but the promise of colder weather was in the air, and I was anxious to get to Philadelphia before winter set in. Mrs. Stearns gave me a cloth bundle with sausages, fresh bread, and dried apples for my trip. I thanked her for her hospitality and shook Mr. Stearns's hand.

"You're a good worker, Henry. You're welcome to come back here anytime."

I started walking north and soon came to Gettysburg. The beautiful town I had first seen at the end of June had been rendered nearly unrecognizable by the battle. The buildings and trees had been gouged by musket and cannon fire, and the once lush farmland trampled by the passage of thousands of men. Though it had been two months since the conflict, the stench of death and decay clung to the place like a shroud. I picked up my pace, having no desire to remain any longer than necessary.

My plan was to walk the thirty-five miles to Harrisburg and, once there, to make my way to Philadelphia. Mr. Stearns had told me to follow the Emmitsburg Road through town until I came to a three-way fork. The road on the right would lead to Harrisburg. I was very thankful for his guidance, as any road signs that might have existed before the battle were now gone.

It took two days to walk to Harrisburg, which was on the far bank of the Susquehanna River. A covered wooden bridge more than a half mile long spanned the river. The bridge was called the Camelback because of its humps, and I had to pay three cents to cross. When I finally got into town I found the train station easily. It was a large brick building, dominated by a tall central clock tower and two tunnels that resembled dark, sunken eyes. I quickly learned that Mr. Stearns had been right— no Negroes were allowed to book transit on the Pennsylvania Railroad. Unsure of what to do next, I approached one of the Negro porters.

"Excuse me, sir, do you know someplace in town where I might spend the night?"

He looked me up and down. "Where are you from, son?"

I was tired and hungry, and I resented being questioned by this man. Particularly after I had just been told that there was no place for "my kind" on the train. But I heard Sam's voice in my head and smiled. "I just came from Gettysburg."

He whistled. "Gettysburg, huh. Were you there for the fight? We could hear the cannons all the way up here. I heard the Rebs got whipped good."

I winced at the memories. "I was there, and thousands of men died on both sides."

"I reckon that's true," he said, rubbing his chin. "Now, what was it you asked me?"

"I asked if you knew someplace where I could stay."

"That's right. Well, the only place I know of is a boarding house on Tanner's Alley. It's not too far from here."

Thanking him, I set out in the direction he indicated and was able to smell my destination long before I saw it. Tanner's Alley was a narrow, foul-smelling lane, hemmed in on both sides by decrepit, wooden buildings built so closely, one against the next, that sunlight rarely reached the muddy ground.

I found the house the porter had recommended and knocked on the door, which was opened by a large woman holding a broom. Her hair was covered with a scarf and her skin was a beautiful shade of brown. I suspected that if she smiled, she would be a handsome woman. She was not smiling.

"What do you want?" she asked brusquely.

"Sorry to bother you, ma'am. Are you Miss Millie?"

"I am," she said, looking me over. "What can I do for you?"

"I was told you might have a room to rent."

"I might, but I don't take charity cases. Do you have any money?"

"Depends on how much it is," I said.

"It's twenty-five cents a day, in advance. Comes with breakfast and dinner. You won't find a better price in Tanner's Alley."

The money I had received from Mr. Stearns, more than forty dollars, was well hidden, but I had put a few coins in my pocket that morning. Not sure how long I would be in Harrisburg, I gave her enough for two nights. She took the money and deftly deposited it into her apron pocket.

"Well, come on in, Mr. . . . ?"

I had often thought of what I might call myself if I were ever given the chance to choose. "Freeman, ma'am. Henry Freeman."

"Pleased to meet you, Mr. Freeman," she said, closing the door behind us. "I'm Millie Long, but everybody around here just calls me Miss Millie. Let me show you to your room."

The house was more well-appointed than its appearance from the street had suggested. There was a large parlor to the left of the door, with two sofas and an armchair, and behind that the dining room. I followed her up the staircase and to a door at the end of the hallway. The room was well worn but clean, with a narrow bed, a faded rug, a small chest, and a blue-and-white basin with a matching pitcher. There was one dirty window that faced out over Tanner's Alley.

"Is this all right?" she asked.

"Yes, this will be fine. Thank you, Miss Millie."

"Dinner is at seven every night; you'll hear me ring the bell. If you miss it, the next chance to get something to eat will be breakfast."

After she left, I put down my bag and looked around the room. It was far from elegant, but I couldn't help thinking that it would be the nicest place I had ever stayed. Until then, I had only slept in slave cabins, barns, or tents. I lay on the bed, closed my eyes, and thought of Gloria. I wished she was with me.

I heard a bell ringing and sat up, disoriented. I had fallen asleep. I washed quickly, put on the only other shirt I owned, and made my way downstairs. There were already two men sitting at the dining room table. They both looked up at my approach. Miss Millie entered from another room and set two dishes on the table.

"This is Mr. Freeman. He'll be staying with us for a spell."

They watched as I took a seat and helped myself to a bowl of potatoes. Finally, one of the men said, "Where are you from, Mr. Freeman?"

"I've been working for the last couple of months on a farm near Gettysburg," I said, putting a forkful of the potatoes into my mouth.

"But where are you from originally? No offense, but you don't sound like you're from around here," he said, smiling.

Before I could answer, the other man said, "He looks like a runaway to me."

I turned to face him. "Why do you say that?" I asked.

He shrugged. "You got that look is all."

"What if he is?" the other man said, putting a large spoonful of beans on his plate. "He must have some money, otherwise no way he would have his feet under Miss Millie's table." Then, turning to me he said, "I'm Nate, and this is my brother Micah."

"Pleased to meet you," I said, still looking at the other man.

"Micah and I haul freight between here and Philadelphia."

"That's where I'm going," I exclaimed. "If you don't mind me asking, how might I arrange transport there."

They looked at each other, and Nate said, "We're taking a wagon there in a couple of days. We might be able to find some room for you in the back, if you have five dollars?" Nate was studying me intently and I could see that Micah had the look of a cat before the kill. They were trying to cheat me.

"Five dollars!" I said, feigning shock. "I don't have that kind of money. I barely had enough to pay Miss Millie for two nights."

Nate frowned. "I thought you said you've been working for the last couple of months."

I didn't know these men and wasn't comfortable admitting to them that I had any money. Looking down, I said softly, "I'm ashamed to say that I lost most of my wages in a card game. I don't have much left."

Nate looked sympathetic. "You got to be more careful with your money, Mr. Freeman. Some of the folks around here will steal you blind."

"You're right, thank you, and please call me Henry."

We ate quietly for several minutes, until Nate broke the silence. "I've got an idea, Henry. If you help us load and unload the wagon, we could give you a ride to the city."

"What?" Micah sputtered. "Why would we carry him anywhere? Philadelphia is already full of runaways, with more coming in every day."

"What you got against runaways, Micah?" Nate asked. "I don't recall any of them ever doing anything to you."

"I've never been a slave, nobody in our family has, but because of swamp-running Negroes like him, white folks look at us all the same now."

I put down my fork slowly, as a cold fury washed over me. In that moment, I didn't care if they gave me a ride or not. I gave Micah a hard look. "Yes, I was a slave," I hissed, "been a slave my whole life. I was born on a plantation in North Carolina." I leaned toward him. "I've experienced my share of hatred and bigotry, but until today it had never come from another Negro. I'm sorry if my freedom is inconvenient for you, but slavery was so much more than an inconvenience for me. For me, it was a matter of life and death."

"I never said—"

"But I'm interested in your opinion, I really am," I snapped, cutting him off. "What do *you* recommend that I do? If a city like Philadelphia is off-limits, where do you think folks like *me* should live? Or maybe you think we should stay down south and take our chances, is what you mean?" I glared at him across the table until he looked away.

"I apologize for my brother's rudeness, Mr. Freeman," Nate interjected quickly. "You're clearly an educated man."

I shook my head. "No, unfortunately I've never had the privilege of an education."

"Well, you speak better than either of us, that's for sure. We would be glad to help you get to Philadelphia. Isn't that right, little brother?" he said, nudging the other man.

"That's right," Micah whispered. "You're welcome to come with us."

"Good, we leave the day after tomorrow," Nate declared, reaching for the plate of chicken Miss Millie had left while we were talking.

* * *

It turned out that the brothers weren't actually going to Philadelphia, but were taking cloth and furs to a nearby town named Cheltenham. There they would be made into clothing that they would take back to Harrisburg and sell at a profit.

It took three days to get to Cheltenham, traveling through beautiful, wooded hills and picturesque green valleys. Nate drove while Micah sat next to him with a shotgun at his feet.

Following my gaze, Nate said, "There are a lot of bad people on the roads these days, especially with the war."

It was mid-September when we arrived on the outskirts of Philadelphia, and I was overwhelmed by the immense size of the city and the vast number of people.

"There sure are a lot of people here," I remarked.

Micah, who had become a great deal friendlier since the first night at Miss Millie's, laughed. "We're still a few miles outside of town. This is nothing compared to how many people you would see if you went into the city."

"And that's why I never go there if I can help it," Nate quipped.

We got to Cheltenham and unloaded the wagon at the home of their father, a severe man that looked at me with suspicion. When we were finished, I thanked Nate and Micah for the ride, and prepared to start walking toward my ultimate destination, the Byberry Meeting House, some ten miles away.

"Why are you going to Byberry anyway?" Micah asked. "Do you have family there?"

"No, I was told by a Union captain to ask for a man there by the name of Robert Purvis. Have you heard of him?" They looked at each other with surprise.

"Heck, Henry, everybody around here has heard of Mr. Purvis."

* * *

After stopping twice for directions, I managed to locate the Byberry Meeting House. It was a white two-story building with a covered porch that wrapped around two sides. The building itself sat gracefully among green lawns and tall shade trees, giving the entire scene a pastoral feel. I asked one of the attendants, a tall, gaunt man, if he knew where I might find Robert Purvis. He pointed to a farm on the other side of the road, saying I would likely find Mr. Purvis there.

A smooth dirt lane led to a small but stately home, set well back from the road. A sign at the entrance read *Harmony Hall.* The house was framed by neat rows of corn and wheat, swaying in the gentle breeze. There were several other buildings to the left of the house, and a small grove of fruit trees on the right. As I walked up the path, I could feel my heart pounding. I had good reason to be nervous. I didn't know this man or if he would even receive me. Nonetheless, after coming so far, I was determined to see it through.

I knocked on the door, which was soon answered by a young woman.

"Can I help you?"

"Yes, I'm looking for Mr. Robert Purvis. I was sent here by Captain Thaddeus Jenkins."

Her eyes widened at the mention of Captain Jenkins, and she told me to wait a moment before closing the door. I turned to look out over the well-tended fields, relaxing somewhat at the familiarity of the scene.

The door opened again, and I saw a trim, well-dressed man, with dark, wavy hair that was beginning to gray at the edges, looking at me quizzically. "I'm Robert Purvis. I was told you asked for me."

"Mr. Purvis, thank you for seeing me," I said haltingly. "I was directed to you by Captain Thaddeus Jenkins, who sends his regards."

He nodded. "Yes, I know Captain Jenkins. I hope he is well."

"He was, sir, when I last spoke to him, just outside Gettysburg in early July."

He nodded. "And how may I help you, Mr. . . ."

"Freeman, sir. Henry Freeman."

"Ah," he said with a slight smile. "How may I help you, Mr. Freeman?"

"Captain Jenkins asked me to deliver a message to you. May I proceed?"

"Yes, by all means."

I closed my eyes and began to recite the words Captain Jenkins had relayed to me, more than two months earlier. "Dear Robert, I hope this message finds you well and that your work proceeds apace. I met this young man a few days after the Battle of Gettysburg. It was an awful, bloody business, as by now I'm sure you've heard, but thank God, we prevailed. When I met Henry, and learned of his extraordinary abilities, I immediately thought of you and your critical work. If used correctly, I believe he could be an important asset to the cause of abolition. But, of course, you are the expert in these matters, so I entrust his care to your hands. Please give Harriet and your children my regards, and I look forward to seeing you again in better times. Your friend, Thaddeus. P.S., I could have written you a letter, but I thought you would find this method of delivery much more intriguing. Exodus 3:7."

He stared at me, clearly nonplussed. "Well, Mr. Freeman, you certainly have my attention. Why don't you come in and tell me more about these extraordinary abilities Captain Jenkins spoke of."

CHAPTER 29

METROPOLIS

1863–1864

M r. Purvis led me to a small room and indicated I should sit in one of the armchairs. There were three large west-facing windows, filling the room with a late afternoon glow. He disappeared, returning a moment later with a tray containing a pitcher of water and two glasses. These he placed between us on a low table. He settled himself comfortably in the remaining chair.

"Where did you meet Captain Jenkins?" he asked casually, as he poured a glass for each of us.

"We were picked up by his men in early July on the Chambersburg Pike, just south of Gettysburg."

He nodded. "And how did you come to be on the Chambersburg Pike?"

"My friend, Louis, and I had escaped from the Confederates just the day before."

"Escaped? Were you being held against your will?"

I looked at him sharply, thinking he might be mocking me, but his face conveyed only kindness. "Yes sir, we were enslaved," I managed, feeling shame at having to say it aloud.

"I suspected as much when you said your name was Freeman. Also, Exodus 3:7 tells the story of how Moses led the slaves out of Egypt. Thaddeus knew it was one of my favorite passages."

"Yes sir, I enjoy it too."

"How did you manage to escape?" he asked, taking a sip of water.

"The Union cavalry attacked as we, sorry, as the Confederate Army was retreating from Gettysburg."

"And what did you do for them?"

"My owner, Dr. Robert Parker of Charlotte, North Carolina, ordered me to accompany his son to war. I had no choice in the matter."

He nodded and made a sweeping gesture with his hand. "Well, that's in the past now. I commend you on your flight to freedom, and for having the perseverance to make your way to me. And don't feel bad about your attachment to the Confederate Army. As you say, you had no choice in the matter. Over the years we've had the privilege to assist many people like you, men and women and some children, as they passed through here on their way to freedom."

"Yes sir, thank you."

"But please, tell me more about yourself. Like me, it appears that you might be of mixed parentage."

Shocked by his matter-of-fact admission, I looked at him more closely. His skin was very fair and, until then, I had assumed he was a white man. Though my complexion was lighter than that of many other Negros, no one would have mistaken me for white.

"Yes sir, my mother was a Negro, and my father was white."

Nodding, he took a sip of water. "I was luckier than you. My mother was also a Negro, but my father did not abandon us. Indeed, when I was a young man, he moved my brothers and me from Charleston to Philadelphia to ensure that we received a good education."

"Yes sir," I said quietly, thinking of how differently my life might have turned out had my father done the same.

"But enough about me, tell me of yourself. I would be interested to learn where you've lived, the type of work you've done, everything really. In short, I want to hear all about your life until now." He sat back expectantly and waited. Somewhere in the house I heard the soft tic, tic, tic of a clock.

There was something about Mr. Purvis's calm demeanor that made me want to unburden myself to him. So I told him of my time on the plantation, of my mother and my work in the fields. I recounted how Dr. Parker had first learned of my gift, as well as my subsequent testing and removal to Charlotte. I told him about all the people that lived at the house on North Tryon, including Sam, Nellie, and the others, and of my early friendship with Matthew. Then I started to describe the work I had done with Dr. Parker in the laboratory, and how I had taught myself to read and perform simple calculations.

At some point during my recounting, he picked up a nearby lap desk and started writing. "Please, go on, Mr. Freeman. I just want to capture your story accurately. My memory is not nearly as well developed as yours," he said with a smile.

Nodding, I continued my account, including my recitations of Coleridge, Dickens, Dumas, Hawthorne, Melville, Shakespeare, and many other writers at dinner parties and soirees. Finally, I recounted being made to memorize the Bible by Mrs. Parker.

He stopped writing. "I'm sorry, do you mean to say that you have memorized the entirety of the Bible?" he asked incredulously.

"Yes sir."

"The King James Bible?"

I told him that I had.

"Can you recite the verse Captain Jenkins mentioned, Exodus 3:7."

"Yes sir." I closed my eyes.

> *And the Lord said, I have surely seen the afflic-*
> *tion of my people which are in Egypt and have*
> *heard their cry by of their taskmasters; for I know*
> *their sorrows.*
>
> *And I am come down to deliver them out of*
> *the hand of the Egyptians, and to bring them up*
> *out of that land unto a good land and a large,*
> *unto a land flowing with milk and honey; unto*
> *the place of the Canaanites, and the Hittites,*
> *and the Amorites, and the Perizzites, and the*
> *Hivites, and the Jebusites.*

"Wonderful," he said, beaming. Then, setting aside his writing desk, he left the room and soon reappeared carrying a worn leather Bible. He leafed through the book until he found the page he wanted. "Can you recite Genesis?"

"Yes sir." I closed my eyes and started speaking.

In the beginning God created the heaven and the earth.

And the earth was without form, and void; and darkness was upon the face of the deep. And the Spirit of God moved upon the face of the waters.

And God said, let there be light: and there was light.

And God saw the light, that it was good: and God divided the light from the darkness.

And God called the light Day, and the darkness he called Night. And the evening and the morning were the first day.

And God said, let there be a firmament in the midst of the waters, and let it divide the waters from the waters.

And God made the firmament, and divided the waters which were under the firmament from the waters which were above the firmament: and it was so.

And God called the firmament Heaven. And the evening and the morning were the second day.

"That's enough, Mr. Freeman. Thank you." He turned to a few additional passages and asked me to recite those as well before finally closing the book. "Your recall is amazing. Captain Jenkins was right; you really do have a remarkable talent."

"Thank you, sir. My mother said it was a gift."

"So it is," he said, seemingly lost in thought. After a moment he continued. "Mr. Freeman, would you mind if I call you Henry?"

"No sir, not at all."

"And please call me Robert. How long are you planning to stay in Philadelphia, Henry? That is to say, do you have any immediate plans?"

I shook my head. "No sir, I don't know anyone here, and I must admit I had no plans beyond finding you."

"I don't know if you've heard but, right here in Philadelphia, not far from this very spot, Negro regiments are being trained at Camp William Penn to fight the Confederates."

"Yes sir, I had heard they were putting Negros into the fight."

"And what about you? Do you have a mind to join up with them?"

I thought about his question. "No sir, not at this time. For the last two years, I've lived among soldiers and seen much of what they endure. The army controlled their every move. I've been a slave my whole life and have only recently gained my freedom, so I'm not prepared to submit to someone else's control so soon. I would like to live as a free man, at least for a time."

"I understand," he said.

"But if I am to stay in Philadelphia, I will need to secure lodgings, and some type of employment."

"I can certainly help you with that," he said, "but I would ask something of you in return."

"Yes sir, how might I be of assistance?" I asked, sitting up straighter.

He hesitated for a moment before answering. "You may not know it, but our goal here is the total abolition of slavery in these United States, and like most enterprises, we need money to do our work. Money for publications, meetings, resettlement and education of newly freed men and women, and many other activities. Over the years, we've been fortunate to have a number of generous benefactors support our work. But in addition to our mission, which is certainly compelling, they often like to meet . . ."

"Former slaves like me," I offered.

"Yes, that's true, but don't underestimate the impact you could have," he said emphatically. "Your abilities, your very existence, proves one of our core tenets, namely that, in addition to all its other evils, slavery obscures and extinguishes an individual's God-given potential."

"What would I need to do?"

"Nothing really, other than attend a few receptions. People will be very keen to meet you and to hear your story, and of course, they'll be fascinated to learn of your singular talent."

"I would be happy to help, sir."

"Wonderful! I believe your work here will be every bit as important as taking up arms, perhaps more so. You can stay at Harmony Hall until we find you more permanent lodgings. And as to employment, I would be pleased if you would consider working with me and other members of the Vigilant Committee to help resettle newly freed slaves. The job pays three dollars a week."

I was nearly overcome with emotion at my good fortune. "Yes sir, I would very much like to work with you," I finally managed.

He stood and held out his hand, which I took immediately. "Excellent, then that's settled. I look forward to a long and beneficial association."

* * *

Mr. Purvis found a place for me to sleep in the bunkhouse, a low, narrow building that sat next to the barn. I shared this with six other men that either worked on the farm or were passing through. I would rise with the sun every morning and help feed the animals or tend the crops. I didn't mind the work. In fact, it felt good to be on land owned by someone like me, and with so many other Negros working there of their own volition. In time, I also had the chance to meet Mr. Purvis's wife,

Harriet, an accomplished woman in her own right, and several of their children including Hattie, who was just a few years younger than me, and their oldest son, Charles.

However, my favorite days were those when Mr. Purvis asked me to join him as he worked. At those times I would saddle two horses—his was a beautiful chestnut stallion—and accompany him as he made his way around town. He might attend a meeting, as he was a member of several local organizations, or simply visit a friend or colleague. Sometimes he looked in on former slaves to ascertain how they were doing in their new lives. On several occasions we attended gatherings of local abolitionists at churches, Quaker meeting houses, or private homes. Whenever I met some of his organization's benefactors, he would say, "I would like to introduce you to Mr. Henry Freeman, a truly remarkable young man."

At such times, I would inevitably be asked to say a few words to those assembled. Though I had given many presentations in Charlotte, those were only dry recitations of something memorized. Conversely, the men and women I met in Philadelphia, though certainly curious about my memory, also wanted to know about *me*. I had done these performances many times, but one was far more memorable than the rest. It was August of 1864, and by then I had been working with Mr. Purvis for nearly a year. That day we had been invited to a reception at the Ashton home, a large four-story stone residence on

Rittenhouse Square. A liveried servant showed us into the salon, which was already occupied by more than twenty richly dressed people. I was still admiring, some might say gawking at, the beauty of the artwork and furnishings when a couple approached. They warmly greeted Mr. Purvis, whom they seemed to know well.

Mr. Purvis put a hand on my shoulder. "I would like to introduce you to Mr. Henry Freeman, a truly remarkable young man. Henry, these are our hosts, Mr. And Mrs. Ashton, who have supported the cause of freedom for many years."

Mr. Ashton reached out and shook my hand. "Welcome, Mr. Freeman. We have been very anxious to meet you. Robert has already told us a great deal about you."

"Thank you for your hospitality, Mr. Ashton, Mrs. Ashton. It's a pleasure to meet you both."

"Well, doesn't he have lovely manners," Mrs. Ashton effused.

A few minutes later, after getting the room's attention, Mr. Ashton thanked everyone for coming and for their continued support. He then ceded the floor to Mr. Purvis, who spoke for a few minutes before introducing me to the assemblage.

I told them of my background and recited a few poems, Bible verses, and selections from literature. I could see that they were impressed by my memory, but

I had done this many times before. A few people asked questions, which I answered. It was all beginning to feel a bit rote, until a florid-faced man asked, a bit rudely I thought, if I understood any of what I had recited, or was I simply parroting back something I'd memorized. Everyone in the room went stock-still, but they were all looking at me expectantly. I knew I had to respond, and I took a deep breath to calm my nerves.

"Sir, that is an interesting question, but I believe what you're really asking is how could someone like me actually understand the meaning behind such lofty words? As I said earlier, unfortunately I have never had the privilege of a formal education. As a slave, education was simply not available to me. In fact, it was illegal. So, without the benefit of having someone with whom I could discuss these passages, I admit that I have had to find my own way. In quiet moments, when I'm alone, I often re-examine what I have memorized, repeating the words, and turning them over in my mind until, I think, I began to understand.

"For example, Captain Ahab in *Moby-Dick* said, 'Better to sink beneath the yoke than to live forever as slaves.' Though no one has explained it to me, who among us wouldn't understand that sentiment. In *Gulliver's Travels*, it is said that 'Every man desires to live long, but no man wishes to be old,' which never fails to make me smile. And, in *The Count of Monte Cristo*, Edmond

Dantès says, 'when we have suffered a long time, we have great difficulty in believing in good fortune.' I must admit that, at first, I didn't understand what Dantès was trying to say. But over the years I've thought about this passage many times and have eventually come to recognize the sad truth of his words.

"However, I will readily acknowledge there is still much that I don't understand. For example, I know that a day is twenty-four hours long, an hour is sixty minutes, and a minute is sixty seconds, but I don't know how a clock keeps time. Scientists believe that ocean tides are controlled by the gravity of the moon, but how? And what is gravity really? And in humans, when limbs must be amputated, why do they not grow back, as they do in some species of lizards? Having recently come from the battle at Gettysburg, such an ability would have been very useful indeed.

"So, as you've said, though I've learned a great many things, there is still much that I don't understand. But I don't feel discouraged in the least by the gaps in my knowledge. In fact, it's quite the opposite; it only encourages me to want to learn more."

For a moment, no one said anything, then one after another they all started to applaud. Even the man that had asked the question was clapping. It was all quite overwhelming, and suddenly Mr. Purvis was at my side.

"Well done, Henry, well done," he whispered over the applause. "Our path forward couldn't be clearer. You have done remarkably well on your own, and the Friends at the local meeting house say you are a brilliant student, but we must now see to it that you get a proper education."

CHAPTER 30

SCHOLARSHIP

1864–1865

T rue to his word, Mr. Purvis arranged for me to attend the Ashmun Institute, a school founded specifically for the education of Negroes. On the morning of my departure, I went to his home to say goodbye. I found him standing outside the barn talking with some of the farmhands.

"It looks like you're ready for your trip," he said, smiling.

"Yes sir, I'm leaving in a few minutes."

"Please be sure to give Reverend Dickey my regards when you see him. Although he doesn't believe in the cause of abolition, he's a good man." I was shocked by this admission and the surprise must have shown on my face.

Mr. Purvis sighed. "Abolition is a . . . difficult issue for many people, even some with the best intentions. So ironically, although Reverend Dickey founded the first institute of higher education in the United States for Negros, he does not support abolition. He will, however, see to it that you receive an excellent education."

"Yes sir," I managed, "I'll be sure to give Reverend Dickey your regards."

"Excellent. Harriet and I are very happy for you. I know you'll make a great success of it."

"Thank you. I will write often to keep you informed of my progress." We shook hands and, suddenly choked with emotion, I added, "I will never forget your kindness, Robert."

"I was happy to be of assistance," he said, placing a hand on my shoulder. "My only request is that one day you help someone in return."

* * *

The Ashmun Institute was in Hinsonville, Pennsylvania, a small town fifty miles south and west of Philadelphia. Hinsonville had been founded by free Negroes and, being situated only six miles north of the Mason-Dixon Line, had for many years served as a haven for those fleeing slavery.

The institute itself sat amid acres of beautiful grounds and consisted of several stately brick structures. The main building, four stories tall and surmounted by a central cupola, was flanked by the president's home on one side and accommodations for the institute's instructors on the other. After unloading my bags, one of the students directed me to Reverend Dickey's home, which was in the nearby town of Oxford.

Before I had left, Mr. Purvis informed me that Reverend Dickey had resigned his role as president of the Ashmun Institute but still chaired the board of trustees. I found the house easily enough and knocked on the front door. Soon, a Negro woman appeared.

"Yes?" she asked, somehow managing to turn this one word into an accusation.

"My name is Henry Freeman. I'm a new student at the Ashmun Institute and I was told to call on Reverend Dickey when I arrived."

She frowned. "Is he expecting you?"

"No, but I've just arrived, and I hoped he might see me."

"Wait here. I'll see if he's available," she said, closing the door. She returned a few minutes later and grudgingly showed me to Reverend Dickey's office. He was sitting behind a large desk and looked up at our approach.

"Ah, you must be Mr. Freeman."

"Yes sir."

"Please, come in and take a seat. I'll just be a minute."

I sat in one of two chairs facing his desk and waited for him to finish whatever he was writing. He was perhaps sixty years old, with a square chin, a long, sharp nose, and a high forehead. His hair, almost completely white, was long but well kept. I noted that his office was neat and uncluttered, unlike Dr. Parker's. The most prominent feature of the room was a large bookcase that was filled with dozens of elegantly bound volumes. I would have liked nothing more than to get up and look through those books, but I willed myself to stay seated.

Putting down his quill, he picked up a nearby sheaf of papers and regarded me over a pair of bushy white eyebrows. "Mr. Purvis says that other than sporadic tutorials from the Quakers you've never had formal schooling. Yet, despite this, he and several others give you their highest recommendations. Do you realize how unprecedented that is?"

This was not the way I'd imagined my first encounter with Reverend Dickey. "No sir."

"Well, it is. In fact, in all the years I've been associated with the Ashmun, I can't recall anyone making a similar request, and if they had, it's very unlikely that we would have granted it."

No, this was not at all how I'd pictured our meeting. Had I traveled nearly one hundred miles only to be turned away? Since he had not asked me a question, I decided to stay silent and wait him out.

He put down the papers and gave me a sympathetic look. "I must warn you, Mr. Freeman, if you decide to stay, your time here will not be easy. In fact, the current president, John Martin, was very much opposed to your enrollment. Ultimately, Mr. Purvis and some of our other more generous benefactors prevailed. But even with their entreaties, your acceptance here is still provisional. I'm not trying to discourage you, but I wanted to make certain you understood the situation. If I were in your place, I would want someone to do the same for me."

Reeling from his words, I closed my eyes for a few seconds to collect my thoughts. I considered what he had said: "If you decide to stay, your time here will not be easy." But when had my life been easy? More resolute than ever, I looked at him again and said, "I will endeavor to do my best, sir."

He nodded slowly. "Very well. Get settled in at the dormitory and report to President Martin's office at 9:00 tomorrow morning. I will pray for your success, Mr. Freeman."

"Yes sir. Thank you." As I was leaving, I turned and said, "My apologies, Reverend Dickey, I'd almost forgotten. Mr. Purvis asked that I convey his regards."

* * *

Having been forewarned by Reverend Dickey, my meeting with President Martin became little more than a formality. Though he asked me several pointed questions, I remained calm and cordial throughout. When I left his office, I was officially enrolled as a provisional student at the Ashmun Institute with classes in geography, history, mathematics, natural science, religion, and rhetoric.

The seventy students enrolled at the institute were a diverse group, as there were few places in the country where a Negro could receive a higher education. Determined not to fail, I threw myself into my studies. I attended every lecture given, read scores of books, and devoured every scrap of knowledge made available to me. In my free time, I would often seek out instructors for additional information and discussion.

Much to the consternation of President Martin, I'm proud to say that I did well in all my classes, and my provisional designation was removed after the first academic term. I enjoyed every subject, but my instructors felt I had a particular facility for mathematics. I'll admit I loved both the beauty and rigor of numbers, and just as reading had revealed the world to me, mathematics had the potential to explain its inner workings.

Every day, several copies of the *Philadelphia Inquirer* were delivered to the dormitory, and I read every issue. The war was still raging, with major battles being fought in the west at Chattanooga and Chickamauga and in the east at Cold Harbor, Fort Wagner, Spotsylvania Court-house, and the Wilderness. In March of 1864, President Lincoln promoted General Ulysses Grant and gave him command of all Union armies. Grant traveled to Washington a few days later, met with Lincoln and his cabinet, and vowed to bring the war to an end within a year.

That summer Negro troops of the 54th Massachusetts Regiment distinguished themselves in a failed attempt to take Fort Wagner, which guarded the entrance to Charleston Harbor. I was proud of the courage displayed by the men and prayed that my friend Louis, wherever he might be, was safe.

True to his word, after capturing Petersburg and Richmond in 1865, Grant accepted Lee's surrender on April 9, 1865, at a small Virginia town named Appomattox Court House. After four years, hundreds of thousands of deaths, and untold suffering on both sides, the war was finally over. But cruelly, less than a week later, in the very midst of our jubilation, an actor named John Wilkes Booth assassinated Lincoln while he and his wife were enjoying a play at Ford's Theatre.

On April 21, his body was loaded onto a funeral train that would carry him back to his home in Springfield, Illinois, making stops in several cities along the way. In Philadelphia, his body was placed on a large, covered hearse, drawn by eight magnificent black horses. I traveled into the city with a group of students from the Ashmun and we were greatly moved by what we saw there. The streets were choked with people, everyone vying for a glimpse of Lincoln's body, or simply wishing to pay their last respects.

The next morning, I made my way to Byberry and met with Mr. Purvis. He looked like a man that was in the throes of grief as, I suppose, we all were.

"Much has happened since we last spoke," he said. "The Union won a great victory, the slaves are free, and President Lincoln is dead."

"Yes sir. Some of us from school traveled to Philadelphia to view the funeral procession."

He nodded slowly. "Very good. But that isn't why you've come to see me, is it?"

I swallowed hard, knowing this would be a difficult conversation. "No sir. I appreciate all you've done for me, I really do, but I need to leave school and go back to North Carolina."

"You intend to get your mother?"

"Yes sir, and Gloria, the woman I hope to marry. I have no way to contact them and, if I wait too long, I'm afraid I may never see them again."

He looked tired and didn't say anything for a moment. "I understand your desire to return, but you must know that this is a very dangerous time to travel. There will be thousands of soldiers on the roads trying to get back home. Making your way to Charlotte in such an environment would be difficult, perhaps impossible."

"Yes sir, I'm sure you're right. This is not an easy decision for me, but I've given it a great deal of thought. I recognize the journey will be arduous, and perhaps dangerous, but I have no choice but to try."

We were standing on the front porch of his home. Without responding, he walked to the railing and looked out over the fields, just beginning to show signs of new life. Finally, he said, "Well, if you must go, I would not recommend traveling south through Maryland and Virginia. That route could be perilous. It would be safer to travel to North Carolina by ship, and then overland to Charlotte. If you agree, I can make some inquiries and arrange transport for you."

Overwhelmed with emotion, I managed to say, "Thank you, Robert, that is very kind, but you've already done far too much for me."

He waved away my objection. "Nonsense, I'm happy to help. I will send word to you at the Ashmun when everything has been arranged."

"Thank you very much. I will reimburse you for my transport."

"Keep your money for now. You can pay me back when you're settled. But I must ask you, what will you do once you've found them? Is it your intention to remain in Charlotte or return to Philadelphia and resume your studies?"

"Honestly, I'm not certain. I love the Ashmun and would very much like to resume my studies, but I don't know what I will find in Charlotte or when I might return."

He turned to face me and extended his hand. "Then this may be goodbye, Mr. Freeman. It has been a pleasure. I hope to see you again, but if that is not possible, I wish you a blessed life."

CHAPTER 31

DEVOTION

1865

In August I received word from Mr. Purvis that, in return for my labor, he had managed to secure my passage on a cargo ship heading to Wilmington. Almost a year earlier, after many failed attempts, the Union had finally overrun Fort Fisher and captured the city. The ship, which had been leased to the navy by a Philadelphia businessman Mr. Purvis knew, was scheduled to leave in early September. That gave me less than three weeks to prepare.

Mr. Purvis had been right—traveling to North Carolina by sea would make the trip much easier. But, of course, that would only be the first leg of my journey.

After arriving in Wilmington, it would still be more than two hundred miles to Charlotte, and I would probably have to walk the entire way. I knew that I would need to travel light, securing provisions on the road. In the end, I decided to take only a bedroll and one small bag containing a jacket, two changes of clothing, some dried meat and fruit, a map, and a hunting knife. The clothing, specifically chosen for its unobtrusiveness, was obtained from a local secondhand store. I didn't want to attract any undue attention. Before I left Philadelphia, I had read that there were many men roaming the countryside, both whites and Negroes. Most were just trying to get home or reunite with their families, but others seemed intent on causing trouble, as if the violence of the war was not so easily left behind.

For added safety, I also purchased a .22-caliber Smith & Wesson revolver. I had seen many guns in my lifetime, particularly during the war, but I had never actually learned how to use one. One of my instructors took me to the woods behind the school and showed me how to shoot. When we were done, he gave me a serious look. "One lesson doesn't make you a marksman. Keep the gun well hidden and don't ever pull it out unless you're prepared to use it. And if that happens, make sure you don't miss."

Two days before our scheduled departure I reported to the ship's boatswain, a short, ill-tempered man with badly bowed legs. The ship itself, an old one-hundred-sixty-foot coal-fired steamer, was being used to ferry troops and supplies to Wilmington. I was the last-minute replacement for a steward that had quit unexpectedly the month before. During the voyage, I would be expected to attend to the officer's needs, much as I had served Dr. Parker and Matthew. I resented having to resume such a role, but I told myself it was only for a short time.

We pulled away from the dock on Thursday, September 7, traveling down the Delaware River and the Delaware Bay before turning south into the Atlantic Ocean. Three years earlier I had seen the Atlantic from the North Carolina shore. But being on the ocean, many times too far offshore to see land, was a truly terrifying experience. At the pier the ship had appeared large, but on the water, it was tossed to and fro like a child's toy. One of the men was new to the sea, as I was, and he suffered from terrible bouts of seasickness. Seeing his distress, I prayed that I would not be similarly afflicted.

Traveling at a maximum speed of nine knots, it was estimated that, depending on wind, weather, and current, our trip to Wilmington would take just over two days. I won't spend time here describing the indignities of the voyage, my threadbare sleeping hammock situated in the lowest level of the ship, or the ever-present vermin. However, suffice it to say that I doubt there was anyone onboard that was happier than me when we finally docked at Wilmington.

It had been three years since I was last in the city, during the 1862 outbreak of yellow fever. Thousands of residents had fled then, trying to avoid the pestilence, leaving Wilmington little more than a ghost town. But as I walked through the streets, I could see that life had returned to the city.

After several false starts, I finally managed to find the road to Charlotte and estimated it would take nearly two weeks to get there by foot. But I wasn't in a hurry. I reasoned that it was better to travel slowly and safely than to take unwarranted risks. After all, I had been away for more than three years, so a few more days wouldn't matter.

One afternoon, after I had been on the road for two days, I saw two white men approaching from the opposite direction. I couldn't yet see them clearly, so I retrieved my pistol from the cloth travel bag I carried and put it in the pocket of my jacket. I hoped I wouldn't need it, but if I did, it was within easy reach.

The sun was behind me and as I got closer, I could see them more clearly. Their dingy and threadbare clothing couldn't hide their identity. They were ex-Confederates and one of the men was struggling to walk. They didn't seem to be carrying anything other than bedrolls, so I was immediately on guard.

When we were still ten yards apart, the taller of the two men called out to me. "Hey boy, we're mighty hungry. You wouldn't have any food, would you? We're just trying to get home."

I studied each of them and concluded that, if an attack came, it would likely come from the man that spoke. "No sir, I don't have enough for myself, and I still have a long way to go."

"Well, why don't you hand your bag over and let us take a look for ourselves," he said with a crooked smile.

I appeared to think it over, then lifted the bag over my head and handed it to him. In his haste to go through my belongings he didn't notice that I had pulled out the pistol, which I pointed at the middle his chest. I was pleased to see that my hand was steady.

He took a step back and put up his hands. "Whoa, don't get nervous boy, I didn't mean any harm."

"Drop my bag and move on then," I said in a firm voice, "I already told you I don't have anything to spare."

He face reddened. "You see that Davey; the nigger pulled a gun on us? This is what comes from setting the darkies free."

"Let's go Mike," his companion said in a weak voice, "I just want to get home."

He nodded, "OK Davey, we're going." As they moved away, he turned and pointed at me. "Don't get too comfortable boy," he yelled. "Mark my words, one day soon we're going to put you and all your kind back in your place."

I watched them walk away until they were nearly out of sight, before retrieving my bag and heading in the other direction. I had broken my instructor's primary rule and pulled out a gun without using it. It was a stupid thing to do. Though I had been angered that he planned to rob me, the truth was there was nothing in my bag worth a life.

Not knowing if they intended to double-back I stayed off the road as much as possible, walking mostly at night. On the fourth day after leaving Wilmington, as I was nearing the town of Lumberton, a wagon carrying a Negro man and woman approached on the road. As they passed, I noted that the man was holding the reins in one hand.

"Excuse me, sir," I called. A moment later he stopped and turned to look at me. I took an involuntary step back when I saw that he was cradling a shotgun on his lap.

"Yeah, what do you want?"

"Begging your pardon, sir, but would you be heading toward Charlotte?"

"That's my business, isn't it," he snapped. "Why are you asking?"

"Well, sir, I'm trying to get to Charlotte to find my family and would appreciate a ride. I could help you drive the rig. I'm a good hand with horses."

The couple spoke to each other briefly. "We don't have any food for you. You would have to take care of yourself."

"Yes sir, that's fine," I said, trying to hide my excitement. "I don't need anything except a ride. My name is Henry. I've been walking since I left Wilmington and my feet are getting mighty sore."

They shared a long look and a moment later he said, "Come on up here and take the reins. But if you try anything or lied to me about being able to handle a rig, you'll be walking again before you can say Jack Robinson!" His wife got into the back of the wagon and, still holding the shotgun, he slid over.

I took the reins and asked, "What's the horse's name?"

He snorted derisively, but from behind me I heard his wife say, "Belle. Her name is Belle."

I rubbed the horse's neck and let her see and smell me. "Hello, Belle. You're a good horse, aren't you girl." She bobbed her large head in response, and after a moment I climbed up onto the bench and got the wagon moving again.

Over the course of the next few hours, I learned that their names were Mason and Josephine, and they were going to Monroe, North Carolina, a small town just outside Charlotte. Josephine had been born in Monroe but was sold away five years earlier when she was eighteen years old. Before that, she'd lived on a small farm with her mother and brother. She had no way of knowing if they were still in the area, but she hoped that they were.

Mason, who was sold when he was very young, did not know where he was from or remember anything of his family. His left hand had been injured working in a blacksmith's shop, rendering it almost useless.

During the ride, I told them something of my life. They were particularly fascinated by my accounts of the war and asked a good many questions. At night they slept in the wagon while I found a patch of grass for my bedroll. On the second day, Mason relaxed somewhat and put the gun down, although it stayed within easy reach. On the sixth day we arrived on the outskirts of Monroe, having been delayed by a cold, driving rain two days before. I climbed out of the wagon and collected my belongings.

"Thank you," I said, shaking Mason's hand. "I can't tell you how much I appreciate the ride. And Josephine, I pray that you find your family."

"Thank you," she said, smiling. "Good luck to you too, Henry."

Mason held up his mangled left hand. "It was our pleasure. Truth is, I'm glad you came along when you did."

Charlotte was less than fifteen miles away. I was anxious to get there, but the sun was already hanging low in the sky, and it promised to be a cold night. I started walking, keeping an eye out for someplace to bed down. I found a small stream in a wooded area, perhaps fifty yards from the road. I studied my surroundings intently but saw no sign of anyone other than me. Relaxing somewhat, I took off my shirt and washed as best I could in the frigid stream. Putting on a clean shirt, I filled my canteen, sat against a tall pine tree, and covered myself with a wool blanket. I would have liked to make a fire, but it was too risky. Closing my eyes, I fell asleep quickly, my mind filled with memories of Gloria.

* * *

Charlotte was much as I remembered it, except for the presence of Union soldiers everywhere. I estimated that there were hundreds, perhaps thousands of them. I couldn't imagine that the townspeople were pleased to have so many Yankees in town.

The house on North Tryon was unchanged, though the grounds didn't look as well tended as I remembered. I walked around the side and headed for the kitchen house. There was smoke rising from the chimney, and my heart soared at the smell of fresh bread. It had to be Nellie or Gloria. After all I had been through, the thought of seeing them filled me with emotion.

I opened the door excitedly and was surprised to come face-to-face with a middle-aged woman I didn't recognize. She grabbed a nearby knife and pointed it in my direction. "Who are you?" she yelled. "What do you want here? We don't have any handouts for vagrants."

Confused, I held up my hands. "I'm sorry, ma'am, I didn't mean to startle you. I was looking for Gloria or Nellie."

She seemed to relax somewhat but kept the knife in her hand. "You need to leave. There's nobody here but me."

I could tell from her reaction that she'd recognized the names. "Where have they gone?" I asked, trying to keep my voice calm. "They were here when I left in '62."

She narrowed her eyes. "Who are you?"

"My name's Henry. I grew up here."

"I heard about you, but like I said, there's nobody here but me."

Taking a deep breath to tamp down my rising anger, I asked, "Well, do you know where they went?"

"No, I don't know where Gloria is. She might be in town somewhere. But Nellie is dead."

I fell against the wall as if I'd been struck. "Nellie's dead? How?"

Her expression softened somewhat. Lowering the knife, she said, "I don't know exactly. They say she was sick, and she just fell out one day." Then, looking toward the house, she added, "But you really need to leave. Mrs. Parker would have my hide if she found you in here."

I felt terrible about Nellie and hoped she hadn't suffered. But my grief would have to wait. If Gloria was still in Charlotte I had to find her. I took a last look around the kitchen house and, as I turned to leave, she said, "I heard you were up north."

"That's right, I was."

She shook her head. "What in the world did you come back here for?"

* * *

I walked to the back door of the main house and knocked softly. I waited for a full minute but there was no response. Just as I was preparing to knock again, I heard footsteps approaching. The door opened and Roxanne let out a shout. "Henry," she said, embracing me warmly, "I can't believe it's you. When did you get back? Does Dr. Parker know you are coming?"

"Roxanne. It's good to see you. No, no one knew. I was in Pennsylvania, but once the war was over, I decided to come back."

Smiling, she gave me a knowing look. "There must have been something mighty important here for you to travel all that way."

I smiled too before becoming serious again. "I stopped by the kitchen and the woman there told me about Nellie."

Roxanne lowered her eyes. "I'm sorry, Henry, I know how close the two of you were. I still miss her."

"When did it happen?"

She frowned in concentration. "It must have been almost two years ago. Her and Gloria were cooking dinner when she died."

Neither of us said anything for a moment, then, fearing what she would say, I asked, "Do you know where Gloria is?"

Roxanne lowered her voice. "She left this summer. Mrs. Parker offered to pay her, but Gloria told me she'd had enough of this place. Last I heard she was working in the kitchen at the Mansion House hotel."

Relief washed over me at the thought that she might still be in town. "Thanks, Roxanne." I looked toward the front of the house. "Is he here?"

She nodded. "Yeah, he's here. You want me to tell him you're back."

I nodded. "Thanks, I might as well get this over with."

She left and a few minutes later Dr. Parker came out onto the porch and closed the door behind him. He didn't look happy to see me. "I'm surprised you would show your face around here. What do you want, Henry?"

"Nothing, sir. I just came to tell you how sorry I was about Matthew's death. As I said in my letter, if you want to bring his body home, I can tell you where he's buried."

"What use is his body to me," he spat. "My only son, my heir is dead and you're alive. Even you can't think that's a fair bargain. What did you really come back here for? Do you want your job back? Is that it?"

"No sir."

"Then I'll ask you again. Why are you here?"

"I came back to find my mother and Gloria." Then, when he said nothing, I added, "We've been separated long enough."

"Well, they're not here, so get off my property before Mrs. Parker sees you. She took ill when the news of Matthew's death reached us and, even now, hasn't fully recovered her strength."

"Yes sir, I'm leaving. I only wanted to pay my respects. I didn't mean to cause any trouble." It seemed to me that our conversation was over, so I was startled when he spoke again.

"I was surprised to get a letter from you. Who wrote it?"

"I did," I answered simply.

He looked puzzled. "Who taught you and when did you learn?"

"I've known how to read for years. I taught myself when I worked for you."

He was clearly taken aback by what I'd said but quickly regained his composure.

"Well, that's all in the past," he said breezily. "I'm a forgiving man. If you want to come back, I might be able to find some work for you."

I smiled my best Sam smile, all the while thinking there wasn't a chance I would ever work for this man again. "Thank you, Dr. Parker, that's very kind. But when my business here is done, I'm not sure I'll be staying."

"Well, think it over. You'll soon discover that living on your own is difficult. You know that I've always looked out for you and your mother. For Gloria too. But don't think about it too long or I'll have to give the job to someone else."

"Yes sir," I said. "I promise I won't think about it for long." Then, without looking back, I walked down the stairs and away from the Parker home.

* * *

The Mansion House hotel, a massive four-story brick building, covered an entire city block. From a distance I saw at least ten Union soldiers in front of the hotel. As I thought about how I might reach Gloria, I saw a Negro man walk past the soldiers and turn the corner into the vestibule that hid the service entrance. I noted with excitement that they hadn't challenged him in any way.

Hiding my belonging in some bushes, I lowered my head and started walking toward the hotel. I could hear the men talking as I approached, but they didn't pay any attention to me. When I was past them, I breathed a sigh of relief until I heard one of them call to me.

"Hey, boy, where are you going?"

I cursed under my breath. Turning toward him, I asked, "Are you talking to me, sir?"

"That's right, I'm talking to you," he said, walking over to me. "I asked where you were going." The other soldiers seemed uninterested in our discussion, but I knew that could change quickly if I didn't give this man an answer that would satisfy him.

"I work at the hotel, sir, in the kitchen."

"In the kitchen, huh." I nodded, afraid my voice would somehow betray the fear I felt. "You don't want any trouble, do you, boy?"

"No sir," I managed. "I don't want any trouble."

He looked toward his friends, who were now paying attention. "Well, if you don't want any trouble, you'd best bring some pie out here for me and my friends."

"Pie, sir?" I sputtered.

"That's right—bring us an apple pie. I know there are pies in there, we can smell them cooking. Isn't that right, fellas?" There was a general murmur of assent from the other soldiers.

"Yes sir, apple pie. I'll see what I can do," I said, hurrying away.

When I got to the servants' entrance, a Negro man was standing outside smoking. He looked up at my approach. "I've never seen you before. You new here?" he asked.

I looked around to make certain we were alone. "No, I'm looking for somebody."

"Looking for somebody," he repeated, on guard now. Who?"

"I'm looking for a woman named Gloria that works in the kitchen. I'm her brother and we haven't seen each other for years."

"I know Gloria, but you don't look much like her family," he said, spitting a piece of tobacco from his tongue. It was clear that he wasn't inclined to help me. I would have to take a different approach.

"You're right, I'm not her brother, but I need to see her. I can pay you if you help me."

He looked skeptical. "You don't look like you can pay anybody," he said with a smirk. Besides, I've got to get back to work. You had best get going; if the manager finds you back here, he'll have you arrested."

"I can give you a dollar if you help me," I said, pulling a coin from my pocket.

He examined it in the dim light of the alley. "Make it two dollars and I'll see what I can do."

I shook my head. "I'll give you the rest when I see Gloria. Tell her Henry is here."

He thought it over for a moment before slipping the dollar into his pocket and disappearing into the hotel.

Not wanting to be seen, I pressed my back against the far wall and waited anxiously. I was taking a risk. He might alert the manager that a stranger was in the alley. Or he could simply keep the dollar I had given him and do nothing. If Gloria didn't come out within ten minutes I would need to leave. I said a silent prayer and held my breath. A couple of moments later my prayer was answered when she walked out of the hotel.

Looking around frantically she said, "Amos, you said Henry was here. Where is he?" I stepped out of the shadows.

"I'm here, Gloria." She rushed to me and collapsed in my arms, crying. I was crying too. I looked toward Amos, prepared to pay him the other dollar, but he only smiled before going back into the hotel.

Still holding on to me, Gloria pulled back and looked at my face. "You came back. I can't believe you came back."

"I came back for you," I whispered, kissing her. "I plan to marry you if you'll have me."

She nodded fiercely, beginning to cry again. "Of course I'll marry you, Henry, of course I will. I kept the money safe, just like you asked me."

"I knew you would," I said, smiling. "But listen, Gloria. I'm going to be gone for a few days. I have to go to the plantation to find my mother."

She laughed. "Henry, your mother is in Charlotte—I've seen her! She lives in the same part of town as I do."

"My mother is here?" She nodded and I wanted to scream at my good fortune. At twenty-nine years old, all my dreams were coming true. Now we would need to make our own way in the world. I knew it wouldn't be easy, but with Gloria by my side, I felt I could do anything. She told me where she was staying, and we arranged to meet later.

I looked toward the street and thought about the soldiers waiting there. "Is there another way out of here other than the street."

"No, not without going through the hotel." She looked at my clothes and wrinkled her nose. "But I don't think that would be a good idea."

I thought about my options. "Well, if that's the only way out I have to ask you for a favor."

"What?" she asked, composing herself to return to work.

"I need an apple pie."

EPILOGUE

1888

Gloria and I talked about settling in Philadelphia, but after listening to my accounts of the city, she wasn't keen to move there. And I had to admit that although I had met many good people in Philadelphia, the city also had its share of bigotry. I wrote to Mr. Purvis to let him know of our decision and, I'm happy to say that we still correspond with each other.

In the end, Gloria and I bought a small plot of land on the west side of Charlotte, near the new Freedman's College of North Carolina. Jackson was still in town, and with his help, we built a small home there.

We've been blessed to have two children, a daughter named Sadie, and a boy named Arthur that everyone calls Skip. My mother and Toby settled near us and, until his death ten years ago from influenza, they were very happy. She lived alone for many years, but after much persuasion, finally agreed to move in with us. Unlike the cabin we once shared on the plantation, there are no plants on the shelves in her room. Instead, they are filled with dozens of Toby's intricate wood carvings.

The year after the war ended, an ex-slave named Kathleen Hayes protested that Negroes still had to sit in the balcony at First Presbyterian Church. Because of her efforts, the presbytery purchased land for the establishment of a new church, the Colored Presbyterian Church of Charlotte. We attend service there every Sunday, proudly sitting in pews on the main floor.

During the day I work as a doctor, treating my patients with a blend of new and old medicines. I don't have a license from the state medical board, but I only treat Negro patients, so no one bothers me. I also earn extra money by assisting Jackson from time to time in his busy carpentry shop. I'm happy to say that over the years we have become good friends. In the evenings I teach reading and writing to students in the church basement.

On Sundays the children come to the house for dinner. Sadie is twenty-two and married to Barry, a wonderful young man. They have a two-year-old girl named Bessie. Skip is nineteen and is enrolled at the Freedman's College in Charlotte. He wanted to attend the Ashmun Institute, which had changed its name to Lincoln University shortly after the assassination, but we couldn't bear to have him so far from home. He's also courting a very nice young lady. Gloria says he's too young to be so serious about a girl, but I'm happy for them. You never know where life will lead you, so when something good comes along, you need to take hold of it.

I can hear everyone in the house laughing and talking, and the sound is comforting to me. Gloria and I have built a home and family we can be proud of, and I love her as much now as I ever did. Life in Charlotte has its challenges, but I'm pleased to say that because of Gloria's calming influence, the anger that used to so often plague me is now only a distant memory.

My daughter and granddaughter come out to the front porch. Bessie climbs into my lap. "Dinners ready dad. Mom said you should come inside."

I lift Bessie into the air, and she squeals with delight. "All right, you got me. Let's go in."

As I stand, I see a hummingbird near the porch that looks exactly like the one I saw so many years ago outside Dr. Parker's office window. I can't help but smile. "It's good to see you again, little bird," I whisper. "We're both free now, aren't we."

AUTHOR'S NOTES

In the novel, Henry has the gift of what might now be described as photographic memory. Although this is a rare trait, it is certainly not unheard of. There are a number of historical figures that were purported to have a photographic memory, including Napoleon Bonaparte, Leonardo da Vinci, Wolfgang Amadeus Mozart, Sergei Rachmaninoff and Nicholas Tesla.

Dr. Parker's character is based on well-known natural scientists of the eighteenth and nineteenth centuries, such as Benjamin Banneker, Robert Boyle, Benjamin Franklin, Luigi Galvani, James Joule, Carl Linnaeus and Florence Nightingale.

The main characters in the novel are fictional, but many of the historical elements referenced throughout the book were real. Should you wish to examine further this period in history, the following is a partial list inspired by actual people and places mentioned in this novel.

NOTABLE PEOPLE

Benedict Arnold – American Revolutionary War General that defected to the British

Archimedes – Greek astronomer, engineer and mathematician

Louis Napoleon Bonaparte / Emperor Napoleon III – Emperor of France

John Wilkes Booth – Actor and murderer of Abraham Lincoln

John Brown – Abolitionist that led raid on Armory at Harpers Ferry

Ambrose Burnside – Union general

Augustus Caesar- First Emperor of Rome

Claudius Caesar- Roman Emperor

Julius Caesar – Roman general and dictator

Tiberius Caesar – Roman emperor

Henry Clay – U.S. politician and Presidential candidate

General Thomas Clingman – Democratic Senator from North Carolina

Samuel Taylor Coleridge – English poet

Jefferson Davis – President of Confederate States of America

Charles Dickens – English author of numerous works

Alexander Dumas – French author of The Count of Monte Cristo and The Three Musketeers

Richard S. Ewell – Confederate general

Ulysses S. Grant – Commander of Union army and 18th President of the United States

Nathaniel Hawthorne – American author

Henry Heth – Confederate general

Thomas J. Holton – Owner and publisher of the
Charlotte Journal

John Irwin –Trustee of First Presbyterian Church

Robert E. Lee – Commander of the Army of
Northern Virginia

Collett Leventhorpe – Confederate general

James Longstreet – Confederate general

J. Johnston Pettigrew – Confederate general

Ambrose Powell (A.P.) Hill Jr. – Confederate general

Daniel Harvey (D.H.) Hill – Confederate general and
Commandant of N. Carolina Military Inst.

Kathleen Hayes - https://fupcc.org/our-history/

Abraham Lincoln – 16th President of the United
States

John Bankhead Magruder – Confederate general

Herman Melville – American author

Paracelsus (Theophrastus von Hohenheim) – Swiss
physician

William Phifer – Planter, reportedly hosted last
Confederate Cabinet meeting at his home on North
Tryon Street

George Pickett – Confederate general

James Polk – U.S. politician and presidential candidate

Robert Purvis – American abolitionist

Dr. Francis Ramadge – American scientist and author

Egbert Ross – Confederate major

William Shakespeare – English playwright

Dred Scott – Enslaved man that unsuccessfully sued for his freedom

Ignaz Semmelweis – Hungarian physician and scientist

John Snow – English physician and scientist

Roger B. Taney – Fifth Chief Justice of the United States

Nat Turner – Led slave rebellion in 1831

George Washington – Commander of Continental army, 1st President of the United States

John Wheeler – North Carolina State Treasurer, first Superintendent of U.S. Mint, Charlotte.

Dr. William Withering – English physician and scientist

NOTABLE PLACES

Appomattox Court House, Appomatox, VA

Ashmun Institute, Oxford, PA (Renamed Lincoln University)

Bethel Church, near Hampton, VA

Byberry Meeting House, Byberry, PA

Camelback Bridge, Harrisburg, PA

Camp Davis, North Carolina

Camp Mangum, North Carolina

Camp William Penn, Pennsylvania

Camp Wyatt, North Carolina

Colored Presbyterian Church of Charlotte, Charlotte, NC

First Presbyterian Church, Charlotte, NC

Fort Fisher, North Carolina

Fort Hatteras, North Carolina

Fort Monroe, Virginia

Fort Wagner, South Carolina

Freedman's College of North Carolina, Charlotte, NC (Renamed Johnson C. Smith University)

Harmony Hall, Byberry, PA (farm of Robert Purvis)

Lutheran Seminary, Gettysburg PA

Mansion House Hotel, Charlotte NC (Renamed Central Hotel)

Mecklenburg Iron Works, Charlotte, NC

North Carolina Military Institute, Charlotte NC

Rittenhouse Square, Philadelphia, PA

Rudisill Mine, Charlotte, NC

Tanner's Alley, Harrisburg, PA

U.S. Mint, Charlotte, NC

ABOUT THE AUTHOR

For many years, Dr. Douglas Young has had an interest in American history, particularly the "peculiar institution" of slavery and the Civil War. In addition to always being a history buff, Douglas studied biology in college and graduate school. He combined his love for both history and science into the writing of this book.

Douglas spent his professional career in medical research and as a business executive. Though he is the author of more than thirty-five scientific publications, this is his first novel. He currently lives in Cornelius, North Carolina with his wife, Pam.